FLESH FLESH

'Vasilka,' I said, my voice unsteady with the pleasure of dominating and humiliating our victim thus, 'look at the slut. I am performing a standard medical procedure, entirely in her own interests, and look: she responds to a large firm object up her small tight bottom with –'

'*Pleasure!*' Joanna completed for me, her voice dripping expertly with disgust. As I continued to pump the thermometer in the girl's bottom, Joanna released a hand from the now mostly redundant task of holding her body up for my assault and stuck a finger in her leaking pussy, twirling it to collect some of her juice. Then she lifted it slowly clear, and the two of us watched the thread stretch and stretch.

'Pleasure,' she repeated. 'The girl is an anal pervert, my dear Lidiya, an anal pervert of the worst and, well, most perverted kind. Listen to her!'

Little gasps of ecstasy were escaping around the girl's gag and, scarce though I could believe it, she was positively rocking her bottom at the instrument invading it. The thread of pussy-juice Joanna was stretching snapped at last and I felt a drop of it hit my face.

FRESH FLESH

Wendy Swanscombe

This book is a work of fiction.
In real life, make sure you practise safe, sane and
consensual sex.

First published in 2006 by
Nexus
Thames Wharf Studios
Rainville Road
London W6 9HA

www.nexus-books.co.uk

Typeset by TW Typesetting, Plymouth, Devon
Printed and bound by Clays Ltd, St Ives PLC

ISBN 0 352 34041 X
ISBN 9 780352 34041 2

DAIRY. A woman's breasts. 'She sported her dairy', she pulled out her breast.

> Francis Grose, *Classical Dictionary of the*
> *Vulgar Tongue* (1785)

MISS J–NSON No. 17, Willow Walk, near the Dog and Duck. This pretty filly is of a middling size, near twenty. Norfolk gave her birth. Her countenance is rather pleasant, with fine black eyes that are very attractive, good teeth, and a fine skin; the *dairy hills* of delight are beautifully prominent, firm and elastic, the *sable coloured grot* below with its coral-lipped *janitor* is just adapted to the sons of Venus.

> Anonymous, *Harris' List of Covent Garden Ladies,*
> *or Man of Pleasure's Kalendar* (1788)

The attitude of the two had a terrible resemblance to a child forcing a kitten's nose into a saucer of milk to compel it to drink. As we burst into the room, the Count turned his face, and the hellish look that I had heard described seemed to leap into it. His eyes flamed red with devilish passion.

> Bram Stoker, *Dracula* (1897), chapter 21

Brînză de Burduf (Romania)
Strong, pungent, spreadable cheese ripened in an animal skin bag (a *burduf*). Has a yellow paste and a grey rind spotted with mould. Traditionally eaten at the end of Lent.

> Sandy Carr, *The Simon Schuster Pocket Guide*
> *to Cheese* (1981)

Words marked with an asterisk are defined in the glossary at the end of the book.

Introduction

The previous novel, *Vamp*, describes a maleless alternative Europe of nocturnal, insect-eating lesbians who give birth by parthenogenesis. The Romanian lawyer Joanna Harker travels to the mist-shrouded island of Transmarynia to assist a Countess Caradul prepare a move to Bucharest, where the Countess intends to run an Academy for Underprivileged Young Women of the Lower Classes. To her horror, Joanna discovers that the 'Countess' is in fact a 'Count' – a monstrous survival of an older race of semi-human beings known as 'men', who are nourished by sunlight, drink female breast-milk, and are able to induce pregnancy in women by impregnation with a foul sexual fluid known as 'sperm'.

Having escaped from the Count's castle in Wales and spent many days recovering in London, Joanna returns to Romania to join her lover Mina and her friends Artemisia, a soldier, and Caliginia, Artemisia's betrothed, and Dr Helsingvill, a scientist; and discovers that Caradul has travelled there himself and been *sperm-training* Caliginia, or accustoming her body to sperm, to prepare her for eventual impregnation. As *Vamp* closes, Joanna and her friends are trying to hunt down the rooftop glass coffins the Count has scattered across Bucharest to assist him as he re-establishes the domain of men using his 'Academy' as cover. They intend to survey Bucharest from the air by balloon, detecting the coffins by the sunlight they reflect and smashing them one by one. But the Count has tracked them down with his sex-betraying female agents, and while Joanna and her lover Mina are aloft in the balloon, he launches an attack on the ground party.

Joanna Harker's Journal, 21 September.

Early afternoon. I am writing on the map on which so many of our hopes rested. Mina and I are being carried away the Goddess knows where, to land the Goddess knows when. Ah, we are cursed, and the Count has foreseen and forestalled every step we have taken! Save the very last, taken, as I shall shortly describe, by Artemisia, and even that may prove unavailing against him. After our misfortunes in the past, the very ease with which we inflated the balloon for our ascent might have warned us; but we took it for a harbinger of success, and as Artemisia winched us to height, Mina positively sang. (Now only her sobs sound in the basket, and I might echo them myself had I not determined to record how our misfortune came about.) The air of day was still and unpleasantly warm about us, and even through the darkened glass of my spectacles it seemed bright and full of menace, showing the city I love in an unfamiliar and unlovely clarity. I reassured myself with the thought that strong sun meant strong reflections and when we were fully aloft I picked up the telescope and began work, scanning the likeliest spots with minute care: towers and the roofs of the tallest buildings. Success was almost immediate: I spotted a flash of sunlight from an old tower across the river, and recalled seeing documents in the Count's files for the purchase of a property there.

I scanned the district, searching for a familiar street, then described the sighting to Mina, who soon had the tower marked on the map. We shared a smile of what I now see was *hubristic* triumph, though I could barely see her face and knew she could barely see mine; and then I raised the telescope to my eye again. Even as I did so, however, the basket lurched beneath my feet and I heard the hawser twang on a deep note, as though the winch had been violently shaken. For a moment I was too concerned to keep my footing to be able to turn the telescope downwards, but Mina was already leaning over the edge of the basket and her cry of horror told me that something was amiss. When I was able to direct my artificially sharpened gaze downwards, I could see much more clearly than she, but I believe my despair can have been no greater.

Far below, in the clearing in which, for precaution's sake, we had inflated the balloon and set up the winch, a fierce struggle was under way between our hopelessly outnumbered side – Artemisia, Caliginia, Dr Helsingvili and Artemisia's two military friends and helpers – and a group of fifteen or more sun-muffled interlopers, who had plainly waited in ambush until the odds were best in their favour. The outcome was inevitable, but even as the jaws of defeat closed upon her, Artemisia – whom I salute as the noblest of warriors and truest of friends – managed to toss out a crumb of victory. Not for herself and her friends and her own lover, my dearest darling Caliginia, but for us, her friends aloft in the balloon.

It was undoubtedly the intention of the interlopers to overpower those on the ground before winching the balloon back to earth and overpowering us two

3

at their leisure. Seeing this, Artemisia called upon all her strength and managed to throw off the four burly women who were battling to bring her to earth. For a moment, Mina and I, watching horror-stricken from above, thought she meant to run for freedom; and that is what a lesser-hearted and lesser-witted woman might have done, thinking to save at least herself though her friends were lost. Artemisia, great-hearted and great-witted, did nothing of the kind. Instead, though she knew she herself lost all chance of escape by it, she flung herself to the winch and I heard Mina cry out with the pain of a bright flash of light that burst suddenly in Artemisia's hand. Suddenly I realised we were ascending swiftly and silently, for even through the telescope the scene below was shrinking rapidly. Artemisia had cut the hawser and set us free, realising that Bucharest, even if she had been able to escape in the instant that offered itself to her, would be swarming with the Count's agents, while we might be carried far beyond its limits.

As yet we are still above the city, but we are drifting steadily southwest, and I hope that a stronger breeze will pick up when night falls. Our best hope, I believe, is to be carried beyond the borders of Romania altogether, for I fear that the Count's silver has corrupted very many officials in my homeland, rendering it unsafe for us to set foot there again. In Bulgaria or Iugoslavia we shall be able to tell our tale without immediate fear, but I know there is a hard road ahead of us if ever we are to rouse the world against the menace already established in the heart of its greatest city. Mina's sobs are lessening now, but a perverse impulse comes upon me to start them afresh with a description of what last I saw as I stared down

4

at the ground through my telescope, when all our friends were borne to the ground and a tall figure came stalking from under the trees in the bright sunlight. I should have recognised its size and gait anywhere, even had its head not been carelessly uncovered to the sun, and I half-expected the sardonic glance upwards and arrogant salute that came next. Even without aid of a telescope, Mina caught the salute through her smoked spectacles, I know, for I heard her cry out; but I feel sure she did not catch the Count's next gesture, else she would have cried out again, and more loudly. No, it was only I who saw that his hand fell to his crotch and the flash of white as he released his 'cock'.

I tremble now with thoughts of what Artemisia, Caliginia, Dr Helsingvili and the two others have endured in that sun-blasted clearing, as they were held down and stripped by his agents (whom I know from their sun-muffling to be women, though I can scarcely call them so, given whom they assist and what they assist him in). He will undoubtedly have wished to punish his captives for their effrontery in sending a balloon up against him, and Artemisia may know for herself now the horrors of sperm-training, if the Count has – μη γενοιτο!* – pushed his cock into her mouth or, worse, her bottom. Her pussy will remain unviolated for the time being, but I have no doubt that he will try to impregnate her before the year is out, and that his Bucharest 'Academy for Underprivileged Young Women of the Lower Classes' will be up and running within the month. Then, I believe, he will call his suns across the ocean to him from Transmarynia, and milk-slaves will groan below the streets of Bucharest while all the horrors of prolonged sperm-training take place above. Only Mina and I stand between him and fulfilment of his evil ambitions: to establish a vampiric empire – a *vempire* – of bright and twisted sensuality, and to bring womankind out from under the cool shadow of nocturnal freedom and back into the eye-searing light of enslaved day. I pray that we shall not fail in our sacred trust.

Later. The breeze that I prayed for has appeared, and the rumble of night-awakened Bucharest is fading fast on the northern horizon. Mina, exhausted by her emotion, is sleeping on the floor of the basket, and my resolve to defeat the Count is heightened by the mumbled cries that occasionally escape her lips. She is plainly in the grip of a nightmare induced by the events of the day, and perhaps, in her scourged imagination, finds herself in the Count's castle of horrors in Wales. I did ill, perhaps, in describing what I endured there so vividly to her, and I have pondered whether to wake her. But no, I believe that the nightmare may prove cathartic and will anyhow fade soon into undisturbed sleep, so she wakes refreshed and renewed for the battles ahead. Goddess forgive me if I do wrong.

Joanna Harker's Journal, 23 September.

We have landed safe and sound, and I continue my journal on the paper of a cheap Bulgar inn with a pen that squeaks like a *liliac*.* Mina, who has just left me to send a telegram to an address given us by Dr Zdravkova (of whom more anon) in Sofia, has already joked about the pen, and I am heartened to see that my thoughts anent her nightmare have proved correct. I questioned her gently when we arrived at the inn, but it is plain she remembers nothing of it and that her sleep has greatly refreshed her. I think I myself will snatch a few minutes of sleep before Mina's return, and I pray that I too am not plunged into a nightmare of my own about the Count, or even, perhaps, about the landing of our balloon, which proved trickier by far than I anticipated. More of that later, perhaps, and of the sweet sequel – or should I, with a smile of my own, say 'coda'? – to our adventure.

Later. Mina has returned from sending the telegram and now ... well, the unsteadiness – and occasional (oh!) illegibility – of my pen will tell the tale as eloquently as my words. Yes, her sweet head is entombed between my trembling thighs and her smooth soft tongue renewing its acquaintance, for the ten- or twenty-thousandth time, with the swollen folds and crannies of my delighted pussy. But I must retain sufficient of my attention and wits to write of our landing and its sequel, and to read aloud what I write to my industrious cunnilinctrix.*

Who has now (oh!) gone to work harder than ever, the minx. Yes. The landing. Trickier by far than anticipated, as I noted previously. We had flown most of the night, my watch chiming off the hours as we passed silent as a *buhă** above empty country, with only an occasional farmhouse or village to interrupt its monotony. I preserved strict silence, not daring to shout questions to those women I heard below me at the latter sites, for I feared that if I spoke in Romania news of a *vox e caelo** would be conveyed to the Count, and he would be able to deduce our exact route and send his silver-corrupted huntresses on our track.

At last, however, I began to believe, from some subtle *je ne sais quoi pas* in the air, that we had passed the borders of our homeland and were floating above

Bulgaria. I determined to test my belief at the next farmhouse or village we passed over; and when one arrived (a farmhouse), I leaned over and shouted, heart hammering in my breast, to the woman whose movements I had heard below. To my inexpressible relief, the accent and broken Romanian of the voice that answered me were pure Bulgara, and I knew that, for the nonce, we were beyond the Count's power.

Now to . . .

Five minutes later. My minx interrupted the tale with orgasm, judging her tongue-gallop cunningly to my remembered excitement and relief. Now she canters again on the lush pastures of my pussy, threatening to break into a gallop at any moment, but I have promised her a thorough bum-warming if she interrupts me again without permission. So. To resume. Yes, I shouted into the darkness below and gasped with relief to hear the voice that answered me. Now I could bring the balloon to earth and seek help at the farmhouse – but imagine my distress when I realised that the excitements and alarums of the previous day had quite driven Artemisia's instructions about landing from my head!

Now it was that I woke gently Mina, to ask her whether *she* remembered what cord it was one pulled to bring the balloon safely back to earth; but her mind, though filled with a delight as keen as mine at the fact of our escape across the border, was quite blank too. We had to trust to luck and divine favour; and so, breathing a prayer to the Goddess, I took hold of a cord at hazard and pulled. Nothing happened, and the noises of the farmhouse were behind us now. I pulled harder, and when nothing happened again, positively wrenched on the thing.

8

Still nothing, so I seized another and hauled for all I was worth.

A sudden hissing of released gas from above spoke of my success, but in the next moment my heart, leaping joyfully at the thought we would soon be safe on Iugoslav soil, was plummeting into my tightened belly, for it was plain that we were descending too fast! Crying a frantic instruction to Mina, I began to jettison the balloon's ballast (*that* part of Artemisia's instructions were easy enough to recall), but it was a close-run thing and I fear we should have had more than a severe bump on landing had I or Mina been a second slower to react.

As we climbed from the basket into a field of young grain, laughing weakly from relief and reaction, the farm-girl whose voice I had heard came running to find us with a hastily snatched lamp. The mysterious landing of a balloon was no doubt a highlight of the year for her, and her atrocious Romanian grew more atrocious still in her excitement. I was curt with her, for her evident youth and innocence were swiftly transforming the heightened emotion of safe landing into lust.

'Where is your mistress, girl?' I asked, interrupting her congratulations.

'She be goed at the town, my lady-good, for to sell –'

' "Gone", not "goed", you fool,' I interrupted her again. 'The *preterit* of the intransitive verb "go" is "gone".'

'I be sorry, my lady-good. She be *gone* at the town, for to sell –'

'She *has* gone, you ignorant slut. Are you deliberately insulting us by the abuse you heap on our mother tongue?'

'I believe so, Joanna,' I heard Mina murmur beside me, and I grinned, knowing that she had joined the game and would need no prompting when I pounced.

'I be true sorry, my lady-good,' the poor farm-girl stammered. 'She *have* g–'

'Enough!' I roared, and pounced on the slut, my pussy already moist beneath my trousers, and positively bubbling with juice as my hands fastened on her sturdy limbs and coarse but thankfully clean garments. Mina joined me a second later, helping me strip her before we dragged her to the basket and tied her in place for correction. It was a relief to discover that she was well washed, smelling only of youth and recent exercise, and my hardened nipples were soon aching as we grappled with her. Ah, but she was a strong one, well muscled from her farm work, and for all that I overtopped her by head and shoulders, I believe I should have been hard-pressed to strip and subdue her soon on my own. With Mina's help it was a matter of a few minutes, but even so, when we had finished and her pale form was gleaming against the basket, lashed tight to it with torn strips of her own clothing and illumined by the rays of the lamp Mina held up beside her, I had to allow a further minute for my breath to return.

The girl, by contrast, was swearing most fluently in her own mother tongue. Its barbarous cadences heightened the excitement I felt at the punishment that would soon descend on her buttocks, which writhed most beguilingly with her struggles to break free. When I was ready, I swung back my arm and lashed at them – *thwack* – with our improvised whip: the waist cord of her own skirt, now lying tattered on the ground at her well-tied feet.

Thwack.

'Shut up, you slut!'

Thwack.

I delivered another for good measure.

'When you address us, you will do so in a civilised tongue. Do you understand?'

But she hesitated a moment and I whipped her again – *thwack* – noting with pleasure that the lamplight that fell on her was now quivering with the lust-induced shaking of Mina's hand.

'Do you understand? Answer at once!'

'Yes, my lady-good. I is –'

Thwack.

'Shut up. Even now, when you have already experienced some – though but the fringes – of the chastisement that awaits you, you persist in your insults to the world's noblest language. I will now question you again on your mistress's whereabouts, and for each mulish error of grammar or pronunciation you will receive a stroke of rebuke. Do you understand?'

Again a fraction's pause and again:

Thwack.

Her bum was nicely marked now, trammelled with my cord strokes, like plough lines on a virginal field into which I had sown the seeds of slow-blossoming pain.

'Also –' I was panting from the excitement of the whipping '– for each *hesitation* you shall receive a stroke of rebuke. Do you understand?'

'Yes, my lady-good. I is –'

Thwack. Thwack.

My p . . .

Five minutes later. But again Mina has brought me to orgasm, timing her tongue-strokes to the excitement of my memories, and that bum-warming I threatened is threat no longer, but certainty. To resume:

My pussy was now positively glued to my undergarments with juice, and I could wait no longer before attending to it.

11

'But –' I had to swallow away my lust before I could continue '– first, we will ensure that you are sufficiently *sturdy* to endure the travails that may await you, should you persist in your insults. You are privileged, slut, to be in presence of one of the finest physicians in Bucharest, Madame Eugenie Krakowa.' (Even in the midst of my lust, I returned enough sense to give Mina a false name, whereby to buy us, perhaps, extra time should the tale of our landing filter into wider Bulgaria.)

'Dr Krakowa, if you please, would you examine the, ah, patient, and pass verdict on her fitness to endure what awaits her?'

'But certainly, Madame Leona,' Mina replied (I smiled at her quickness of wit, for she had rechristened me); and setting down her lamp she positioned herself ready for my instructions.

'Where shall I begin?' she asked.

'Bum first,' I said. I had laid the improvised whip on the grass, dragged up my skirt, and now, averting my gaze from the examination, held my finger poised at my straining clitoris. A gasp from the farm-girl told of Mina's eager hands fastening to her bum cheeks, and I began to frot myself, slowly, luxuriantly.

'Are they . . . are they *firm*?' I asked.

'Ind . . . indeed they are,' Mina said, her own voice unsteady with lust. 'Deliciously firm, but sensitive withal.'

'And her bum skin –' with an effort I slowed my clit-frotting, which threatened to bring me to orgasm too soon '– is it smooth? Is it tender?'

Another gasp from the farm-girl.

'Aye,' Mina said. 'Smooth. Very smooth. And *very* tender. I feel the glow of the strokes we have already visited on her.'

'And are they . . . are they fit, in your pro . . . your *professional* opinion, to endure a further dozen strokes?'

'Most certainly,' Mina said. 'And a further dozen atop that, should need arise.'

'Ah, excellent,' I murmured, almost lost in the deepening well of my impending orgasm.

'Please repeat that, Madame Leona,' Mina said. 'What do you wish me to examine next?'

I cleared my throat, struggling to slow my finger again.

'I said "excellent", Dr Krakowa. But please examine next . . . her *tits.*'

The gasp that broke now from the farm-girl's lips, as Mina's eager hands lifted and clasped her breasts, was too much for me, and I sank to my knees, sobbing with pleasure, as my pussy-juice splashed my hand, spurting from my orgasmically writhing pussy.

'. . . irm,' I could finally hear Mina say through the thunder of blood in my ears. 'Very firm.'

I shook my head, trying to refocus my attention.

'And . . . and her tit skin. Is it –'

'Aye,' Mina interrupted, running ahead of me in her eagerness. 'Smooth and tender. But her nipples –' more gasps from the farm-girl '– puzzle me.'

I pushed myself back to my feet, working on my pussy-lips now, for my clitoris, so recently triggered, was too sensitive for direct stimulation. Through further gasps from the farm-girl, I asked: 'Why do her nipples puzzle you?'

'They are swollen, Madame Leona, and seem *excessively* tender. Hear how she gasps as I manipulate them.'

And she fitted her actions to her words, exciting still louder gasps from the farm-girl.

'And what do you think explains this, Dr Krakowa?'

13

'I confess that I am at a loss, Madame Leona.'

'Then question the slut. Chew her ear if she refuses to answer.'

But the farm-girl was already stammering out the cause.

'It be my mistress, my lady-goods. She wash and scrub all servants with her own hand each morning, and be very cruel on our *gerdi*, our teeties, with scrub bru–'

' "Cruel"?' I broke in. ' "Cruel" do you call your mistress? You ungrateful slut. Dr Krakowa, have you completed your examination?'

'All but her private parts, Madame Leona.'

'Then examine them, if you please, and deliver your verdict on her fitness to endure further punishment.'

'At once, Madame Leona.'

And with a further gasp from the farm-girl that spoke of a final two-handed squeeze at her tits, Mina stooped to push the farm-girl's thighs apart from the rear and examine her pussy. I heard Mina cry out with mock disgust, and smiled again.

'Wh .. what is it, Dr Krakowa?' I asked, having begun to frot my clitoris again.

'The state of her vulva!' Mina said. 'Positively drenched with *jus amoris*.* Her thighs are inundated as far as her knees. It is evident that those tales of Bulgar perversity are based on a firm foundation of fact. The girl's a pervert!'

'What manner of pervert?' I asked, feeling my knees weaken again as a second orgasm swelled inside me. The farm-girl moaned as Mina's skilful fingers slid and tickled at the swollen tissues of her pussy.

'She evidently derives pleasure from pain.'

'Then we must beat the perversity out of her,' I said. 'And run the risk that we will merely add more fuel to the fire.'

'Aye,' said Mina a little distractedly, still exploring the farm-girl's pussy with her fingers.

'Then she is fit for punishment, in your professional opinion?' I prompted.

'Aye. Oh –' she withdrew her fingers and stood back '– aye. She is fit. Do your worst, Madame Leona.'

I withdrew my fingers from my own pussy, denying myself another quick orgasm that I might heighten the next, and grabbed up the cord from the grass.

'I will, Dr Krakowa, I will.'

And th . . .

Five minutes later. For the third time my minx has interrupted my chronicle with orgasm. How she will suffer for it when I lay my pen aside. To resume:

And then, as Mina held up the lamp in one hand and frotted herself with the other, I set to work both punishing and beating the perversity out of the farm-girl as she tried – in vain, alas for her – to complete a sentence in good, grammatical Romanian telling of her mistress's whereabouts and the likely time of her return.

Entry on a separate sheet in Joanna Harker's private shorthand. I am risking much by committing this to paper, even in such a form as this, but Mina is willing and the risk heightens the excitement both of the remembering and of the recording. So: when we had completed the farm-girl's punishment, purchasing four or five orgasms apiece at the cost of her pain and humiliation, she had told us that her mistress would be back within the hour and began to beg us, whimpering with the blaze in her buttocks, to release her, that she might have her work completed before that time.

'She be cruel to I, very cruel to I for all times, but more still cruel when I be . . . I know not how you say . . . when I be . . .'

'When you are idle,' Mina said. 'When you are sluttish, slovenly, and disobedient. And quite right too. But we have not finished with you yet, my toothsome morsel of tender-bummed girl flesh. Not by a long . . .'

And with this she leaned over the rim of the balloon's basket, her own tender bum straining at the cloth of her dress in the lamplight, and straightened with a long shape in her hand that I could not recognise for a moment, still slack witted with the last orgasm I had wrung from the farm-girl's punishment.

'Not by a long *telescope*,' she resumed, walking behind the farm-girl, kneeling behind her, and seeming to lift the eyepiece of the telescope up between the girl's thickly glistening thighs.

'Eh, my fine slut?' she said, and the farm-girl's gasp of horror and my own were simultaneous.

'Mina!' I ejaculated, forgetful of our role playing in my shock. '*What* are you doing?'

Mina's beautiful face, alight with an unholy glee of conscious sin, glanced back at me to the accompaniment of further gasps from the farm-girl. She was pushing the eyepiece gently home, inserting the telescope into the girl's pussy while preserving her maidenhead with a skill worthy of the medical role she had been playing and which she, at least, had not forgotten.

'She is a Bulgara, Madame Leona,' she said, her shoulders jerking slightly as she began to rock the telescope in the forbidden valley into which she had inserted it. 'And 'tis no perversion to pervert the perverted. Listen to her, Joanna. Just listen.'

She too had now forgotten our role playing in the excitement of hearing the farm-girl's love song: those

16

gasps of horror and affront were changed now to gasps of pleasure and lust, and Mina's shoulders jerked harder as she worked the telescope deeper and more vigorously in the girl's pussy.

I paused, torn between unparalleled disgust and unwilling delight: disgust at the perversity being enacted before me; delight at the sounds of pleasure and lust filling my ears – aye, and at the squelch and pop of the instrument whereby Mina brought them forth. I stepped forwards, undecided even as I moved whether to drag Mina by main force from her wickedness or to seize the telescope and assist her in its commission.

The farm-girl's loud and prolonged descent into orgasm countervened, and I stood irresolute. Mina, having gently rocked the last drops of pleasure out of the girl, withdrew the telescope with more pops and squelches of pussy-juice and turned to me, one of her sweet white fingers marking a point on the thickly glistening barrel.

'As high as this, Madame Leona,' she said. 'It is evident that the girl has been –' and a moment before she said the word, I saw a scalding blush irrigate her face '– *dildo'd* before.'

'Mina!' I cried, stung again to forgetfulness of our role playing as those forbidden syllables assaulted my disbelieving ears. 'How *could* you?'

'As easily as you could yourself, my darling,' she said, and held the telescope out to me, looking more beautiful and desirable than ever as the blush faded in her exertion-moistened cheeks. I heard my mouth, opened ready to heap more opprobrium on her, close with a snap, and my gut rolled with a rarely before experienced access of lust. Mina smiled with triumph as she saw my hesitation.

'Take it, my darling. It is thoroughly lubricated for the *next* stage of its journey.'

17

For a moment, I could not catch her meaning, and then my mouth fell open with horror to the accompaniment of Mina's silvery laughter. For if my mouth signalled my horror, my eyes signalled my lust, for they had flown involuntarily to the farm-girl's firm, stroke-marked bum cheeks, still quivering and twitching with the orgasm Mina had induced.

Silently, swallowing hard at a knot of commingled disgust and delight in my throat, I walked forwards, accepting the telescope from Mina's hand and kneeling behind the farm-girl. When I spoke, my voice trembled for a moment, then grew firm and unyielding, acquiring the surety of purpose of the fingers of my left hand, which were working between the girl's thighs, coating themselves thoroughly before working their load into her second and even more forbidden entrance: her lightly furred bumhole.

'Open for your mistress, girl. I am going to *dildo* your bottom.'

The girl's wits, still wandering in orgasm-haze, sharpened in an instant as I placed the eyepiece of the telescope on her anus, and she came to voluble life as I pushed slowly but relentlessly.

'*Ne! Ne!*' she wailed. 'Not *zadnik*! Not bummyhole! *Ne! Ne!*'

But the lust-thunder of blood in my ears was too loud for me to catch her words, which were twisted more barbarously than ever in her emotion, and mingled more and more with her uncouth mother tongue. Mina, watching with delight as I inserted the telescope, later said that the girl was rejecting the anal assault not on moral grounds but on the grounds that violation of her bottom was reserved for her mistress; and it certainly seemed true that she was nearly as familiar with a dildo in her bum as with a dildo in her pussy, for the deeper I slid the lubricated length of the

18

telescope, the more her cries of protest were interrupted with gasps and moans of pleasure.

When I began to diddle her clitoris in accompaniment with the insertion, seeking to brush aside the remaining thorns on her path to anal pleasure, all pretence seemed to be discarded: she positively began to *rock* her bottom at the firm length of the invader, seeking, it seemed, to welcome it more deeply more quickly, till suddenly, with a wail of surrender, she collapsed into orgasm again and I felt the telescope shift in my grasp as the sturdy muscles of her bottomhole fastened tight around it. Behind me, I heard Mina, who had evidently been frotting hard as she watched my assault on the girl's most intimate and forbidden orifice, gasping her way through an orgasm of her own.

Joanna Harker's Journal, 23 September (continued).

When we had wrung the time of her mistress's return out of the girl, the knowledge was already redundant, for her mistress interrupted a tonguing I was forcing her servant to perform on my inflamed pussy. But interrupted only for a moment: the mistress, whose Romanian was almost accentless, waved aside my polite offer to return the girl to her rightful service at once.

'Let the slut tongue you to your heart's content, my lady,' she said, having been directed across the field to our balloon by another of her farm-girls. 'I will in fact be most interested to hear what you make of her technique, for I have devoted some time to training her, and believe I have beaten her free of her earlier *bêtises*. "More pain on the bum, more pleasure through the tongue", as the old country saying runs.'

'I . . . ah . . . am most gr . . . ah . . . grateful to you, mistress,' I said, clutching the farm-girl's head more closely between my thighs. 'And may I ... ah ... congratulate you ... ah ... on the *cleanliness* of your farm-girl.'

'Why, thank you,' said the Bulgarian. 'You will find it holds true also of my other sluts, if you care to honour me by accepting my hospitality for a day or two before going on your way. When friends visit me from the city, I do not wish them to return with news that I have let my standards slip simply because I have exchanged urban life for rural.'

I tried to reply but was gasping too much now to succeed, and it was Mina who took up the slack of the conversation.

'Then you have not lived here long, mistress?'

Even as I rocketed into orgasm – truly the girl's technique was of surpassing excellence for a Bulgarian country slut's – I noted the reply and sent up thanks to the Goddess, for it seemed a stroke of unhoped-for luck.

'No, my lady. I am but recently retired from an administrative post in the Bulgarian Ministry of Education –' here her voice politely increased in volume to overtop my groans of deepest orgasm '– where I oversaw scientific training in our universities. My retirement here was long-planned, and grants the chance, after a gap of too many years for me to enumerate, to resume basic research.'

'And your speciality, mistress?' Mina asked.

'Sex and reproduction among the lower animals, my lady. I am a long-standing correspondent of the famous Georgian researcher Dr Helsingvili, of whom perhaps one or both of you may have heard.'

The news was enough to trigger a second orgasm in me even as I trembled in the after-throes of the first.

Joanna Harker's Journal, 24 September.

And now we find ourselves in Sofia, better positioned than we had dared hope to commence our campaign against the Count. Mina still regrets that we had to decline the offer of hospitality from Dr Zdravkova (the retired university administrator of the farm), but I have refrained from echoing her regrets, lest I encourage that too-strong hedonistic side of her nature. Certainly, it would have been delicious to continue acquaintance with that firm bottom we so mistreated on landing, and to extend the acquaintance to those as-firm breasts and scrubbed-tender nipples, but business must come before pleasure (my pussy remoistens at memory of the girl's tongue), and even Dr Zdravkova's promise that *all* of her girls were handpicked for firmness of bottom and breast and flexibility and size of tongue could not shake me.

Accordingly, having thanked her for her help and the money she willingly lent, we left the farm at dawn to travel in her pony-trap to the nearest station and catch a day train for Sofia. Dr Zdravkova selected our balloon-slut as driver, and Mina and I hugged, nipple-tweaked, and pussy-stroked each other with delight to observe how uncomfortable her bottom was on the trap's seat. When we arrived at the station, the girl sprang quickly down to help us descend, and both Mina and I, as we kissed her goodbye, took opportunity to seize and knead those ultra-sensitised bum cheeks, breathing in her gasps of pain and protest like perfume.

'Obey your mistress in all things, my girl,' I told her, now stroking and soothing the firm buttock flesh I had seized. 'And I prophesy that your tongue will prove your fortune. I will enquire your name when I write to thank her, and you may be sure that should

I return to Sofia in five or ten years' space, I will look you up in the cunnilingarium* in which I expect to find you. I almost pray, for your sake if not for mine, that I am unable to make a booking without protracting my stay to a month.'

And so we left the girl flushed chelce* with my compliments, and hurried to buy tickets for the Sofia day train. The yawning girl on the ticket counter, as slow-witted as she was large-breasted, was unable to understand our Romanian, and had to call for her overseer, whose eyes exchanged a flash of complicity with us even before we made our complaint and urged speedy punishment for the delay the girl had caused us. As we trotted hand in hand for the platform to which we had been directed, the overseer was bundling her already-weeping charge into her office; and as we began to descend the steps of a subway we heard the first crack of punishment begin behind us.

'A broad leather strap,' Mina pronounced, her hand tightening on mine in her excitement. She fell silent, waiting for the next crack to follow us down the steps, carried across yards of air from the purposefully left ajar door of the overseer's office.

'Yes,' Mina continued as it sounded. 'A broad leather strap, but it is being used at first on a *clothed* bottom. Later, I suggest –' her hand tightened again on mine as a third crack, distant now but perfectly distinct, came to our ears '– she will strip the slut's bum bare and use a *narrower* strap or –' she gasped with pleasure, for the blows sounding behind us were coming faster and faster, as though the overseer were unable to master her bum lust '– a *tawse* or *quirt*.'

When we reached our platform – too distant, alas, for Mina's prophecy to be confirmed – my darling began to describe how the counter-girl's bum would now be reddening beneath the blows of the strap, and though the train arrived within a few minutes, the pussies of both of us were oozing thickly as we climbed into a compartment. I pondered kidnapping a guard to service us as we travelled to Sofia, but was unsure whether a Bulgarian station would maintain sufficient staff to meet passengers' whims that were common enough in Romania.

When the train departed and no fellow passenger had joined us in our compartment, to be invited to sample our pussies if *bourgeoise*,* or forced to do so if *proletarienne*,* we stripped and soixante-neuf'd, Mina rudely – and calculatedly – commenting, as we neared repletion, that the altitude we had attained in our balloon flight seemed to have *weakened* the already thin flavour of my pussy-juice. That was the cue for the spanking for which I knew she had been longing since she heard the first blow land on the counter-girl's bum. So we passed the hour and a half *most* pleasantly that brought us to Sofia, where the first coin I spent was deposited on the palm of a *petite* station guard, with careful instructions in pidgin Romanian to lick the seat of our compartment clean of the pussy-juice with which it was streaked and stained. Mina wanted to stay and watch, but I was impatient for our hotel and the sleep with which we would refresh ourselves for the next stage of our campaign against the Count, and dragged her away almost by main force.

But it was she who fell asleep faster in our double bed, cradled in my arms, lips still pressed to the nipple she had been sucking, and I who sought sleep in vain for a time, pondering the events of the past twenfer* and seeking in them an overlooked vein of ore with which to forge further weapons against our unspeakable Enemy. Then I too slipped into sleep, to

23

awake most deliciously with Mina's lips and tongue gently roaming my thigh-hollows and pussy. When I had responded in suitable fashion (having discovered that we had slept a full further twenfer away), we rose, dressed, and broke fast before hastening to consult the Bulgarian official to whom Dr Zdravkova had given us a letter of introduction and who would, if Dr Zdravkova's promise held good, already be alerted to our presence in Sofia by telegram.

So it proved: when we had communicated our arrival, A–'s personal secretary (I employ a false initial to throw investigators off her track, should the worst come to the worst and the Count find some way, having laid hold of this journal, to visit retribution on those who have assisted us in Bulgaria) took us personally to the office in which A– awaited us, and we were soon discussing our . . . *mission*, should I call it? Campaign? Nay, best: crusade, for it is a holy task we have set our hands and our hearts to, to rid Romania – and all Europe, Transmarynia inclusive – of the foul contagion of the Count.

'Dr Zdravkova's telegram was cryptic, I must confess,' A– began, speaking Romanian around her pipe with a thick but by no means impenetrable or unpleasing accent, 'but I trust her implicitly, and if she recommends you to me, I will do all that lies in my power to assist you. You are but new-arrived from Bucharest, I take it?'

'Yes, mistress,' I returned, exchanging a glance of relief with Mina, for we had both already divined that our interlocutrix was, despite her somewhat ponderous manner and formal dress, no officious bureaucrat, but a woman of quick wit and ready sympathy. 'Or better say, but new-*fled* from Bucharest. We reach the shady haven of Bulgaria from a glare of evil that even now brightens to noonday brilliance in our capital.'

A– nodded with a puff at her pipe, her lips quirking momentarily with amusement at my extravagant but unrevealing rhetoric, and tossed across the table a newspaper dated the month before.

'Does what you speak of have some connexion, perhaps, with the advertisement on the front page?'

I took up the paper, which was evidently Sofia's Romanian-language daily, and the gasp that escaped me as my eye fell upon the bottom right corner of the front page was adequate reply to A–'s question. Mina's hand fell comfortingly to my shoulder a moment later, and I handed the paper back with an involuntary shudder.

'Yes, mistress. In fact I . . . I helped prepare the text for him, for *her*.' I corrected myself as I saw puzzlement in A–'s eye at the first pronoun I had employed. 'It was in Transmarynia only a few months back. But how did you guess that it would have some connexion with our flight from Bucharest?'

A– tapped the 'advert' with the mouthpiece of her pipe. 'This "Academy for Underprivileged Young Women of the Lower Classes" has interested my department for some time past,' she said, sucking on the pipe again with an incongruous squeak and cocking a benevolent eye at Mina's smile of amusement. 'It had the look – and I speak in strictest confidence, you both understand, of course? Good, good – the look of a *revolutionary* or *anarchist* enterprise. You hear little of it in Romania, perhaps, but we in Bulgaria have had much trouble with disciples of that pernicious hedge-philosopher Karla Marx. They are forever fomenting disorder and discontent in our serving classes, and though the rank and file are drawn from Bulgarian "natives" –' she grunted sardonically around her pipe '– the leadership is almost invariably of foreign extraction. Our suspicions were that the academy was to be a training school for a native generation of leaders all across Europe, Bulgaria too, but our investigations in Bucharest soon convinced us that it was no "socialist" –' another sardonic grunt '– enterprise we were dealing with, though neither did it seem the wholly charitable enterprise it presented itself as.

'There matters rested,' she went on, 'till Dr Zdravkova's telegram recalled the case to my attention. An enigma recalling a mystery, you might say, and I dug out the file on my arrival here this morning. We had plans, you know, to plant an *agent* in the academy. Indeed, our suspicions were so grave that my own secretary – when I tell you that her wits match her beauty you will gain some inkling of her calibre – would have taken on the role.'

Mina's gasp of horror and my own were simultaneous, for A–'s young secretary, whose crisp and confident typing we could hear through the closed door of A–'s office, had impressed us both deeply in the scant minute we had had in her company, and the thought of her in the hands of the Count, those firm breasts perverted to his nefandous usage, that fresh face soured with the misery of milk-slavery, was almost too much to bear. A–'s eyebrows lifted with surprise.

'What I say shocks you, my dear ladies? But I served myself as a foreign agent in my youth, like all of my senior colleagues, and no woman enters this branch of public service in ignorance of the dangers she may have to face for her motherland, be they at home or abroad.'

I had Mina's hand in mine, squeezing it comfortingly, and shook my head in response to A–'s words.

'No, mistress, we are both familiar, in principle at least, with such work; it is just that we know . . . we

26

know what your secretary might have faced should she have undertaken the task of infiltrating the academy – and believe me, it is a horror beyond the imagining, though not, alas, beyond the remembering.'

'Then you yourselves have experience of some similar academy?' A– asked.

'No.'

I bowed my head for a moment, bright memories overwhelming me, and now it was Mina's hand tightening in comfort on mine.

'No, mistress,' I resumed. 'I speak of the proprietrix, not the property. Of the . . . the *woman* who will run the place. I endured a captivity by her in Transmarynia, and have a ready sympathy born of heavy experience for all her victims, past, present and to come.'

'But what actually is it that she *does*?' A– asked me. 'And why is the criminal law helpless against her if it involves mistreatment of others as severe as that I read in your face, my lady? Why, too, did you hesitate when you spoke of her as a "woman"? Do her crimes place her beyond the pale of human nature?'

'"No, mistress. Say rather that her *person* places her beyond the pale of human nature. When I speak of her as a monster, I do so in a double sense: as a prodigy of wickedness, and a prodigy of nature.'

'I am afraid you speak in riddles, my lady. Do not fear to confide in me: I have handled many a weighty matter of state involving our two nations, and have never brought either to harm by indiscretion.'

I glanced at Mina, asking her permission to proceed, and she nodded fractionally.

'But perhaps,' said A–, pressing a bell on her desk, 'we would all three be better for a glass of *mavrud*.'*

27

The typing in the next room stopped and we heard the secretary stride across the floor. The door opened, and there she was, more attractive than ever now that we knew of the peril she had narrowly escaped. That one so young, so beautiful, so firm-breasted might have fallen into the Count's hands tightened my throat and positively brought tears to Mina's eyes (she has informed me) as we gazed upon her.

A– gave instructions in Bulgarian, and I heard Mina sniff as the secretary swung efficiently on her heel, her excellent bottom swaying at us for a moment in the doorway, and strode away to fetch the *mavrud*. Soon we were sipping at it, Mina cocking half an ear (she later revealed) to the resumed typing in the next room, as I described the nature and deeds of the Count in greater detail. As I spoke, I saw horror and understanding come over the face of A–, who soon laid down her glass, as though sickened with my recital of the Count's crimes. Then she held up her hand for a halt.

'No further description is necessary, dear lady. I extract as much understanding of this monster from your own expression, and your beautiful femme-wife's,* as from your words. Either alone would suffice; together, they doubly convince of your truth and of the peril Romania and my nation – all Europe – presently face. As much as is in my power to do, I will do, but that seems little, I confess. My official writ does not run across your border, and if all you say of this countess's w–'

' "Count",' I interrupted her gently. ' "Count" is how she denominates herself, mistress, or rather how *he* denominates *himself*. I had a bitter lesson in language in that Welsh castle.'

'Aye,' said A–. 'Foul words from a fouler past. This "count", then, if all you say is true of her wealth

28

and the corruption it has already brought about in your countryfolk, then what little power I possess in Bucharest dwindles further. We – and I must request that this confidence go no further? Thank you – we have agents, of course, in your capital, but none are high-placed, and though Romania herself is aware of all of them –' a flicker in her eye told me that this was perhaps not strictly true '– by international convention she pays no official heed, just as we pay no official heed of your agents in Sofia, should they remain within limits of acceptable espionage. So there can be little hope of help from that quarter. What, may I ask, had you planned to do against this, this count, on arriving in Bulgaria?'

I looked at Mina, and snorted ruefully.

'We have looked little beyond our escape, Mistress A–,' I said. 'But our chief hopes rested on a swift exposure of his schemes. If it becomes known widely what he purposes, what *manner* of being he is, then his plots are bootless. His staff and students will watch him with a suspicious eye, deserting him or reporting him to the authorities at the slightest misstep.'

'For that you need the press,' A– said. 'And the press of Bucharest herself. But would they not demand proof of your claims? You might, with my assistance, get up an agitation on Bulgarian soil, but would the rumour carry so far as Bucharest, and last long here, if the "Count" works to suppress it, as surely he must? But what has struck you, my lady? I see from your face that some new dismay is upon you.'

'I have recalled the heavy advertising he has run in our press, mistress, and the promises made of further to come, when he opens a second and third academy in our provinces. Our papers will not be anxious to offend a source of ready income, and I guess, knowing his cunning and unscrupulousness as I do, that he will already be hastening to befriend the editors of Bucharest. With so many young girls at his disposal, I fear he will find it no difficult task. Alas for our decadence! In cleanlier days he would have found it impossible to gain a foothold as he has, and my stomach still revolts at the thought of those countrywomen of mine assisting him in his . . . *deeds* in that clearing.'

'You think he plans to prostitute the students of his academy?'

'Aye. Half brothel, half milking-shed, that is what it will be. The jaded sensuates of Bucharest will flock to it like wasps to spoiled fruit. There is nothing like a fresh face and a foreign accent to spark tired loins, Mistress A–, as no doubt you learned on your own sojourns abroad.'

A– nodded, half in response to my words, half in abstraction as she followed some memory of her own. Then she looked up, her eye sparking with sudden authority.

'Advertising, you say. He spent heavily on advertising.'

'Yes,' I returned, wondering where the point led.

'For students?'

'Yes.'

'But not students alone.'

'No. N . . .' Then it struck me. 'No. Not students alone. Also for *teachers*.'

A– nodded. 'My thoughts exactly.'

She jabbed the bell on her desk again, and the typing stopped again in the next room. When her secretary opened the door, A– spoke swiftly in Bulgarian and she nodded, replied, '*Da*, Madame A–,' and left us again.

30

'I have asked her to fetch today's copy of this –' she tapped the paper lying on her desk '– Romanian-language daily. If this count of yours – nay, forgive me, I forget our European common peril – of all ours is still seeking Bulgarian teachers for her academy, then there is your opportunity. You can apply, and with the references I can supply for you, I have strong hope that you will be accepted and, in suitable disguise, be able to enter his service.'

'Then he has advertised for teachers here?' I asked, hearing the tremor in my own voice, for I confess that the prospect of entering the Count's employ again awoke painful memories.

'Yes, my lady. But with what you have told me, I fear it is no tribute to the excellence of our teachers' training or steadiness of their professionalism. Bulgaria has, half to our sorrow, half, alas, to our secret pride, a certain . . . *reputation* outside her borders, has she not?'

'It is true, mistress,' I admitted, not daring to meet Mina's eye, for it doubtless glowed with mischief at the thought of our shared farm-girl. 'All the pain-brothels *de luxe* of Bucharest offer two or three Bulgarian dominants to their submissive customers. "As thirsty earth for summer rain, so hungry bum for Bulgara's pain", so our saying runs.'

A– chuckled, relighting her pipe, which she had put aside when the *mavrud* was brought in.

'There was a police case not so long ago,' Mina added in her clear sweet voice, in which I – and plainly A– too – could catch a throb of excitement, 'when one such dominant carried her domineering . . . to excess.'

Her eyes were fixed on A–'s as she spoke, as A–'s were fixed on hers, and I wondered jealously for a moment if she were gauging the dominance that lay within, and imagining the out-of-hours relationship between A– and her beautiful young secretary. But A– broke their locked gaze with a glance at me and a puff on her pipe.

'No injuries, I hope?' she said, returning her gaze to Mina.

'None,' said Mina, with faint disappointment. 'Only use of certain . . . instruments.'

'Ah,' said A–. 'Our reputation goes before us. I have no doubt that this count has counted on it in her recruitment from our schools. It is possible – for your national honour's sake I hope probable – that these masked women who assisted him in that clearing were Bulgarian, the scum of our sea ports or of our slums in Sofia. He has no doubt been recruiting for his academy through channels both legitimate and illegitimate.'

At this point there was a soft knock at the door, and A–'s secretary entered with the newspaper A– had requested. A– motioned her to hand it to me.

'It will fill a quarter page if it is there, like all the others,' she said.

I scanned the front page, then the second and third, and there it was, the bold type in the heading tightening my throat with fear and disgust, for it spoke to me of the cruelty and dominance of the Count himself.

'Yes, Mistress A–,' I said. 'He is advertising still for Bulgarian staff.'

'Excellent,' said A–. 'Then are you prepared to apply for posts in his academy, and to seek a way of overthrowing him from within?'

I exchanged a glance with Mina, and she swallowed, then nodded slowly and with evident reluctance.

'We are, Mistress A–,' I said. 'Though I believe that a series of anonymous letters despatched to public figures with denunciations of the Count should also be tried.'

'It can do no harm,' said A–. 'And if it succeeds – I must confess to doubts – it will save you entering the lioness's den. But they must be worded carefully, to carry conviction, and I believe it would be most unwise to despatch them from Bulgaria, lest this count, with all her bestial cunning, sniff some connexion with your job applications. Despatch from Transmarynia itself might be best, do you think?'

I thought a moment, then nodded. 'Yes. What they might lose in immediate prestige, coming from such a barbarous realm, they would gain in verisimilitude. She who writes of a Transmarynian from Transmarynia might be expected to know whereof she speaks.'

'Then if you will undertake to write them within the week, I will undertake to have them in your homeland within the fortday.* No, do not concern yourself: they will be copied in another's hand before they are sent in the diplomatic bag to London, for the personal attention of the *chargé d'affaires* whom my department employs.'

I smiled and nodded, for she had read my thoughts exactly from my face: I *had* quailed at the prospect of the letters bearing my own handwriting, so well known to the Count, or Mina's, also known to him. It seemed likely that one of the public figures at least to whom they were despatched, or members of their personal staff, were corrupted by the Count and that the originals themselves would soon be in his hands.

'Your *curricula vitae* you must leave in my hands,' A– continued. 'You will both be natives of Lom, on the Romanian border, where Bulgarian is little spoken, but you must both acquire a minimum vocabulary and grammar in our tongue before you leave, and be trained in a suitable accent. I will place our entire school of espionage at your disposal, and I beg that you match my willingness to assist with a willingness to apply yourselves hard to your studies. I have overseen many missions before, and none I can remember presented my agents with a tenth of the danger of this.'

'None could know it better than I, Mistress A–,' I said.

'Perhaps so. But you must impress the danger firmly on your charming femmewife here, for I confess I recoil at the thought of sending one so young and beautiful into the hands of such a monster.'

Mina beamed at this, the minx, and I could see that her tale of the police case had awoken A–'s lustful interest in her.

'I will certainly impress the danger on her, Mistress A–,' I said. 'And reimpress it, lest the initial marks fade.'

Mina's beam was replaced with a look of apprehension as the meaning of my words sunk in, and A– chuckled heartily, puffing hard at her pipe.

'I intend that your curricula vitae will, for any normal employer, disqualify both of you with hints, and more than hints, of a criminal record. But please, my dear lady Joanna, do not acquire in actuality what I intend to bestow on you in scheming fantasy.'

Mina snorted. 'I am not so easily dominated, mistress,' she said. 'And "Soft rump may outstay strong hand", to quote one of those old-fashioned sayings Joanna is so fond of.'

'I know it well,' A– replied, with a glance at the door to her secretary's room that told us both our speculations anent their relationship were correct. 'But strong hand has the sweeter side of it, even when leaving the fair field with struck colours.'

34

'So the dominant believe,' Mina said, with that familiar toss of her small round chin. 'But the field wherein thorns are sown may yield roses in despite.'

A– laughed now, removing the pipe from her mouth and stabbing the mouthpiece at my little spitfire.

'She challenges us, thee and me, my lady Joanna,' she said, 'and we dominants of Bulgaria are not accustomed to let such challenges pass unmet. I promise my secretary will not disturb us – unless it be by way of assistance – so may I invite you to "Play your pawn", as *our* saying goes?'

'*După a locului obicei* . . .'* I said, and sprang upon my beautiful young femmewife. Her shriek stilled the typing in the next room for a second, but it resumed the second after, and I realised that Madame A– must have often conducted such sessions in her office. Aye, often, for the easy skill with which, leaning forwards over her desk, she seized Mina's wrists and pulled her torso flat atop the desk spoke of frequent practice. I had already gripped Mina's knees between my thighs and was lifting her skirt and petticoats, exposing the ivory and silk of her bottom and rear thighs and sending a ruthless hand to roam and stroke their curves and hollows as she jerked and struggled, with muffled screams against the baize of A–'s desk.

'If you are prepared to begin your lessons in Bulgarian *now*,' remarked A–, having to raise her voice a little above Mina's commotion, 'then count off the strokes after my example.'

'A most excellent suggestion,' I said, sniffing suspiciously and pushing a finger up between Mina's thighs and testing the state of her pussy. It was already gaping and flooded, and anger flared up inside me at the thought of how long she had been anticipating this spanking, and manipulating us two dominants into administrating it. Well, we would see how pleased she was with herself when it was done, for my jealousy of A– was quite dissolved in my anger, and I was resolved to invite her to top my own spanking with a spanking of her own.

'Then I shall recite the numbers,' said A–. 'And you shall repeat each after me. Very well? Very well, then. I shall begin when you nod, one to ten.'

I allowed myself a moment's more stroking of Mina's silk-skinned bottom, then raised my hand, drew a breath, closed my eyes with a prayer to the Goddess for strength, opened my eyes, and nodded.

'*Edno*,' said A–.

I brought my hand down with a thunderclap.

'*Edno*,' I repeated.

'No,' said A–. '*Edno*.'

I brought my hand down again, *thwack*.

'*Edno*,' I repeated.

The typing stopped once more in the next room before beginning again, though it was oddly slower as th–

'*Dve*,' said A–.

Down my hand came for the second (ha!) time.

'*Dve*,' I repeated.

The typing was definitely slower, and oddly unco-ordinated, and my nipples, already peaked hard with bum-lust, throbbed painfully as I realised what A–'s beautiful young secretary must be doing in the next room, one ear cocked to the sound of Mina's chastisement.

'*Tri*,' said A–, her face beginning to sweat faintly with the effort of holding Mina's wrists to her desk.

'*Tri*,' I repeated.

The effort of holding Mina in place with only *one* hand; the other was busy, like her secretary's, be-tween her thighs as she gorged her ears on the sounds of firm palm meeting soft bum.

'*Ne, tri.*'

Down came my hand again, *crash*, and now Mina cried out with her first genuine pain-plea.

'*Tri*,' I repeated, my breast flooded with envy of the two masturbating Bulgaras, for I could not devote a hand to my own thickly oozing pussy.

'*Chetiri*,' A– said.

My sob of frustration and the crash of palm meeting buttock were simultaneous.

'*Chetiri*,' I repeated.

'*Pet.*'

Down came my hand for the seventh-time-that-was-only-the-fifth. '*Pet*,' I repeated.

'*Ne, pet.*' A– said, and I could hear little, if any, difference between her pronunciation and my own.

Thwack.

'*Pet*,' I repeated. The rhythm of A–'s moving hand was quickening now, and in the next room the typing had slowed to almost nothing. I wondered how many errors A– would find in the documents her young secretary was preparing, and what penalty she would inflict for each.

'*Shest*,' said A–.

'*Shest*,' I repeated, and *thwack* down came my hand. But through the echo of Mina's wail there was a squirt of liquid meeting the carpeted floor of A–'s office. I sniffed, drawing the unmistakable aroma of piss-spice into my nostrils, but I had to cough to attract A–'s attention: her head had gone back and her tongue was writhing in one corner of her mouth as she masturbated harder and faster.

'M– my lady?' she said.

'She has pissed on the carpet on your floor, Mistress A–,' I told her. 'A regular trick of hers, when the throes of pain overwhelm her. Ah, no, you don't, you slut!'

37

This last was addressed to Mina, who, fastened at knee and wrist, was attempting to rub herself out an orgasm by shuffling and squeezing together her thighs. The sound of A–'s own masturbation ceased, and she rose in her seat, still clutching Mina's wrists with one strong hand as she tried to see what Mina was doing.

'She is thigh-frotting herself, Mistress,' I told her, trying to prevent the unlawful deed by thrusting my hand between her thighs and keeping them apart. 'Have you perchance straps or ropes, with which to restrain her?'

A–'s free hand descended hard on her bell, but the disjointed typing continued in the next room till her hand descended again. My hand was fully between Mina's thighs now, squeezed and slimed as she struggled to satisfy her criminal desires. Now the door to A–'s office opened behind me, and the secretary's voice said something unsteadily in Bulgarian. A– replied in the same tongue, there was a brief pause in which I could hear the secretary opening a drawer in the next room, and then the feet of the secretary were returning to A–'s office.

In a moment she was assisting me to lash Mina's feet apart with slender but unbreakable cords fastened to the feet of A–'s desk, and my nipples throbbed again as I smelt the sex-scent from her, sharp and distinct through the familiar reek of Mina's now exposed pussy, and felt the moisture on her right hand as it brushed against mine. A– had to speak sharply to the girl before, with evident reluctance, she left the office, closing the door behind her, and I listened for her typing to resume as I readied myself to continue beating Mina.

'She has soiled your floor badly, I am afraid, Madame A–,' I said. 'And continues to do so now.

There is a steady drip of pussy-juice into the piss-patch. She is positively flooded. See?'

I rummaged between Mina's splayed thighs, tormenting her with a vigorous but too brief fondling, then held up glistening fingertips for A–'s inspection.

'Aye,' said A–. 'And I *smell* the slut.' She drew in air heavily through her nostrils. 'Tobacco has never destroyed my nose for a ripening pussy,' she said complacently. 'And I could smell *hers* from almost the minute you entered my office.'

I made no reply to this for a moment, and Mina's buttocks, already heavily marked with my palm print, quivered with telepathic dread as my eyes flashed to them in threat.

'Yes, mistress,' I said. 'You will see how her odour heightens even further as I continue. But which number had we reached? Four, was it not?'

'Aye,' said A–. 'Four. On your nod, my lady.'

I took another deep breath, holding my hand an inch above Mina's buttocks, feeling the heat that was radiating from them. How the poor dear must already have been suffering! And yet greater still must be her suffering of mind, as she reflected that she had barely surmounted the foothills of her ascent to the peak of pain whereto we would raise her, A– and I.

Another deep breath.

I nodded.

'*Chetiri.*'

Thwack.

'*Chetiri,*' I repeated.

'*Ne, chetiri.*'

Thwack.

'*Chetiri.*'

A– had resumed her masturbation, her eyes half closed as she rocked in her chair, her other hand locked as firmly as ever on Mina's wrists.

39

'*Pet.*'

Thwack.

'*Pet,*' I repeated through Mina's moan of pain, and suddenly A– was groaning too, but with orgasm. As though some psychic sympathy existed between the two of them, I heard a near simultaneous groan from the next room, where A–'s secretary too had apparently orgasmed, delighting on the mere sound of Mina's chastisement.

A– was lifting her left hand from between her thighs now, still gripping Mina's slender wrists firmly with her right. She dipped its glistening fingertips in the pool of tears shining on the desk beneath Mina's face and she sucked them cleanly one by one, savouring the musk of her own pussy and the brine of Mina's tears, then dipping them again in the pool.

' "The salt of her tears is sweeter than honey",' she said. 'A quotation from a favourite poetess of mine. It is a sure sign of a born submissive. But please do not let me delay our session any longer. At your nod, my lady.'

I had seized the opportunity to assault the overflowing well of my own pussy, tweaking the lips and thrumming at the aching little tower of my pussy-horn; but I disciplined myself, vowing not to orgasm till the first tranche of spanking had been completed. Another deep breath, and I nodded.

'*Shest,*' A– said.

Thwack.

'*Shest,*' I repeated.

'*Sedem.*'

Thwack.

'*Sedem,*' I repeated.

'*Ne, sedem.*'

Thwack. A squeak of protest from Mina, and I heard the cords lashing her ankles to the table twang as she struggled.

'*Sedem*,' I repeated.

'*Ne, se-dem.*'

Thwack. The cords twanged again, and now A– had to seize Mina's wrists in both hands.

'*Sedem*,' I repeated.

A– nodded with satisfaction. '*Osem*,' she said.

Thwack. More twangs from the cords.

'*Osem*,' I repeated.

'*Devet*.'

Thwack.

'*Devet*,' I repeated.

'*Ne, devet*.'

Thwack. Now Mina raised her head, mewing something I did not catch to A–.

'*Devet*,' I repeated. 'What is she asking, Mistress?'

'*Deset*,' A– said. 'I am afraid . . .' *Thwack*. My palm-stroke on Mina's bum drowned her words for a moment '. . . catch it.'

'*Deset*,' I repeated. Mina was repeating her words, too, and now A– grunted with surprise.

'It is *Bulgarian*, my lady Joanna. She is asking – in a commendable accent but with the most uncouth vocabulary – for her pussy to be serviced. Orgasm, if you please, and the spanking nowhere near its end.'

'Did you say Bulgarian?' I asked.

'Yes. Bulgarian. Were you aware that she had ever taken a Bulgarian lover?'

'She never spoke of it before I left for Transmarynia, and I am certain that there has been none since I returned. And in the interval she was, she assured me, chaste as a statue.'

'Plainly, then, she has lied to you,' A– said. 'Or concealed some episode in her past. She has been suffered at the hands of a Bulgarian dominant at least once in her past, and been taught those words by her.'

41

'Then we will get to the bottom of this before we take our leave of you, Madame A–. If you would care to take over spanking duties, while I watch and wank as you have done?'

'Certainly, my lady Joanna. But might I suggest that we have my secretary in to prepare her for my unworthy efforts on her bottom?'

'She too is a spanker?' I asked, somewhat surprised to hear it.

'Ah, no, you mistake my meaning, my lady. She is spankee, not spanker, and I suggest that we set her to work on your femmewife's overexcited pussy with tongue, lips and teeth.'

'If it is the Bulgarian custom,' I said, 'so early –'

A– held up her hand.

'No,' she said. 'Again you mistake my meaning. My secretary will not bring your femmewife to orgasm. No, she will set to work on her overexcited pussy . . . and overexcite it still further. Your femmewife will be moaning for release, I promise you. My secretary is an expert in pushing girls to the brink of the gulf of ecstasy, and leaving them there, stranded, a tormenting inch from the endless fall.

'Then she draws them back, and again pushes them to the brink. Then again, if I choose to command her. And again. And again. And again. Then we pause, and then I set her to work on the girl's breasts and nipples, if it be necessary.

'But it rarely is. I promise you, we have had girls broken completely after no more than half an hour's acquaintance with her mouth on their pussies. They exchange all they know for the orgasm she has repeatedly allowed them to approach but not to embrace. To watch her is to see a truly great artist at work, my lady Joanna. But this must, of course, go no further.'

I nodded, tapping my mouth with a Mina-musked forefinger.

'I see. This is part of her professional duties?'

'Yes. She is already our most prized torturess, and yet she uses *pleasure* to torture native criminals and the captured agents of foreign powers. But pleasure is a means to an end, my lady, a road to the palace of orgasm, and it is better never to travel than to travel endlessly and never arrive. As you will see, if you grant me permission to call my secretary in.'

I looked at Mina's bottom and the glistening splay of her thighs beneath it. 'Madame A–,' I said, maliciously slipping my hand between those thighs and delicately tickling her pussy. 'I shall be delighted to grant you permission for your expert to torture my deceitful and carpet-soiling minx to the point of madness with this orgasm-denying mouth of hers.'

A– clapped her hands with pleasure as Mina moaned in protest and began to struggle again to free herself from her bonds.

Joanna Harker's Journal, 24 September. Evening.

The above was written on our return from A–'s office, when poor Mina was still to recover fully from the attentions of A–'s young secretary. Ah, young, but infinitely wise in the ways of a pussy, like a dolphin herding silver fish for a fisherwoman in a tale of ancient Greece, and able to direct them precisely where it chooses. Poor Mina was brought to the brink of orgasm seven times, five times via her pussy, once via her nipples, once via her pussy again, and each time was plainly worse than the last, till she was moaning with tear-stained cheeks for release! I was almost ready to call off the torture and twiddle her to rough-and-ready orgasm with a finger on her clit, but

A– shook her head as she sent her secretary back to her typing duties with a solid palm on her bum. She began to roll up her sleeve, ready to begin the spanking.

'No,' she said. 'Now we wait a minute, and I spank an orgasm out of her. It will be stronger than any she has known before, I promise you, but the worst of it, for her, is that it will leave her unsatisfied. The nerves of her sexual centres have been stretched too tight by my secretary's tongue, and will not relax again for hours. You will have to bring her to orgasm several times more after you leave, and then allow her to soak in a cool bath and frot herself to several more. But I must thank you most sincerely, my lady Joanna, for allowing me such a sight as this.'

She spoke of Mina strapped face down to the table, palm-burnished bum bare, thighs splayed, pussy swollen and oozing like a huge split fig, but smelling sweeter than a fig by far. A– stepped forwards and gently, with the merest edge of a fingernail, began to trace the curves of Mina's bum, murmuring throatily to herself in Bulgarian. Then she stepped back, beginning to flex the fingers of her spanking hand.

'*Magnifique*,' she said. 'Such a bum as this I have not seen for many months and –' she sniffed long and lovingly '– such a sweet-scented pussy has not crossed my path for two years. It was that of a Romanian submissive then, too, my lady Joanna, fresh across the border. I believe it is something in your diet, or in your water. And now, if I may begin?'

'Certainly, mistress. But you will forgive my curiosity if I ask what it was you were saying to yourself just now, as you inspected the *champ de bataille*?'*

'It is a little ritual of mine,' A– said with a half-embarrassed laugh. 'I was a mountaineer in my youth, and now, when I encounter a fresh pair of breasts or buttocks, I like to imagine them as

44

identical peaks, and myself leading an assault with a team of eager novices. I climb one; I plant my flag; I conquer. And then –' she stepped to spanking range, turning her head to raise her eyebrows at me for final permission '– I climb the other.'

I granted permission with a nod.

Thwack.

Her hand descended on Mina's twin peaks, then darted in again to pinch and knead. Now it swung back, and

Thwack.

Only a single pinch as the hand darted back in, and she held her fingers together as she withdrew her hand, so that a ridge of soft bum flesh came with it, then was released before

Thwack.

It was a virtuosa performance, a veteran spanker of exceptional skills at the height of her powers working on a bum worthy of her finest efforts, and I could only swallow my envy and watch, hoping to pick up hints of technique, and praying that Mina would not find my own efforts inadequate after this. The pinches, the kneadings, the speed and weight of the spanks A– delivered seemed to vary capriciously, but from Mina's ever-growing state of agitation – her sighs and groans, the tremors that ran through her body, the increasing thickness and scent of her pussy secretions – I knew that A– was skilfully manoeuvring her to orgasm, sliding her back to the brink of the abyss over which her secretary had refused to push her.

But what was this? Panting, with glowing eyes and quivering bosom, A– was stepping back and gesturing forwards at Mina's bum with that well-practised instrument of gluteal torture: her sturdy right hand.

'My lady Joanna, only yours can be the honour of firing the train that blows your darling to atoms. But quick – delay would be dangerous for her, and might leave her requiring medical attention. A firm stroke must be delivered to her buttocks within ten seconds, of medium strength but with a tightly locked wrist. Can you supply it?'

I hesitated a moment, and with a click of her tongue she seized and dragged me into position, holding me from behind, taking hold of my right wrist and swinging my hand back, ready to deliver the spank of which she had spoken. Dominant though I am, I confess that A–'s strong hands and the solidity of her body and breasts against my back shook me with a secret delight of submission, so that for a moment I wished *I* were in Mina's place, moaning with the pain of A–'s palm in my buttocks, my dripping pussy on humiliating display for all to see.

But I was shaken only a moment, for sight of Mina's buttocks, ready for my hand, brought me back to myself, and I breathed deep with sudden resolution. Evidently feeling the quiver that ran through me, A– released hold of me and stepped back with a breathy murmur.

'Strike,' she said. 'The ten seconds are nearly up.'

But I waited, asserting myself in face of her order, believing that I could judge Mina's state of arousal as well or better than she. My darling was dangerously aroused, her pussy and her breasts heavily engorged with blood, but she could boil a moment or two longer. And then I was seized by sudden joy, fiercer and stronger than that aroused by A–'s hands on my body, and it was the Goddess Herself breathing 'Strike!' in my ear. Such an order I could not disobey.

Thwack.

Ah, never have I been prouder of a blow: it fulfilled A–'s instructions to the letter, but I added a caress and pinch as I drew my hand back, breathless with excitement at the sequela, my ears still ringing with Mina's almost piglike grunt of ecstatic pain. She has told me before that in being spanked one of the most potent spurs to extra pleasure is the humiliation of having her pussy on full display between her splayed thighs; but never has she spoken the words with such fervour as on our return to our hotel. The thought, she tells me, of both her butchwife and a Bulgarian official feasting their eyes on her pussy caused her more acute shame than she has ever known before, and deepened and widened the abyss of orgasm into which my final blow tumbled her.

I have told her in my turn, tickling and teasing the object of my remarks, that never before have I seen her pussy writhe and spasm with such abandon, or seen the tendons in her thighs so sharply and clearly defined, or smelt the musks of her pussy-juice and sweat so powerfully and nipple-stiffeningly compounded. This was an orgasm of orgasms, something to treasure in memory for both her who experienced and her who brought about, and I send a thousand blessings to A– for granting me the opportunity to land that final blow. Though Mina is breathless in her admiration for the skill with which A– spanked her, she tells me she experienced no true worship for the hand that fell on her buttocks or tweaked and pinched them: the pain-joy she had of it was all of the head and not at all of the heart.

But that final blow, delivered, she somehow managed to learn through the pounding of blood in her ears, by the hand of her own true Joanna – ah, she worshipped *that* hand, and fell screaming into the abyss treasuring the memory of its loving cruelty and its cruel love. Yes, A– is a shrewd reader of women's hearts and minds, and I am very glad that she puts her wisdom to good ends and not ill, for I have little doubt that she could have driven a wedge between Mina and me with her spanking. Mina laughingly denies it, and tries to kiss away what she calls my doubts of her eternal affection, but she who has experienced true evil – as I have done in the castle and dungeon of the Count – cannot easily be free of its taint. Yes, already the lightness of heart in which I left A–'s office has begun to evaporate, for I feel that blazing Sun beat upon me from Bucharest, where the Count plots and meditates upon his future evils. We must and will defeat him – and my lightness of heart returns a little when I consider that he now has A– ranged against him. A foe of such calibre might cause momentary doubt in even one as arrogant as he. But Mina here demands that I extend my praise to A–'s secretary, whose tongue and lips will, she says, live as long in her memory, though not as powerfully, as the hand of the mistress.

Entry on a separate sheet in Joanna Harker's private shorthand. Again I risk much by committing this to paper, but again Mina is willing and again the risk heightens the excitement of reminiscence. Yes, I have not told all that took place in A–'s office, for there was a sequel to that final and most shattering of Mina's orgasms. And yet it was not the final, for A–, with a loving pat and caress to Mina's bum as she passed it, returned to her chair and unlocked a secret drawer. The bat's squeak as she slid it open, eloquent of infrequent use, took my eyes away from Mina's quivering flesh and dripping pussy for a moment; and then they were held by what A– was lifting forth: a narrow leather case battered and stained with a century's usage.

I watched as A– laid the case on her desk, put her thumbs on the twin catches, and looked up at me. A smile lit her face for a moment, and then, as she winked, her thumbs sprung the catches and the case jerked open. I sniffed, catching a sudden sharp and for a moment unclassifiable scent. Then I felt my mouth fall open at what A– lifted forth: a giant ivory d– (even in this code I feel a horror of committing the name to paper), knobble-lengthed and bulb-ended like some nightmare instrument of perverted torture, and fitted at the other end with straps of new leather – this was the sharp scent I had caught as the case was opened. A– looked up at me again, and her smile broadened at the emotion on my face.

'The more the thing disgusts you now, my lady Joanna, the more delight you will have in its use.'

An urge to flee the room flared up in me, over-whelming even the knowledge that to do so would leave Mina at A–'s mercy, but my legs seemed paralysed and I could but swallow dryly as A– rose from her chair and carried the blasphemous instrument to me.

'Strip, my dear lady. It must be strapped to your loins before you –' her voice sank to a lascivious whisper, sharp and sin-inviting as the serpent's voice in Eden '– *penetrate* her. Here, I will help you.'

The straps of the d– rattled as she laid it on her desk and began to help me out of my clothes – or rather, to strip my clothes from me, for I could lift not a finger to assist. My paralysis had passed into shivering, and my will to resist or flee had melted into a daze. A– was still whispering to me, sewing her purpose to my brain and tightening the stitches with merciless hands.

'Ah, I see you are a virgin to this, my lady, but I promise, you will never have felt –' her fingers were busy on my collar and sleeves '– the likes before. If you think you have tasted the joys of domination before, think again. You have but –' off came my blouse '– sipped at the rim of the cup, never quaffed fully. Ah, my lady Joanna –' down slid my skirt '– to know that I am initiating you into this mystery gives me joy almost as deep as if –' her fingers were busy on the ribbons of my knickers '– I were to *fuck* your femmewife myself. As I have –' she stooped to slide them down, breathing in deep of my pussy-scent '– *fucked* so many girls so many times before with my . . . instrument.'

She turned from me on the word and lifted her 'instrument', stooping again to begin strapping it to my loins. My body shivered uncontrollably as the leather straps brushed my skin, and even a murmur from Mina, as she began to surface from her orgasmic swoon, could not return me to full awareness of myself. A– was looping two of the straps around my waist, and binding them fast behind me. Now she reached between my thighs, seized a third strap, and tugged it up hard against my pussy and perineum. The cool ivory base of the d– butted against my upper pussy as the third strap was bound into place, and now A–'s skilful hand was adjusting it to my pussyhorn, jiggling it as she asked with whispers whether it was comfortable.

I swallowed again and managed to croak out a reply. She nodded, made the final adjustment to the base, then gave final tightenings to the three straps that held the nefandous engine firmly to, and jutting from, my lustless and shrivelled loins. And yet I realised to my horror, as A– stepped back from me, that they were *not* lustless, *not* shrivelled, but on the contrary throbbing with new and unholy life. A– spoke again, and this time at normal volume, in a voice of congratulation and friendly command.

'She awaits your pleasure, butchwife. Her pussy gapes for you. Unleash your lust on her and know domination beyond your brightest dreams.'

I tried to avert my eyes, but they fixed despite myself on Mina's bottom and splayed thighs, and on the oozing slit beneath the one and between t'other: her sweet pussy, ah, Goddess forgive me, her sweet *tight* pussy. The thought could have swung me one of two ways: into retching nausea; into flaring lust. For a moment the balance was exact and my mind hung poised; and then A–, reading my mental struggles with consummate and loving skill, tipped the balance with a whisper. 'Plough her, farmer.'

With a growl of lust, I advanced on my helpless victim, one hand seizing the solid head of the d– as with the other I unfolded her slick and swollen pussy-lips.

'Lady Mina, prepare to receive thy mistress,' A– intoned. 'Lady Joanna, prepare to thrust.'

Mina stirred and struggled, feeling the bulbous head of my monstrous loin-engine brush her pussy. She was starting to emerge from her orgasmic daze, and I could see her trying to look behind and see what I was doing.

'Lady Mina: receive. Lady Joanna: *thrust*.'

I thrust, but in my inexperience and excitement the d– head slid at an angle, barely penetrating Mina's pussy before sliding forth and prodding harmlessly at her thigh. A–'s loving laugh soothed away my chagrin and I put the bulb-head back in place.

'If at first you don't succeed,' A– chanted, 'thrust, thrust, and thrust ag–'

But her voice was drowned by Mina's cry of shock, horror and protest: the head of the d– was inside her, firmly lodged, and with another jerk of my hips I could slide deep inside her. My head was singing with excitement, my heart pounding like a steam hammer, my lips, fingertips, and nipples tingling and smarting, but my loins

51

had become like ice, inert and irresponsive, as though they were finally resisting my perversion, offering me one last chance to withdraw and leave Mina's inner depths unviolated.

But now my darling was struggling, moaning with anxiety and protest, trying to jerk her pussy off the bulb-head lodged firmly between its lips, and at the thought that my tender *fluture** might escape its pin, my toothsome morsel its skewer, cruelty and lust surged up within me, and with a grunt of triumph I thrust again, driving the knobbled length of the d– fully home into my darling's tight-walled and oozing cavern of love. Mina's wail of protest climbed in pitch in exact synchrony with the passage of the d–'s head up her pussy – she tells me now that the sensation of it was like nothing she has experienced before, as though she had acknowledged domination before only with her lips and felt it only on borders of her being, and now was forced to her knees as she felt it invade her core. I thrust until I felt the d– meet final resistance, and paused, gorging my ears on Mina's whimpers of submission and surrender.

'Now,' said A–, whom I could hear frotting hard at her own pussy, 'withdraw a little, and thrust again. And repeat. You will soon have the way of it, and your femmewife's response will guide you. Yes –' Mina gasped as I slid the d– out, sending its knobbles sliding in reverse down the walls of her pussy, and thrust again to the limit '– that is the way. And again. And again. Yes . . . yes . . . yes . . . yes . . .'

But now A– fell silent, for it was Mina who was affirming my thrusts, and even – in the midst of my own perversion I trembled with the shock of it – thrusting herself *down* to meet the upstrokes of the d–. Oh, my sweet and salacious slut, my pinned and tender moth, my toothsome and skewered morsel, oh,

52

oh, oh, for my ice-bound loins had melted as I thrust and my clit-thorn, rubbed again and again against the ivory of the d–, was lifting me towards my own ecstasy.

'Call her a slut,' A– advised suddenly in my ear. I realised with a shock that she was behind me, her mouth pressed to my ear as she clasped herself to me naked, for I felt the pelt of her pussy rasping silkily at my buttocks and her hard nipples rubbing at my back. Her left hand was fumbling at the juncture of the d– and Mina's pussy, reading the depth of penetration as I thrust and withdrew, thrust and withdrew, while her right hand worked at her own clit-horn.

'Slut,' she repeated unsteadily. 'Call her . . . call her a slut.'

'Mina, thou art a slut,' I groaned, sending the d– sliding to its limit in Mina's pussy.

'A filthy slut,' A– elaborated, tracing the curves of my buttocks with pussy-wet fingers. 'A filthy slut. To submit to such . . . such *bestiality*.'

'Mina . . .' I began again.

'She has no name,' A– interrupted me, and now she was tribading me, rubbing her clit-thorn on my buttocks, dominating me as I dominated Mina. 'She is lower – ah – lower than the beasts. She . . . ah . . . no, this *thing* has lost all *right* to a name. Slut is all it can be. Slut.'

The rhythm of my thrusts was quickening, and the three of us seemed to be melting together, like a dish of three ingredients blending skilfully in the skillet of a master chef.

'Slut,' I told Mina, my gasping mouth full of her sweat scent and pussy aroma. 'Filthy slut. To submit to this. To *welcome* it. To *collaborate* with it. Slut . . . slut . . . slut . . .'

A– groaned with pleasure into my ear, and then her teeth were nipping at me, urging me to greater efforts as her pussy ground and smeared at my buttocks. But her urging was unneeded: I was thrusting as hard as I could, and Mina was eager for every millimetre of the d–, thrusting herself down on it as hard as I thrust it up into her, and now beginning to abuse herself as she had so often in the past, approaching her biggest orgasms.

'Slut . . . yes . . . slut . . . I am . . . a slut . . . hurt me, Mistress . . . punish me . . . punish your slut . . . train her . . . train her to your . . . to your will!'

On the last word she was shouting, and I managed to find a spurt of extra effort, a fingersbreadth of extra length, for a final thrust that brought her, and me, and A–, to orgasm. How long I lay collapsed on my darling's back, nailed into her by the full length of the d–, sealed to her skin by our mingled sweat, I do not know, but finally A–'s voice – calm and reassured again – recalled me to myself.

'Lady Joanna, wake up.'

I shook my head, realising that A– was no longer clasping herself to me from behind, that my pussy-juice-crusted buttocks were bare and unridden.

'Wake up, my lady. I have readied another treat for you. Turn and see.'

I pushed myself up on Mina's back, wondering what held me in place there, realising what I had done and that the instrument of my perversion was still thrust to its fullest in her pussy. I groaned, stung with post-orgasmic remorse. What had I done? Why had I allowed this foul Bulgarian dominatrix to persuade me – to *trick* me – into befouling my darling thus? Mina moaned as I tried to pull back from her, and my remorse heightened. What had I done to my darling? The d– squelched in its living socket, and I tried to remember how to move my hips and slide it free. There – it was coming free, and Mina was moaning again.

Oh! But it was a moan of *regret*, a moan of protest that my ivory engine should be deserting her, and what was this she was murmuring, was speaking, was *begging*?

'Again. Again. Fuck me again. More. I want more.'

Sick at heart, I felt the d– come free from her sopping pussy – and worse, *heard* it do so. But simultaneous with my rising sickness and disgust was a rising anger, anger at the woman who had persuaded my feet to tread this well-lit upland path, in the full light of the sun. That Bulgarian bitch A–, doubtless laughing to herself as she heard Mina's protests. When the d– was free I turned as sharply as I could, still dizzy with the afterseethe of orgasm, but with words of reproach and abuse crowding in my head.

'Madame A–,' I began, but then stopped. A– was standing behind me, smiling as she saw the anger on my face, but with one hand held out to indicate the 'treat' she had 'readied' for me – or rather, the treat that had readied *itself*: her secretary, called into the room while I lay dazed on Mina's back, then stripped and ordered to bend forwards, holding apart the cheeks of her pale and shapely buttocks to present to me, glistening with the saliva of her mistress's preliminary tonguing, her . . .

Ah, even the thought of setting down the word brings my sickness and horror flooding back, for it was plain what that poor perverted girl was offering to me at the direction of her monstrous chief, her – Goddess, forgive me – her *anus*. Her tight, round, glistening anus. I was to advance on her, my d– dripping with the lubrication of Mina's pussy-juice, and take her as I had taken Mina, with brutal dominance, but by a different and even more perverted route: not *per vas nefandum*, 'by the unspeakable vessel', as our theologians designate the sin of vaginal penetration in their manuals of morality, but *per vas nefandissimum*, 'by the utterly unspeakable vessel', as they designate the sin of *anal* penetration.

A–'s eyes were fixed on my horror-stricken, lust-tightened face as I hesitated, hauled one way by disgust, then t'other by desire.

'Come, my lady Joanna,' she said. 'Invade her. Penetrate her to the core, and you will hear her sing you a song of thanksgiving.'

I took one stumbling step forwards, then another, the d– pointing at the tight and tender entrance to A–'s secretary's bowels, then reeled and would have fallen, but for A–'s quick movement to seize hold of my shoulders and hold me up. Her cool breath fluttered at my ear.

'*Bugger* her, my lady. Bugger the slut. She surrenders herself to you in defiance of all laws of feminine purity, and must be punished.'

She assisted me forwards, unaware of the thought that had struck me like a thunderbolt, loosening my knees and my very hold on consciousness. This deed that some part of me, deaf to all pleading, purposed with unspeakable lust and perversity, I could not claim that it placed me on a level with the animals, for such things were unknown amongst them, not consciously abhorred but rather utterly alien to the wholesome, unreasoning instinct by which they obeyed Mother Nature's sexual commandments. No, it did not place me on a level with the animals, but far, far above, on a sun-scalded peak occupied by – deadly sickness seizes me by the throat as I prepare to write the name – occupied by the *Count*.

Yes, I could disguise it from myself no longer, and I recognised its foul lineaments in the horror I had just perpetrated on my own poor femmewife. That which I had done to Mina was that which the *Count* would have delighted to do, and that which A– urged me to perpetrate on her secretary was that which the *Count* would have performed with double delight. Domination and conquest by penetration and thrusting: his foul psychology reeked from every pore of it. But it was as though my intellect, and my will, were sealed off inside my skull, unable to affect or influence my apostate limbs and pussy. A– guided me forwards to the pagan altar of sacrifice – the secretary's smooth and rounded buttocks – and my trembling hand was guiding the head of the d– to the portal that waited between them.

The secretary murmured and trembled as she felt the head pressed to her flesh, nudging first at her buttock cleft, then sliding down a little to press at her sphincter, but when A– spoke to her sharply in Bulgarian, she stiffened, trying to hold the tremors down in her body by sheer force of will. Poor girl! Poor, poor girl! It was apparent that she faced this 'buggery' – A–'s use of the term had recalled Dr Helsingvili's words to me – with pounding heart and stone-dry mouth, obeying her mistress out of fear and respect, not lustful anticipation. And indeed, how could any sane woman face the prospect of being anally invaded with equanimity and calm? Even in Bulgaria, surely, where, if tales spoke truly, the foulest perversions were routine in the illegal brothels of ports and market towns, no whore could be hardened to such an assault on her bumhole.

No, even in Bulgaria it was surely rare, and A– had perhaps persuaded the girl to it only by stressing the importance of her visitors, and the necessity of

maintaining good relations between the girl's motherland and Romania by submitting to their base
desires. Yes, all this flashed through my mind in an
instant as the head of the d– lodged in its buttock-
dell. Then A–'s voice was whispering again in my ear,
instructing me in the task ahead. Another wave of
sickness overcame me as I listened, but my heart was
trip-hammering with lust and my lips, fingertips and
nipples were tingling with that now familiar lustful
anticipation.

'Clasp her around the waist, my lady, then begin to
penetrate her. Press slowly at first, gradually increasing the pressure and forcing your way inside her
bottom. She will struggle and cry for mercy, but I will
hold her firmly in place, should this prove necessary,
and you must not allow your will to weaken even for
an instant. She knows how privileged she is to receive
such an attention from so distinguished a visitor as
yourself, and the pleasure she will reap once you are
fully up her and thrusting will more than compensate
her for the sweat and sorrow of the initial entry.

'For yourself, apart from the physical and psychological rewards of the deed, there is a consideration
that I believe you have already half unveiled to
yourself. From what you tell me of this "Count", she
will have taken many women by the same route with
her monstrous erectile sex organ. The d– you thrust
into my secretary will not, alas, report to you directly
of what it discovers in her tight bowels, but I believe
that you will gain valuable and perhaps even vital
insights into your opponent's mind and modus oper-
andi. You have already placed yourself in her place
by what you have performed on your dear femmewife, dominating a woman *per vas nefandum*; now the
vas nefandissimum awaits you. Do not allow quotinoctial* morality to hold you back: the fate of

58

Europe and of all Europe's women now lies in your hands. If my secretary must be sacrificed to grant you the knowledge by which you save us, so be it. I am glad to pay the price, and so, when she looks back, will she be. Go to it with courage, my lady, and my blessing go with you.'

She kissed my ear, and withdrew, and with humming ears and shrivelling heart I steeled myself to perform that which she urged me towards: the buggery of her secretary. The head of the d– was firmly lodged in her bum-dell, and now I began to apply the pressure A– had advised, pushing with gradually increasing strength. And yes, as A– had predicted, the secretary moaned in protest, stammering out pleas in alternate Bulgarian and Romanian, with the most charming and nipple-tingling of accents.

'My lady . . . ah . . . ah . . . pliz, my lady . . . not my bottom . . . oh, my poor bottom . . . you hurt me, my lady, y–'

A–'s voice broke in, speaking rapidly and harshly in Bulgarian, and such was her dominance over the poor girl that she positively began to push herself back against my pressure, *assisting* me to invade her bowels. In another few seconds, with a gasp of lust from me and a piteous wail of surrender from her, I would succeed, and once again I felt horror mingle with my excitement as part of my mind stood aloof, naming me supreme Hypocrite and Villainess. I, who had suffered so sorely at the Count's hands and heard of worse suffering from his chained and weeping milk-slaves, was about to possess a girl by the most forbidden of her orifices in exactly the manner of the Count.

Oh, but in the instant in which my pressure on her bum bore fruit and the d–, lubricated with Mina's pussy-juice, sank with a jerk into her bowels, accompanied by my gasp and her wail, one thought lanced me worse than realisation of my hypocrisy and villainy, worse than my futile sympathy for her whom I abused – the thought, or rather the regret, that my mode of possession was *not* exactly that of the Count, as A– had noted. No, his d– was *flesh*, and equipped with that bulbous and sensitive head. My invasion of this delightful Bulgara's bottom was by proxy; his would have been at first hand.

But now A–'s voice was whispering in my ear again, instructing me in the next stages of my first successfully completed buggery (aye, even at that moment, sick with horror at what I had done, I named it to myself as 'first', meaning to taste its bittersweet delights again).

'Complete your in-stroke ruthlessly but with care: the bottom is tenderer than the pussy, less well equipped to receive a foreign invader, and must be broken in more slowly. But the fruits you will gather from the thorn bushes of her anguish will be at least as sweet, I assure you. Yes, that is the way. Ignore her whimpers: press her to her limits. Yes. Yes. And before the end she too will share a little of your ecstasy. Yes.'

She broke off to rebuke her secretary in Bulgarian, but the poor girl, with a d– spearing into the tenderest, the most sensitive region of her body, seemed momentarily deafened, and continued to whimper and gasp as I pushed the d– into her, sliding its thick and knobbled ivory shaft through her cringing bumhole and into the vestibule of her trembling bowels. Oh, the sense of possession was overwhelming: I owned the girl as I had owned none of my lovers before, even pussy-pierced Mina, and envy of the Count lanced me again as I imagined how *his* sense of possession must be greater still, magnified by his use not of a *succedaneum*, a substitute, but of his own flesh: that thick and throbbing *cock* of his.

I realised that A–'s voice was whispering in my ear again, encouraging me to complete the in-stroke and withdraw before thrusting forwards again, gradually building up a rhythm and truly buggering my poor whimpering victim. I felt her lips kiss my ear as the d– reached its limit, and my out-stroke was accompanied by her excited words of praise.

'You are a natural, my lady Joanna, and might have been born Bulgarian. Never before have I managed to persuade one of your race so easily to an act of anal penetration or seen her perform it with such gusto. Yes. Now push forwards again. Yes. Ignore her cries: she is your field, and you must plough her. Oh, I relive my own first buggery through you, my lady. Yes, with the laurels of successful pussy-fucking on your noble brows –' here she kissed the brows of which she spoke '– you turn with barely a protest to possessing my secretary *per vas nefandissimum*. Do you know, I have had Romanian visitors faint on the spot when they beheld one of my secretaries holding open their bum cheeks and offering them that puckered hole beyond which a New World lies waiting? Yes, faint on the spot – be silent, you slut! – or throw up. Several have threatened to report me to the Romanian Embassy, and two, to my certain knowledge, carried out the threat.

'But, as I know this is safe with you now, my brave darling, your Ambassadress at the time, yes, now the out-stroke, she was one of those who had *not* fainted or thrown up at the prospect of d–ing one of my secretaries by this forbidden orifice. She, though, had been pussy-fucking for weeks before I judged her ready for this still greater treat. You, I knew, were

61

ready almost from the moment you entered my office. Yes, now forwards again, and begin picking up the speed and force. There are many more where this slut came from –' at this point, from behind us, too, came a cry of protest from Mina, evidently recovered enough from her pussy-fucking to be listening, and indignant, she now tells me, to hear such an expert cunnilinctrix spoken of in such dismissive terms '– though her bottom will be very sore after this, she can do her work as well standing up or crouching as sitting down. Would you like –' and this was spoken more loudly, pitched to reach the ears of her secretary even through the latter's sobs and groans of protest '– to bet on how long it is before she sets bottom to seat again?'

It was a mischievous suggestion, for she well knew that it was in my own hands, or rather with my own hips, how fast and hard I pressed my buggeree, and she evidently wished me to be as ruthless as I could be. But my sympathy for the poor girl was welling up again, brought back to life by her protests, and though it could not prevent me continuing to bugger her, I gasped out a refusal to take part in any bet on how fast the poor girl's poorer bottom would recover.

'I . . . ah . . . I thank you . . . ah, ah . . . mistress,' I gasped out to A–, 'but . . . ah . . . I could not . . . ah . . . could . . . ah . . . not *bet* . . . ah . . . on such . . . ah . . . a thing.'

A–'s lips met my ear again, and I felt her tongue, swollen with lust, lick at my flesh. 'I know, my darling lady,' she whispered, her breath cooling the daub of spittle on my skin. 'I spoke for my slut's benefit. I have sworn to sack her if she fails to recover from one of these sessions of buggery within nine days, and though she knows I love her, and her tongue on my pussy, too much ever to carry out such a threat, the fear of dismissal nevertheless nags at her in her weaker moments, and is a potent weapon when I seek to persuade her to important deeds. Such as *this*, my lady. Oh –' I felt her hand reach to feel the juncture of my loins and her secretary's bottom, her fingers darting to read the relentless rhythm with which I sent the d– sliding into the girl's bowels and out again '– but I never guessed that the task of persuading *thee*, my lady, would be so much lighter.'

My gasps of pleasure, as the base of the d– butted and slid on my engorged pussy-thorn, were beginning to drown the gasps and whimpers of her secretary, in which protest was now mingled with a rising pleasure.

'You are both almost ready, my lady,' A– whispered. 'And it is time to assault her breasts and pussy with your hands. Punish her nipples and pussy-lips. Feel how the slut has responded to your buggery, and your sympathy for her will diminish as you complete your way with her.'

It was difficult for a moment to unclasp my hands from around the girl's waist, where they had held me locked in place as I pounded away at her bottom; but then they were free, sliding on a field of streaming sweat as I sent them in opposite directions: one down, to her pussy, one up, to her breasts. And what they found there caused me to pound away harder than ever, cramming every last millimetre of the d– into that forbidden receptacle, for the slut, as A– had truly named her, was pouring with pussy-juice and was more stiff nippled than I could believe. A true masochist, to respond with such strength to such humiliation and mistreatment, and her gasps and whimpers now, as I set to work punishing pussy and breasts, were those of approaching orgasm, mingling with the grunts that spoke of my own approach to the same.

Then surprise knocked me off my stroke for an instant: breath puffed at my own bottomhole and a moist tongue was suddenly lapping at it, drinking the sweat that trickled there, then working lower, over my perineum to my engorged pussy. It was my darling Mina, unbound by A– as I entered the final straight of my d–'d gallop at that delightful young Bulgara's bottom, and now lending her tongue to the task of heightening the orgasm I purchased therefrom. I had both hands on the secretary's pussy now, tugging the lip-petals wide to slide my fingers deep into her silk-skinned flower-throat, which was already beginning to tighten with orgasm. I heard a slap of palm meeting bum flesh from behind me as A– encouraged Mina to greater efforts, and Mina's tongue jerked on my bottomhole.

It was enough: as I drove the d– for the final time into the secretary's bottom, my loins exploded and I shrieked with ecstasy. It was only later, when we were in our hotel room again, that Mina told me the language I had employed: not Romanian, nor Bulgarian, but *Anglish* – the mother tongue (if so foul a creature as he could be said to possess a mother) of our Transmarynian foe. Mina has said nothing, but I believe she has guessed the reason: that I felt myself in the Count's place, performing one of the Count's deeds, and unconsciously chose the Count's own words to mark my triumph. Aye, but that is only the half of it, for even in the moment of orgasm I was lanced with envy again: that I could not *discharge* as the Count does, firing a heavy sexual fluid into those conquered bowels that would linger there, slowly dripping forth and reminding the girl of what I had enacted on her. Aye, A– spoke truly when she foresaw how the buggery would grant me insight into the psychology of our foe. To do as he does is to think as he does: pitilessly, cruelly, and with no higher ambition than to tread his helpless female prey into the mire and leave her there, a living and weeping symbol of his unholy power and might.

Joanna Harker's Journal, 7 October.

Please excuse occasional illegibilities, my possible future transcriber (I pray that there be one, though I will not be presumptuous and pray that she be *myself*). I write this in the train at an unaccustomed angle, travelling over Bulgarian [tracks?] not so well maintained as the Romanian will be, when we cross the border. Aye, Mina and I are returning to the land of our physical birth and also, unless the Goddess be with us, of our spiritual death. If we fail in our mission and fall into the Count's hands, we can expect no mercy. He will exploit us as 'milkers' or (my heart [quails?] at the thought of it) 'breed' from us, infecting us with an [embryo?] apiece, having conditioned our bodies to his unspeakable 'sperm' by mouth and arse. My stomach rolls at the mere thought of these things, but better to face the truth and be steeled to it than hide from it and lack resolution in a critical moment.

But I can hardly think of a stronger impulse to resistance than my love for Mina, which pierces me anew as I look on her strangely unfamiliar face, sleeping peacefully on my lap. Our disguises were the final stage of our preparation for our Crusade (I ask myself again whether I am too presumptuous to name it thus. No, for it defends that which is Holy against that which seeks to defile it). The Count knows me at first-hand and has seen the picture of Mina that I carried with me to Transmarynia. But I do not believe he will recognize us now: A– has seen to the slightest detail, even down to altering the shape of our eyebrows and bestowing a well-glued beauty spot on Mina. I, as the greater risk, received the greater attention: I have practised new mannerisms and a new carriage till they are first nature to me, not second; my hair is dyed a lighter shade and my hairline raised by plucking (my pussy moistens at memory of the plucker, and I will tell the tale later, if time permits); and I have worn a '[prosthetic?]' in my mouth so that I now, without conscious thought, speak with a distinctive 'slur' of my sibilants. Mina, more solicitous, bless her, for my safety than her own, wished me to wear smoked spectacles as an added precaution, with the excuse of sensitive eyes, but A– vetoed the suggestion, persuading Mina that they would 'over-egg the pudding' and might raise the Count's suspicions. She then made Mina laugh with a tale of a disaster she herself had had in her younger days with an over-elaborate disguise.

I smile myself at memory of it, and though we speed from Bulgaria now, we have both vowed to return and thank A– for the help she has given us and the love with which she sent us on our way. The Count swallowed the bait of our job applications almost too eagerly, and we had an interview with one of his 'representatives' in Sofia less than two days after he received them. (Life is swifter – almost too much swifter – than in our mothers' day, thanks to the telegram.) Both of us played our parts to perfection, A– later told us: the office in which the interview took place was under surveillance, for she wished to know as much as possible of the Count's deep-voiced Bulgarian agent, and watched the whole thing through a peephole. I fear that in the latter stages, when the agent had us demonstrate our 'pedagogic' prowess on the bottom of a cleaning girl whistled up from the street, that I heard A– risk discovery by frotting in accompaniment to the blows we landed on a fine firm bum, but it later transpired that she had recognised the agent as a former convict she herself had put behind bars, thwarting a spectacular robbery in a provincial bank.

The woman and her confederates had attempted to blast open the vault after entering the bank at midday, but A– managed to trick them into buying a less powerful but quicker-acting explosive than the dynamite they had sought, and all five were captured on the spot, dazed and deafened by the premature detonation of their charge. The agent had never recovered full hearing (I had thought she was paying especial attention to our lips), and A–'s frottage had been quite safe. The interview was conducted in Romanian, of course, for we had stated our birthplace and upbringing in northern Bulgaria clearly, but I believe that Mina, so spectacular has her progress been in even the short time available, could have coped with half or more of the questions in Bulgarian. I have accused her of finding herself a 'pillow-tutor' and of paying for her expertise in a new tongue with her own tongue, figuratively speaking – or rather, *un*-figuratively speaking. Yes, I warmed her bum several times for her laughing denial of it and I stir reminiscently in my seat as my pussy wakes and Mina murmurs on my lap. But I know her and trust her too well to have levelled the accusation in earnest. Yet A–, most certainly, and her secretary, would gladly have filled the role.

But Mina may hunger in vain for such mistreatment from me in future, for she too from now on, as a teacher in the Count's 'Academy', will have to take the active part and not the passive. A vision rises before my eyes of the adolescent bottoms that await us two, pale and perfect as full moons before the Fall of Woman, but where the vision excites and entices me, I fear Mina would be less eager. She is too convinced a submissive, and though she will happily participate with me in domination of a servant-slut or farm-girl, her true tastes have always lain elsewhere. Well, perhaps she will acquire the taste for true sadism during our stay. Certainly she must not hold back or evince the slightest reluctance when called upon to discipline her young female charges. The curricula vitae the two of us supplied with our job-applications did indeed hint that we were concealing criminal records, and the look of satisfaction on the face of the Count's Bulgarian agent, when her probing forced 'revelations' out of each of us in turn, said clearer than words what hiring instructions she was operating under. The Count expects a pair of merciless bum-beaters and titty-tormentors, and a pair of merciless bum-beaters and titty-tormentors he will receive. And there, at least, I will *not* be disguising my true identity.

But now my wrist is beginning to ache from the unaccustomed angle at which I am writing, and I must lay my pen aside. A concert pianist would do the same, and could any pianist in the world be as careful of her wrists and hands as one who, like me, expects to perform on the soft and tender bums of young and beautiful women? If I know my Count – and I do, alas, I do – the softest and tenderest bums of the youngest and most beautiful women await this wrist and hand. And so *au revoir*, future transcriber. Your own wrist may be aching soon, for I intend to fill these pages with every dimple of every bum, and deafen your ears, symbolically at least, with the volume and vigour of the spanking I deliver thereunto. If you do not interrupt your transcription with frequent frottings, I will have failed indeed.

Joanna Harker's Journal, 11 October.

Ah, I spoke more prophetically than I knew, for my own wrist aches far worse than on the train and if I could have one prayer granted, it would be for perfect ambidexterity. But I should say 'one *more* prayer granted', for the Goddess has smiled upon our enterprise to date and we are already high in the Count's esteem. Hence, in fact, the soreness of my wrist and my inability to rest it, for this is the first moment I have been able to snatch for resumption of my journal.

Mina, bless her, has taken up dictation at this point, despite the soreness of her own wrist, for she has been hard worked too by our 'employer', curse him. I will begin with our arrival in Bucharest from Bulgaria. How clichéd is the phrase, 'Nothing could ever be the same again', but how very true it can be. The very smell of Bucharest's air was charged with the knowledge that *his* nostrils drew it in and *his* lungs spewed it forth, and the echoing rumble of our incoming train beneath that oh-so-familiar soot-stained station roof repeated the single phrase, 'He is here, he is here, he is here.' Mina's knees gave way as she stepped from the carriage, and I had to hold her up, reading in her face what ailed her, and reviling the Count anew in my heart. We were on Romanian soil again, but our motherland was no longer our own, was sliding helplessly from our grasp. The bustle of our countrywomen around us, so ordinary and so oblivious, merely brightened our horror, and my first action was to take Mina to the station restaurant, where I urged two cuntsful of menstrual wine down her.

Then we went to look for the carriage the Count had promised us by telegram would be waiting. Our vinous diversion had taken half an hour and the driver's greeting spoke of her impatience, but Mina, spirits lifted by her lapping as I had hoped, deftly turned the situation to our advantage by informing the slut in the curtest of tones that we had paused to mete out punishment to an insolent platform guard, whom we had left in a station lavatory massaging her own copious tears into her own stinging bum. The driver swallowed hard and grew noticeably more respectful after that, and I have no doubt that the Count, who will have established an efficient espionage system in his 'Academy', will have heard of the matter before sunrise. Then we were off, clattering down familiar street after street seen in a glare of secret and deadly knowledge.

Mina whispered to me whether we should find an excuse for a genuine assault on the driver to add to our fictional assault on the platform guard, but I judged (and rightly, I believe) that this would be adding thorns to nettles. An effective entrance on the stage is accompanied by *one* thunderclap, not two, and the tale of our fictional session with the platform guard would grow in the telling as a genuine session with the driver would not and could not, for our efforts would be recorded clearly on her bottom and inspected by those to whom she divulged it. And so, instead of setting to work on the driver's bottom, we tickled each other's pussies as we were driven to the Count's lair, that we might arrive with fingers suitably stained and benodorous,* as though from our fictional session with the platform guard.

Our preparations were not in vain, as was apparent within seconds of our meeting with the Count. Ah, how my heart pounded when I heard his well-remembered, well-loathed voice approaching the room to which we had been shown. Mina, reading my emotions with her quick submissive's intuition, caught hold of my trembling hand and squeezed it. As she released it, her hand stuck a little to mine and I flashed a grateful smile to her, for now I could endure even the impact of the Count's heavy feet on the floor. He was giving instructions in Transmarynian to someone, and I wondered who it was. One of his suns? A woman enslaved by him in Transmarynia and brought to Romania to serve him? But then all thought of this was driven from my head, for the door was swinging open and the Count was coming in, having to stoop his head a little to pass beneath the jamb as he threw a final instruction over his shoulder to his apparently departing interlocutrix.

Yes, for he closed the door behind when he had entered, looking at each of us in turn with a wolfish smile that cracked the thick white make-up he was again wearing on his face. And those false breasts of his! How could I ever have been taken in by them? They were too solid and irresponsive to movements; and yet Mina, who has never seen the repulsive *flatness* of his naked chest (and never will, I pray), remarks now that they would have fooled her. Truly, we see what we expect to see, and such a monster as the Count is so far outside our quotinoctial experience that he can move among us freely and be taken for no more than an exceptionally powerful and vigorous dominant woman.

Aye, a dominant, for I saw Mina tremble with involuntary lust as he reached out and shook her hand. The strength of his grip, she told me later, overcame her disgust at the *warmth* of his palm and fingers, and she was unable to rally her reason in time to drive back her instinctive reaction with the thought of what this *Überfrau* truly was: no *Frau* at all, but a *monster*. Then the Count was turning to me, raising

71

his hand to sniff the stickiness he had felt on Mina's hand. My disgust and rage at this uncouth breach of etiquette drove back my fear, which had threatened to rise again, and the hiss of blood in my ears was clearing in time for me to catch the words he spoke as he took and squeezed my hand as he had squeezed Mina's.

'Enchanted, my dear Miss Ignatieva,' he said in his excellent Romanian. 'I am the Countess Caradul, and your new employer.'

As he released my hand, again he raised his fingers to his nostrils, his smile broadening again as he sniffed deeply at them even as I murmured a conventional response and began to apologise for our late arrival.

'Yes, yes,' he said impatiently. 'But my driver informs me that you, ah, dallied at the station with an insolent rail employee. You left her suitably chastened, no doubt?'

My heart thudded at this revelation of the efficiency and speed of the espionage network I had already foreseen, but I believed, and Mina has confirmed, that my voice was steady enough as I answered.

'Suitably but insufficiently, Countess. We had urgent need of another half-hour, and even that would have left the two of us unsatisfied. We like –' I forced a cruel smile to my face '– to leave an *impression*.'

The Count chuckled and clapped his hands, and I was displeased to see Mina tremble momentarily with pleasure at the force with which his palms came together.

'Wonderful!' he cried. 'You confirm my desire to staff the entire Academy with Bulgaras, for the three who are already here have more than satisfied my demands. Romanians –' and here he lowered his

72

voice to a conspiratorial rumble '– are too often inclined to be *fundamentally* lacking in the true spirit of instruction, and my, our, girls merit better.'

I smiled and nodded. 'You will find that we, my dear Countess, are *fundamentally* strong in just this area.'

'*Fundamentally* severe,' Mina chimed in, and the Count chuckled and clapped his hands again.

'Excellent!' he cried. 'But I must not keep you from your unpacking and the toilet you no doubt wish to perform after your journey. Come with me now and I will show you the dormitories you have been assigned, where you must both –' he fixed us each in turn with his gaze, and I noted that I must warn Mina not to pout '– exercise stern discipline over your charges, who have been left unsupervised since the departure of their previous dorm mistresses a week ago. Those two, native Romanian lasses, were sadly inadequate in discipline, but I trust you two will soon erase the memory of their weakness. You have made a strong impression already on my driver, and must follow it up with vigour to make a similarly strong impression on the Academy as a whole. I place discipline at first place, and last, in pedagogy. It is a *sine qua non*, as I am sure you must both agree.'

'Indeed, Countess,' I replied, and Mina chimed in with: 'Spare the rod and spoil the child.'

Did the Count's eyes flicker at 'rod'? Aye, they did, for he smiled and repeated the word with relish.

'Rod. Yes. The rod. It must not be spared, though with these dormitories it has been for a week or more. Their bums have lain fallow, by my special order, in order to allow you both fresh ground to plough. They will soon be wishing that their bum flesh had not been allowed to recover full sensitivity, I am sure. But now come, my dear ladies. Your luggage will already be waiting for you in your cubicles. That is, it *should* be waiting for you; if it is not, at least the bottoms of at least two of my serving girls will pay the price.'

But our luggage was waiting: we had been assigned neighbouring dormitories on the uppermost of the Academy's three floors, Mina's called 'Marigold Dorm' and mine 'Jasmine Dorm'. I confess to a moment of worry when I saw that the initials of the dorms matched the initials of our *true* names and not of our assumed ones (Lidiya for Mina, Vasilka for myself), but it was surely nothing but coincidence: the other dorms, as we soon learned, were all named after flowers (save for the three special punishment dorms, Thistle, Briar and Nettle).

'Your girls are out on the sports fields,' the Count informed us when he had shown us briefly over Jasmine. '*Mens sana in corpore sano** is another of our mottoes. Our sports mistresses will be putting them through some vigorous paces, so you will have plenty of time to wash and prepare yourselves for their arrival. I can return and introduce you formally if you like, or let you introduce yourselves. It is up to you.'

I noted an edge in his voice that spoke of more to the choice than seemed to meet the ear. Accordingly, I exchanged a momentary glance with Mina and was relieved to see that she had noted it too. I let her reply: I had already spoken enough and two dominants, as we were pretending to be, would surely speak on equal terms to their employer.

'It won't be necessary for you to wait, Countess,' Mina said. 'You must be exceedingly busy, and we have already taken enough of your time.'

The Count bowed his head with a smile in which I read more than his usual satisfaction. Mina had replied exactly as a Bulgarian dominant, bursting to be at her charges, should have replied.

'Then I will leave you to it, dear ladies. Marigold Dorm is just along the corridor, as you know, my dear Miss Svetkova.'

He began to bow, but Mina shook her head and said, 'Have you forgotten something, Countess?'

'Hmmmm?'

The Count's thick left eyebrow rose, and my stomach rolled at the thought of the further thick hair hidden beneath his clothing on his chest and belly, thighs and arms.

'The keys to our punishment cupboards, Countess,' Mina said.

I suppressed a smile. Was this another little test of the Count's? I believe so, and I was relieved that Mina had passed it without my assistance, for I confess that I could not have done so: the question of the key to my own cupboard had slipped my mind, so hard was I concentrating on our adversary. The Count tutted with perhaps feigned self-reproach.

'But of course, my dears. Here you are.'

As his sardonic gaze met ours unblinkingly, his large hand slipped under his collar and rummaged between his large artificial breasts, drawing up a bunch of keys from which, after due inspection, he detached two.

'Yours, my dear,' he said, handing Mina one of the keys; and 'Yours, my dear,' handing me the other. It was unpleasantly warm and I suppressed a shiver of distaste as, without another word, he bowed and swept from the dormitory, closing the door hard behind him. Breath whistled from Mina's mouth in a sigh of relief, but I held up a warning hand as I saw her prepare to speak, perhaps of the visible *misalignment* the Count's rummaging had given to one of his artificial breasts. His heavy footfalls were shaking the floor as he departed along the corridor, but I knew him too well to suppose that we had suddenly been left quite alone.

'A most charming woman,' I said, and Mina's look of puzzlement cleared.

'Yes,' she returned. 'Quite as we expected. But I must, my dear Vasilka, be off to my own dormitory, to prepare for my own girls.'

'Good luck, darling Lidiya,' I said, and we exchanged a silent and all-too brief kiss during which I seized and squeezed her buttocks, trying to impress her with something of my own will and energy for her coming encounter with twenty or thirty young women.

For my own part, I was filled with excitement as I washed and changed into some fresh clothes, ringing the bell for a servant to take away the clothes I had travelled in. The girl that came panting into the dorm, evidently having rushed up two flights of stairs, was slender and had a slant to her eyes of just the kind I had most missed in round-eyed Transmarynia. Had I not been preparing myself for my dorm, I should certainly have found an excuse to detain her longer, but I did nothing beyond an inspection of her teeth (all in excellent condition), a two-handed squeeze of first her tits and then her buttocks (of a firmness inviting prolonged future investigation), and an up-skirt grope of her pussy (almost unfledged and reassuringly clean – the Count evidently kept his serving sluts in good order).

She scurried off with flushed cheeks and a squeak at my buttock-slap, and I strolled over to the windows to open one and listen for the arrival of 'my girls' from the sports field, feeling my nipples peak and pussy stir pleasantly as I named them thus to myself. My girls were out there now in the cool darkness, exercising by mellow lamplight under the supervision of those sports mistresses of whom the Count had spoken. I could not see them, for my view of the sports fields was blocked by the chapel, but I could hear instructions ringing out in the distance.

'Melissa, you slut, run harder. Harder! Or I will report you to your dorm mistress!'

I smiled, squeezing my nipples through the cloth of my dress, picturing Melissa to myself and hoping that *I* was the dorm mistress of whom that distant voice was speaking. I leaned out of the window further, looking to my left, for I knew that Mina's dorm was beside mine and wondered if she too was listening for her future charges as I was. Yes! There was her beloved hand, darting out for a moth attracted by the lamplight; and when I rapped on the window frame, her head appeared, and her chewing lips blew me a kiss that I returned with a laugh.

But now whistles were blowing from the sports field, signalling the end of whatever games were being played or races being run, and within a minute, trotting around the corner of the chapel that had shielded them from our gaze, came our lambs. My heart gave a wolfish bound in my chest, for even at a distance I could see that the Count's instructions anent scholarships to his Academy had been followed to the letter – and no doubt the calliper and tape measure too. I had translated his words, and then read them aloud to him three times, for he insisted on making minor changes that I now realise were factitious: he wanted the secret pleasure of hearing me speak of something whose true significance I had no way of fathoming.

But foul as their source was, and sun-scorched as the purpose at which they aimed, I strained to recall his words as I watched my girls trotting up to the main house of the Academy in a silence that spoke eloquently – and paradoxically – of the discipline enforced by the grim, squat figures that trotted on either side of that luscious phalanx of youthful girl flesh. How did they run? Ah, yes: 'The doctor is to pay close and careful attention to the breasts, ensuring that they are above a certain ratio of the girl's height and/or weight, and that the left should deviate in size and sphericality from the right (or vice versa) by no more than 5 per cent.' And yes, I could see the breasts that bounced and shook beneath thin cloth rendered almost transparent by sweat, and they were of an exceptional size and perfection that impressed themselves more and more on me as the girls – some of them *my* girls – approached.

I was almost mesmerised by those bouncing globes, and leaned out dangerously far as the girls passed beneath me and entered the house. As I pulled back, I heard a laugh from the window on my left, and saw that Mina was shaking her head at me. But then she stopped, and my anger at her insolence vanished, for here it came, rushing deliciously into our nostrils on the cool night air: the scent of that girl-phalanx's combined sweat, risen to our height after its generatrixes had passed. I drew it deep into my lungs, feeling my nipples peak again, and then, having shaken my fist in only half-mock threat at Mina, I withdrew my head from the window and closed it. Several moths were in the room spiralling around the lamps, having passed me unnoticed, such was the attention I had been paying to the girls; and I caught one as Mina had done, a rare *Merveille de la Nuit* whose powder I wiped from my lips with a hand tingling for bum.

The other moths I left to spiral: we would soon see if we could entice them from the light with some fresh sweat or fresher pussy-juice. And even as I framed the thought, I heard the light sound of many young girls' feet on the stairs leading to the dormitories, overlain with a growing murmur of voices. I lowered my eyes with a prayer to Maria Profundissimi Spelaei, Mary of the Deepest Cavern, my favourite Madonna, asking her that she assist Mina with the girls of her own dorm; and then raised my eyes to meet the wave of gently steaming young female flesh pouring into my dorm. *My* girls, and, oh, I was right to foretell that the Count would have picked only the ripest and sweetest fruit from the vast female orchard of Europe. And sweet was the word: watching my girls pouring into the dorm, I felt as though I were nine years old again, and watching the proprietress of a sweet shop tip a flood of glistening sweets from a huge jar into her scales.

All were exceptionally beautiful, all exceptionally large breasted, and all, I would soon learn, exceptionally callipygous. Nor, unless my dormitory was the *crème de la crème*, which I could not for a moment believe, would the rest of the Academy's student body be even less delightful to the eye, moistening to the pussy, stiffening to the nipples and hardening to the will. For I felt my appetite for dominance flare up furnace-like as they came flooding into the room, giggling and whispering more than ever as they saw the new dormitory mistress who awaited them. I closed my eyes and drew in breath for a long instant into my nostrils, savouring the fresh scent of innocent sweat that washed over me. Then I opened my eyes and shouted: 'Silence!'

A half-instant later, from the dormitory on my left, came an echoing shout of 'Silence!' It had succeeded my own too quickly to be imitation, and I mentally promised my Madonna a week's worth of candles for the inspiration she had breathed into Mina. But then I thrust the thought away from me; I was concentrating every fibril on the task ahead of me, meaning to savour it to its limit. Gaping mouths and widened eyes faced me, and I gloated inwardly as I saw some flinch when I shivered with mock rage.

'What do you mean by this insolent display of chatter and gossip for your new dormitory mistress? Well? You girl, answer me!'

I thrust a finger at the face of one of the girls nearest me, a tall Nordic blonde who I half hoped was the Melissa I had heard rebuked on the sports field. Oh, and I shivered again, but with lust this time, for her nipples, half visible through the sweat-soaked cloth of her sports vest atop the generous and shuddering mounds of her tits, stiffened to my tone and dominant, jabbing finger.

'Ve . . . ve are s–'

'Shut up, you slut,' I said, suppressing another shiver as her nipples lengthened even further. 'Tell me your name and country first, then offer your pathetic excuse.'

'I am Katrina, mistress, from Stockholm. And I offer you our apologiess for our inssolence. It vos unintentional, for ve vere not told dat ve vould –'

'Yes, a pathetic excuse, as I foresaw. The Countess –' and what was that flicker on both the young Swede's face and that of a dark Mediterranean girl as I spoke the title? '– would expect courtesy towards *all* middle-class women within the Academy, whether they are staff or not. And am I not a *bourgeoise*?'

'Y–' Katrina began.

'All of you,' I snapped. 'I want an answer from all of you! Well? Am I not a *bourgeoise*?'

An uncertain and irregular chorus of 'Yes, mistress' began, and I chopped the air for silence.

'All together, and *loudly*. Am I not a *bourgeoise*?'

'Yes, mistress,' came the chorus again, more regularly this time.

'Louder!'

'Yes, mistress!'

'Then your insolence was wilful and meriting immediate punishment. These are my instructions. Get to the foot of your beds, each of you – hey! You will not move till the instructions are complete. Get to the foot of your beds, each of you, and stand there facing the wall. On my command, you will each take hold of the waistband of your sports shorts. On my further command, each of you will draw your shorts down simultaneously and bend forwards, raising your bare bottom to meet that which awaits it. Very well? Then do it. Quickly! Quickly! The last one standing at her bed will receive a double dose!'

Ah, that sowed panic, and two girls ran into each other as they rushed to avoid the fate I promised, tumbling to the floor with shuddering breasts and coltishly sprawling limbs.

'On your feet,' I said, stooping over them and drawing in the scent of their sweat as I seized each by her hair and hauled. With cries of pain they rose to their feet and scampered for their beds as all the others, already safe at theirs, watched to see who lost the race.

'The rest of you,' I shouted, 'do as you are told and watch the wall!'

Heads snapped round, and the two girls reached their beds in almost the same instant, simultaneously panting and sniffing away tears of pain from the hair-tug with which I had assisted them to their feet.

'I cannot decide which of you was last,' I lied, for the girl I preferred had in fact won the race, 'so you will *both* receive a double dose. It will teach you not to be so clumsy next time. Right, now, all of you, listen for my instructions. First, take hold of the waistbands of your sports shorts.'

I strolled down the dormitory between the double row of beds as my order was obeyed, savouring the fear and apprehension that filled the air beneath the fluttering shadows of the light-hungry moths. My girls had, as yet, I knew, no idea of how stern I was. Was my bark worse than my bite? Or as bad? Or was – and I saw one girl's knees tremble and weaken as perhaps that very thought struck her – my *bite* worse than my *bark*? I reached the large punishment cupboard at the far end of the room, freshly and nostril-tinglingly painted with the cross-ed canes of the Academy's crest above its motto: '*E Puellis Mulieres Facimus*', 'From Girls We Make Women'.

And now, I wondered, would my reading of the Count's character be true again? I had already foreseen the beauty and big-breastedness of his students; would he have ensured the detail, so small but so important, for which I now hoped? I lifted the key he had given me from a pocket, pushed it into the lock, and turned. The wards responded silently and smoothly, and the cupboard was ready to be opened. I took hold of the knob of one door of the cupboard and slowly pulled it open.

And yes, he had ensured that so-small but so-important detail: the punishment cupboard was pre-pared according to the best tradition, for the door swung open with a long, unoiled squeak that was answered with three girlish squeaks of involuntary fear from behind me. Evidently the dorm mistress who had had charge of these delicious young morsels before me had not been entirely remiss: she had instilled a healthy fear of the sound of the cupboard opening in at least three luscious breasts.

I opened the other door of the cupboard with a second squeak that was answered again with involuntary squeaks from behind me. And I? I gasped involuntarily and clapped my hands softly with delight at what I had revealed inside the cupboard. The metaphor of the sweet shop was in my head again, for the cupboard, large as it was, was crammed almost to capacity with the highest quality instruments of puellar* chastisement and torture.

There were canes of every size and thickness, and flexibility too, no doubt, and whips to match them woven from silk and flax and human hair; sturdy bum-paddles and delicate titty-scourges; gags and handcuffs, ropes and cords, and even a pair of bridles; candles for dripping hot wax on quivering bottoms and pussy-mounds, and scrapers for removing it again; silver nipple-caps to be heated and forced over tender young nipples; tweezers for plucking hair from pussies and bumholes; jars of chopped and irritant animal whisker and dried herb for dropping down knickers and rubbing on breasts – oh, a veritable Cornucopia of Cruelty. My pussy squirmed with delight and positively squirted juice as I gazed upon it, and I almost forgot to wonder what was in a still-locked section of the cupboard on the bottom left.

I tried my key in its keyhole, but it was rejected and I shrugged. A mystery for solving later; for now, I had – I turned to look again – yes, twelve bottoms to see to. Let's see . . . yes, *that* would do nicely. I chose a sturdy ivory bum-paddle carved in Gothic script with the motto '*Inter Lacrymas Sapienta*', 'In the midst of Tears, Wisdom'. Oh, it might have been built for me, so snugly did its handle fill my hand, with ridges that exactly fitted my fingers, and when I tested it on the palm of my other hand I hissed softly with pain: it was so well balanced and the air holes in its blade were so scientifically spaced that even the mildest stroke swung harder than one expected. Well, the strokes I was about to deliver to the expectant but unwilling bottoms of my girls would not be of the mildest.

I swung round, feeling pussy-juice beginning to trickle down my thighs, and gazed up the two rows of waistband-clutching insolents that awaited me. Almost half of the girls were trembling with fear or the effort of retaining their position and, as I drew in a long breath, I could smell that the sweat of all them, generated on the sports field, had begun to ripen on their luscious bodies, losing the bouquet of extreme freshness and growing muskier and even more desirable.

'Right, girls,' I said. 'On command, pull down your shorts simultaneously and bend forwards, exposing your bottoms for inspection and –' I paused with consummate skill, then allowed the word to hiss lasciviously from my mouth '– chastisement.'

And now at least two-thirds of the girls were trembling, and in each case, whatever it had been before, the cause was now definitely fear. I was on inspired form that night and believe that one or two of the most susceptible might already have pissed themselves with fright, had they not come fresh from exercise and been sweating heavily.

'Now!' I yelled, and down came their shorts, and they bent forwards over their beds, twelve pairs of firm pale buttocks gleaming suddenly to my greedy gaze like a heaven overstocked with moons. And yet one or two of those pairs ... Frowning, I strode forward to confirm my suspicions, fingering absently at an achingly stiff nipple with my free hand as I bent to examine first one pair of buttocks, then, further

84

down the row, another. The Count had explicitly stated that the bottoms of my dormitory, like those of Mina's, had been allowed to lie fallow. No instruments of chastisement should have met these perfect mounds of tender bum flesh for at least a week.

And in ten cases out of twelve, none had. On the two pairs of buttocks I had just examined, however, there were marks too fresh to have been inflicted more than a day or so before. Plainly, there was a private disciplinarian at work in the Academy, or a teacher disobeying the orders of the Count. I stepped back to the first pair of buttocks again and examined its marks with an expert eye before rubbing my fingers over them, reading their heat and texture.

No, these were the marks not of an experienced professional but of an amateur still learning her trade, albeit not without a certain raw talent. I sniffed at my fingers when I lifted them from the sweat-slicked bum cheeks, and could not resist licking them as I returned to the second pair to confirm my diagnosis. Aye, this too was the work of an amateur, and I would wager a week's bum-swiping to an hour's titty-torture that it was the same amateur. I sniffed and licked my fingers again when I had finished stroking the bum cheeks before me, noting that the sweat here was even more to my taste.

'You, girl,' I said, prodding the bum, 'what is your name and nationality?'

I saw the bum cheeks quiver as the girl swallowed, evidently fearful of what my close examination of her bum portended.

'Julia, mistress,' she said. 'And I am of Ispain.'

Ah. Then that accounted for it. I had always enjoyed the secretions of Spanish girls, who seemed bred for muskiness and brine of sweat and pussy-juice. I dropped my bum-paddle with a clatter on the floor, making the poor girl and her immediate neighbour on the right jump in fright.

'Tell me, Hoolia of Ispain,' I said, seizing hold of a bum cheek in each of my hands, 'where do these marks on your bottom come from?'

Now I heard a suppressed gasp from behind me, and could narrow its source without turning my head to a single girl. Was that my amateur bum-fancier? But Spanish Julia had not answered. I levered her bum cheeks apart and stooped to examine the glistening hollow of her anus, where her dark bum hair was beginning to sprout again after plucking. Ah, I envied her who had performed it, wringing squeak after squeak from this firm-fleshed nymph with each jerk of her tweezers.

'Come, girl,' I said, as though addressing the nether mouth that shone before me. 'Tell me where the marks come from.'

I thrust my face forwards, pressing it close to her bum as I licked first at her anus, then lower, over her sweat-soaked perineum and fourchette, then higher, back over her anus and up her bum cleft. It was delicious: her sweat had not come into its full bouquet but made up in freshness and directness of flavour for what it lacked in depth and subtlety.

Still no answer. Wiping at my lips, I withdrew from her licked-clean cleft, into which further sweat was already trickling. Visions were possessing me that were even more delicious than her sweat, of setting to work on her bum with my paddle, driving the answer out of her; but there would be time enough for that later, and I knew I could impress the girl, and her dorm mates, far more by employing an *indirect* torture.

'You will not tell me, hey?' I said, bending to pick up my paddle. 'Then perhaps you will tell me this, young Hoolia. Who is your best friend in the dorm?'

Silence for a moment, then: 'I ... I have no best friend, mistress.'

'Liar,' I said conversationally, as I strolled to stand behind the girl on her right. Ah, and here was another bum perfect in its own way: slenderer and less full fleshed than the Spaniard's, but just as well proportioned, with the sweetest-lipped pussy peeking beneath it through the thigh-gap.

'You,' I said, prodding at the bum with my paddle. 'Give me your name and nationality, then tell me: who is Julia's best friend in the dorm?'

'I am Cecilia, of Norway, mistress. I ... I do not kno–'

I had already, and silently, moved into position; and now, before the lie had fully left the Norwegian's mouth, I swung. The thunderclap of the paddle meeting bum brought gasps of fear from every other girl in the dorm; Cecilia herself did not simply gasp but shriek, and she almost fell forwards on the bed in her surprise and pain.

'In position again, you little slut,' I instructed her through her first snivels. 'Bottom held ready for a second stroke if you lie to me again. Who is Julia's best friend in the dorm?'

Ah. The Norwegian girl was trying to look sideways at the Spaniard, apologising for the information she was about to supply. I had moved back into readiness and it was all the excuse I needed: *Thwack!* Again my paddle crashed home on those slender buttocks.

'You were instructed to face the wall,' I told her, having to raise my voice, for her snivels were sobs now and I could see her hands clenching and unclenching as she fought to keep them clear of her bum. How the poor dear was longing to squeeze and rub her tormented bum flesh! But my predecessor dorm mistress, for whom my respect was increasing by the minute, had evidently trained that well out of my charges. 'You were also instructed to tell me who Julia's best friend is. An answer, now!'

'Sophia, it is Sophia!'

'And who is Sophia? Point to her.'

The Norwegian risked a quick glance to her left and across the aisle, making sure of her target, then her arm came up. Ah, the plot thickened, for her unsteady finger was aimed at the *other* pair of marked buttocks I had examined. Julia and Sophia had evidently been targeted together by the amateur bum-paddler whose identity I was now tracking down.

'Good,' I said. 'You have seen sense, Cecilia. I will leave you for the moment, but if I catch sight of you attempting to rub or soothe your bottom, I will be back. Do you understand me?'

'Yes, mistress.'

Now I turned and crossed the aisle to the young girl identified as Sophia. When I reached her, I slipped a hand between her thighs and groped her pussy as I purred: 'Nationality?'

She gasped as my fingers began to tickle her; now I felt her swallow as Julia had before her. 'I am from Greece, mistress.'

'And you are Julia's best friend in the dorm, Sophia?' I asked, still purring, still tickling at her sweat-moist pussy, which was already beginning to respond to my fingers. Another nervous swallow, and then she evidently flung all caution to the wind.

'Yes, mistress. I am ... and I am also her best friend of the Academy.'

'Excellent,' I said, withdrawing my hand and stepping back into position. 'Then Julia will not wish *you* to be beaten for *her* refusal to tell me who is responsible for the marks borne by the bottoms of both of you. Will she?'

She hesitated only a moment, but I was keyed to hairtrigger speed and once more the thundercrack of paddle meeting bum echoed through the dorm.

'Will she, my dear Sophia?'

She could not answer for a moment, her hands clenching to keep from rubbing at her freshly paddled bum; and then she said, her voice tight and unsteady with pain: 'No, mistress.'

'Then I ask Julia again: who was responsible for beating the two of you? She has ten seconds to answer. One . . . two . . .'

As I counted off, I slipped my free hand up between Sophia's thighs. Ah, the blaze in her bum had ignited a similar blaze in her pussy: my tickling fingers met a thick seepage of pussy-juice, and my own voice grew unsteady as I stepped back into position, anointing the blade of the bum-paddle with the pussy-juice.

'Eight . . . nine . . . ten . . .'

Thwack!

This time Sophia cried out, acknowledging the extra force with which I had swung, and perhaps feeling the smear of her own moisture left on her bum by the paddle.

'Are you sure, young Sophia?' I purred maliciously, turning to watch the reaction of Julia's bum to my words. 'Are you sure your "best friend" –' I snorted sceptically '– values your happiness so highly? Or will she keep her secret at your expense, and allow you to be beaten again? Let us see. One . . . two . . . three . . . four . . .'

I was back tickling at her pussy, moistening my fingers thoroughly, my heart pounding at the thought of thrusting them ruthlessly deep inside her. Ah, I was truly jealous of the Count and his thigh-organ when I calculated the number of fresh female orifices there were to invade in this dorm alone: twelve mouths, and twelve pussies, and twelve bottomholes between twelve pairs of smooth firm bum cheek. I took a deep breath and stepped back again, completing my count, readying myself to swing the re-anointed paddle.

'Nine . . . ten.'

Thwack!

But Sophia cried something out in the instant before the paddle leapt to her firm bum cheeks for the third time, sealing the pain of the first and second blows beneath its own fresher and hotter pain. For a moment I could not understand what she had said, my ears still rejoicing in the sound of the bum-clap, then I realised that it was 'Please!'

Whom had she been addressing? Myself, or Julia, or both? I turned to watch Julia's bottom, and saw with delight that it was quivering with emotion. My psychology was working as perfectly as I hoped: I might have beaten Julia's own perfect bottom eight or nine times before forcing her secret from her, for in that case I would have been inflicting only physical pain on her. By beating Sophia, I invoked a potent mixture of guilt and, whether Julia was submissive or dominant, envy: guilt that her silence was prolonging Sophia's punishment; envy of receiving the punishment, if she were submissive, or of inflicting it, if she were dominant.

'Poor Sophia,' I said, stepping back to her and tickling her pussy again. My fingers were soon drenched as far as the knuckles and a small pool of pussy-juice was glistening on the floor beneath Sophia's thighs where the drizzle had escaped the net of her sports shorts. 'Poor Sophia. Julia seems unconcerned at your plight. Your bottom pays the

price for her stubborn silence, and she is left un-
moved. Brace yourself, for you are about to pay the
price again. One . . . two . . . three . . .'

I heard a sob from Julia as I rubbed Sophia's
pussy-juice for the third time into the blade of the
bum-paddle. Was she about to break and reveal the
identity of the unauthorised, amateur dominatrix
who had enjoyed this perfect Mediterranean bum
before me? Please the Goddess, no, for I believed that
a fourth bum-stroke, at best, and fifth bum-stroke, at
worst, would bring this delicious girl to orgasm.

'Seven . . . eight . . . nine . . . t–'

'No!'

I grunted with exasperation, swinging on my heel
to face Julia, a drop of pussy-juice from the bum-
paddle flying loose to land on the floor of the dorm
midway between us, where it shone like a little star.

'Yes, Julia? Are you prepared to reveal the name?'

A snotty sniff, and another quiver in her bum
cheeks. I swung back instantly to Sophia, set the
bum-paddle ready, and resumed my counting one
short of the thunderstroke.

'Nine . . . t–'

'Yes! Yes, I will tell. Please. Please I will tell.'

I swung back to Julia. 'Then give me the name. At
once.'

'It . . . it was Ruth.'

'Who? Point her out to me. Quickly.'

Julia's hand came up and pointed to her left, to the
tallest girl in the dorm.

'Ah.'

I strode down the dorm to the accused girl, letting
the bum-paddle fall from my hands as I reached her,
to clatter on the floor in a way that made Julia jump
with fright again. But not the accused girl: her broad
but perfectly proportioned bum was motionless. I

seized hold of it, gripping a cheek in each hand and juddering it mercilessly.

'Are you Ruth, you slut?'

An insolent moment of silence, then a contemptuous 'Yes, mistress.'

My pussy, already seething from Sophia's bum-paddling, writhed and gushed with lust, and I longed to have a magic word to speak that would convert my clitoris into a suitable instrument of chastisement: lengthen and swell it to a fleshy d– I could force brutally up the bum of this gorgeous slut, making her moan and wail as I thrust her own insolence and rebellion up her nether-throat.

'What is your nationality, Ruth?'

'I am Transmarynian, mistress.'

Ah, I might have guessed it: her hair was the lightest in the room.

'And have you been beating girls in your dorm not merely without permission but against the explicit orders of the Countess?'

Another insolent moment of silence, then another contemptuous 'Yes, mistress.'

This was too much: I let go of her, dragged my dress up, and thrust my oozing pussy at her bum, riding her with potent insult and dominance. Oh, and the pleasure of it corrupted my judgment, for I was shocked by the words I spoke next, knowing what they might portend for the girl.

'Then you will be reported to the Countess,' I told her, holding back my orgasm by sheer force of will as I ground my pussy-thorn at her smooth bum flesh. 'And *she* will know what to do with you.'

Analysing my motives for this outburst, I understood that I was vicariously surrendering to my desire to bugger the girl. *I* could not do so, but the Count could and very possibly *would*, for the threat acted on the girl as the clatter of the bum-paddle had not: I felt her bottom quiver with emotion beneath my pussy-thrusts and she moaned involuntarily with fear. Evidently, the Count's reputation as a stern discipli-narian was already well established in the Academy. Realisation of my perversity acted like a douche of warm water on my loins, and I withdrew from my tribadism, leaving the curves of her bum smeared with my pussy-juice. Upon her left bum cheek, curved like a question mark, was one of my pussy hairs. What had I done? What suffering had I assigned to her at the Count's warm and merciless hands?

Yet something in me rejoiced at the thought of it, and longed to be present at the girl's coming inter-view with the Count. But now something else caught my notice: the moth shadows around the lamp were reduced in number and when I looked back at the bending Sophia I saw that her oozing pussy had drawn moths from the light as I had foreseen: two were already crawling down the curves of her bottom and one or two more, to judge from her wriggles, were at work between her thighs.

I slapped at Ruth's bum.

'Sophia has responded too enthusiastically to her bum-paddling,' I said, 'and her pussy is attracting moths. Shut up, you sluts!'

Muffled giggles had sounded from four or five of the girls.

'We will shortly see how well you attract moths yourselves,' I told the dorm, 'for I will shortly be seeing how the rest of you respond to similar blows landing on your bottoms. But . . .'

I broke off for a moment, listening.

'Yes, I thought that would shut you up. But in the meantime, Sophia's pussy and inner thighs need attention. You, Ruth –' I slapped again at her bottom

'– will see to them. Now! Do it. Get your shorts fully off, crawl to her, and begin licking.'

I stepped back and watched the tall Transmarynian girl discard her sports shorts and then begin crawling down the dormitory to the oozing pussy of her victim. Ah, I could not resist it: the way her bottom wriggled swung my paddle back and sent my feet scampering forwards to land – whoosh! – the hardest blow I had dealt yet to the firmest and perhaps most beautiful pair of bum cheeks in the dorm.

And perhaps the most sensitive too: Ruth's yelp of pain rang beneath the ceiling of the dorm and the eleven remaining bottoms jerked with fright and pain. But now I snorted with rage: the slut was positively *rubbing* at the pained spot as she crawled even faster to her destination.

'Stop!' I cried in Transmarynian. 'Stop, you slut.'

Still rubbing, she stopped. I swished the paddle experimentally as I advanced on her, preparing myself to deliver even harder blows on her.

'You are *rubbing* your arse, girl,' I continued, still speaking in Transmarynian, for I knew that eleven pairs of ears would be straining, mostly in vain, to decipher my words. 'How dare you? How dare you seek to ease pain legitimately inflicted upon you by your dorm mistress? Stop it, stop it this instant.'

With obvious reluctance, she dragged her hand away from her bottom, and I bent to examine the mark my paddle had left. Ah, she *was* especially sensitive: seldom have I seen such a strong response to stimulus. One entire cheek of her bum was flushed sowl,* darkening to vace* where the blade of the paddle had crashed home, and the other cheek, in nervous sympathy, was discolouring even as I watched. I held out my free hand and could feel the heat pouring off her bum even before I touched it.

'Beautiful,' I murmured in Transmarynian. 'You have a very beautiful bottom, girl.'

I swallowed and withdrew my hand from her bum with almost the same reluctance she had shown, realising that my fingers were gliding ever closer to the tightly sealed mouth of her delicious bumhole and that contact with it, even with my fingertips, might have prompted me to folly.

'Yes,' I said, raising my voice and speaking again in Romanian, 'a beautiful bottom. And it must suffer for your disobedience. Three strokes, girl, and if I hear a single squeak from you I shall add three more. Do you understand?'

The fingers of my free hand were rummaging between my thighs as I spoke, gathering pussy-juice; now, as she quivered with dismay and answered in a fear-tightened voice, 'Yes, mistress', I reached forwards and marked the left cheek of her bum with three laden fingertips, leaving three glistening vertical smears of my pussy-juice.

'These are the strokes you *will* receive,' I said, rummaging between my thighs again, 'and these –' I added a further three juice-smears to her right cheek '– the strokes you *may* receive, if I catch the slightest squeak or murmur. Very well?'

'Yes, mistress.'

Ah, her courage was returning, I could tell, like that of a batswoman in that absurd Transmarynian game of crucket or whatever it was called: the glistening strokes on her bottom had reminded me of the three sticks erected at each end of the – what was the word? – yes, the *wicket*. Well, this would not be a *wicket* but a *whackit* I was bowling on. Aye, a small voice whispered in my brain as I stepped back and prepared to begin, but would you not prefer *bowelling* to even such a delicious task as *bowling* against this

95

bottom? I shook my head involuntarily, but the voice had spoken sooth: even the delights of beating her bottom seemed insipid for a moment as I thought of sliding a d– home between those splendid cheeks as her sturdy frame, rocking with protest, was held down by five or six of her fellows; and I envied the Count again with a bitter envy. What dominant, in her heart of hearts, would not envy him? Aye, envy him possession of that fleshy rod with which he could pain and degrade his victims even as he received the most exquisite pleasure via the very instrument with which he inflicted that pain and degradation?

But recollection that his 'cock' was equipped with coarse and weakly responding nerves – else, Dr Helsingvili had reasoned, prolonged thrusting and friction would have been unneeded in Caliginia's exquisitely tight and tender nethermouths of pussy and bumhole – forced my envy down, and my appetite for the task in hand surged again. A bum-paddle and a paddled bum would suffice for me, and the thought had no sooner flashed through my re-excited brain than I sent the first of the three promised blows swishing through the air to crash home against that ultra-sensitive Transmarynian bottom. The poor girl almost left the ground vertically, so strongly did the sensation sing through her nerves, and I positively heard her teeth grind as she suppressed the urge to scream. Cruelty flamed up within me, fuelled by the delight of dominating such a long-limbed beauty, and I felt the urge to tell her that it was but a practice stroke, that the true three were still to come, and see her horrified reaction.

But that would not 'have been crucket', as the Transmarynian saying had it. I must match only the strength of my wrist against the firmness of her will to keep silent, and not take any unfair advantage.

'One,' I said as I prepared for my second stroke, then, 'Brace yourself, girl.'

And *swish! thwack!* the second blow flew home. A new metaphor occurred to me now: I was no longer bowling on a whackit, I was the storm-whipped sea of the Transmarynian Channel, hurling giant waves against the White Cheeks of Bendover, that they might crumble and topple. But the metaphor lacked verisimilitude, for the White Cheeks were no longer white but flaring vace, so heated by the punishment they had received that the six smears of my pussy-juice were already dried and flaking. I was in position again, and ready for the third stroke, which would be the strongest of all.

'Brace yourself, girl,' I said, swinging my arm back and up to its full extent and going up on my toes. This would be a thunderbolt descending from Heaven, hurled by Jumiter* against the doors of a blasphemous temple, to blast them flat and force the sheltering priestesses within to repentance. *Swiiish! Thwaaack!* Ah, and *this* time my sturdy Transmarynian priestess acknowledged the blow with a sob of agony that she tried to gulp back even as it forced its way between her writhing lips. But as my fingers flew to my aching clitoris and I began to squeeze and tug for an orgasm far beyond anything that monster the Count could know (I prayed), I coolly reached the decision *not* to inflict a further three strokes from her. There were three parts to my reasoning:

First, that a capricious dominant is even more wearing on the nerves of a submissive than an unswerving dominant. To know to the millimetre what penalty will be exacted for what offence allows the submissive some reassurance and certainty in the midst of her woes. But if she is unsure whether a reprieve will come when punishment is expected, or whether a punishment will be suddenly and capriciously doubled, she is cast adrift into chaos and has no sure footing for either hope or despair.

Second, I was glutted on my big-bottomed Transmarynian's pain and distress for the nonce and required a palate cleanser before I set to work on her again. More pairs of exquisite bum cheek beckoned from all points of the dorm, and I was now longing to sample their response to my bum-paddle, which I already seemed to have owned for years.

Third, Greek Sophia's pussy had now emptied the air of *all* the moths formerly swarming to the lamps, and I could see from her wriggles and suppressed murmurs that their tickling tongues would have her orgasming in another minute. Ruth's tongue on her pussy instead would doubtless have the same effect and even more quickly, but that would supply me with my excuse to return to the big-bottomed Transmarynian after my palate cleansing.

And so, with a snort of disdain, I ordered her on her way.

'Your buttocks are like wet dough,' I told her in Romanian, knowing that her beating would send her sliding to the foot of the hierarchy in the dorm for a day or two, with a new nickname ('Doughbum' or 'Flab-arse') to embitter her stay there. 'I am not wasting any more effort on them. Get licking Sophia's pussy as you were ordered, but beware: if you make her come, I will return to my kneading. Go!'

I reversed the paddle and jabbed at the rim of her sensitive arse-dell with the handle, sending her on her way with an indignant yelp. The shining tear-splatters revealed on the floor as she crawled forwards aroused my lust again and for a moment I regretted my decision to break off the bum-paddling of this tender-fleshed Juno. A glance up and down the dorm reassured me. My girls were still waiting for their punishment as I had ordered, bent forwards with sports shorts down and pale, sweat-moistened bottoms on full display.

I licked my lips and strolled to the head of the dorm, eyes flickering as I judged angles and distances. Could I sweep down the dorm delivering backhand and forehand blows with the paddle, chastising first a bum on the left, then a bum on the right, left, right, left, right, left, right, completing the full set of bums in the dorm in thirty seconds of vigorous work? (Save for Sophia's and Ruth's, of course, which I had already seen to?) *Should* I sweep down the dorm thus? Yes, I thought I should. No doubt my little beauties were already hoping that I was tiring of punishment and that my blows would begin to fall more lightly and infrequently. One sweep down the dorm, and another *up* it would disabuse them, and set me up nicely for my second bout with Ruth's bum: a moan from Sophia told me that the Transmarynian girl had no hope of obeying my command not to make her Greek cunnilinctree* orgasm.

Right. Then to work. I closed my eyes and bowed my head, sending up a prayer to the Goddess for success and visualising myself at work, backhanding and forehanding my way down the dorm. When I opened my eyes and raised my head, I pondered a moment whether to make a practice run, swinging but not landing. No, my girls would hear me pass and guess what I was up to. Better that it was a thunderbolt from a clear black sky. I nodded, swung my arm bac . . .

* * *

[Editrix's note: The MS breaks off here where half the page is burnt away, and resumes disconnectedly overleaf.]

. . . stumbled and nearly fell as I completed the return journey up the dorm, the strokes I had dealt on firm female bum flesh still ringing in my ears. My success had been complete, and my throbbing heart bounded anew as I heard Sophia succumb finally to Ruth's tongue on her juice-flooded pussy with moans and gasps of orgasm. Ruth's bum was mine again to do with as I pleased, and I felt ready to throw not six strokes of the bum-paddle against it, but sixty – six hundred!

After a moment to control my breath, I called out to her. 'You Transmarynian slut! You were ordered not to allow that Greek slut to come, and it is painfully audible that you have disobeyed completely. Come here, and prepare to receive the three paddle-strokes I mercifully rescinded, plus three more to pay for that illegal orgasm.'

I saw the head of the Transmarynian girl drop from between the Greek's glistening thighs, and then, hanging that head, she was crawling to me, wincing as her bottom throbbed in anticipation of the new strokes that awaited it.

'Face up!' I ordered and she obeyed, her fresh young face crusted with tears, her wide mouth shining with pussy-juice. Well, the crusting would be washed away in a minute, and I saw no rea . . .

[Editrix's note: Here the MS breaks off again, and no further word survives of Joanna's first encounter with her dormitory.]

Count Caradul's Diary, 11 October
(Kept in phonograph in Welsh).

Well, I come fresh from meeting our two new young Bulgarian teachers and have, naturally enough, a raging erection to dispose of. A trip to the milk-dungeons is indicated, but my cock will be all the firmer for ten minutes' delay and spurt all the stronger. I am still breaking in the arse of that big Romanian bitch – I forget her name – ah, yes, Artemisia. The pleasure of penetrating her will be heightened by the thought that two of her friends are above me as I slide my cock home. The bird that flew my net has returned of its own accord, and I will soon have it and its companion caged with the rest. My cock throbs at the prospect, but I must admit that – no, I feel a superstitious disinclination to name her till the moment I truly possess her – I must admit that Joanna's femmewife alone could almost satisfy me. That photograph of hers I saw in Wales barely hinted at her beauty, and said nothing at all of the grace with which she moves and the clarity and sweetness of her voice. How I longed to welcome her in traditional Transmarynian fashion, with a stripping and binding, while her enraged butchwife, also stripped and bound, watched and struggled in vain to prevent me forcing a thorough cock-sucking out of her!

But I would not, in tribute to her beauty, have insisted that she *swallow* on that first occasion. No, with consummate chivalry, I would have pulled my cock free and douched her breasts with my salty cream. Then I would have forced Joanna to lick them clean, allowing her to resume the sperm-training that she so wilfully broke off in Wales. Yes, Joanna, if I do not have you pregnant within the year it will not be for want of trying. You will swallow my sperm daily, or as much of it as I have to spare from your femmewife's sperm-training, before I take you *volens nolens** on a gallop down the Bulgarian highway. It will be *nolens*, I guess. [Laughter.] But would I have it any other way?

Later. I return glowing with satisfaction, cock freshly polished, from my session with big Artemisia. Her arse is not so sleekly curved as those of the Academy or as her own dear Caliginia's, but its puckered portal conceals riches of constriction and heat such as I have rarely experienced before. On each penetration she is as tight as ever, and it is as though I am taking her anal virginity for the first time. Nor does her rage at my penetration decrease or her resignation increase: to the sexual pride of a dominant she adds the martial valour of a soldier, and I believe I could bugger her daily for a year and never see her relent a fraction of her struggles and curses as I prepare her to receive my fleshy sword to the hilt. Ah, and I deployed my new trick to torment her today: a description of how Caliginia differs in her response to an identical anal assault.

'Not with struggles and curses, my fine fat-arsed Romanian slut, but with sighs of satisfaction and moans of pleasure! She pleads with me not to relent an inch, but to slide my cock home till she feels the hair of my pubic bush rub the sensitive rim of her sphincter. Like . . . ah . . . *this*, you slut.'

[Grunts and heavy breathing as the Count is lost in the memory of his session with Artemisia for a moment, before recovering himself.]

Aye. Aye. Then Caliginia, chained on the opposite wall and watching as I bugger her lover, bursts out with indignant denials of my calumny, despite the dire consequences I have threatened should she break her silence. But Artemisia, I know, is unsure whom to believe: her femmewife or her tormentor. I always penetrate Caliginia in private now, unchaining her and taking her into a separate cell, where Artemisia is unable to observe how she responds as I knock for entrance on her portals. And in truth, now that Caliginia knows who I am and what it is I intend to make of her, she is no longer the willing lover she was, though I know that she still receives more satisfaction from penetration by my cock than she will ever admit. Later today, when I take Caliginia away again for fucking, I will leave the door of the cell ajar and have Caliginia licked to orgasm by a milk-slave also, that her cries of ecstasy may reach Artemisia's unwillingly straining ears and seem to confirm what I tell her of her response to my cock. Caliginia will reveal the truth when she is returned to their double cell, but all dominants are jealous and possessive at heart, and the seed I have sown today will bear abundant fruit in future. Artemisia positively *vibrated* with involuntary rage and jealousy as I told my lies today, adding greatly to the pleasure I experienced as I buggered her, and I believe her anal chamber clamped on me even more tightly than it has done in the past.

But to other matters now, for my cock is stiffening too hard at these recollections and I worry that I should be forced to descend again and bugger her for a second time if I continue. Not that there would be any harm in that, *ceteris paribus*,* but other things are not equal. My balls are not inexhaustible, large as they are, and while Joseph and Paul are still in Wales and Richard still on business in Georgia, I must ration my sperm. Artemisia has received her dose today, but Caliginia still awaits hers, and I have three new milk-slaves to initiate. Their schoolfellows think they have been returned home, and letters will shortly be arriving for their special friends that seem to confirm this. That is the task I will set them today, in between cock-suckings and breast-nibblings: to write those letters and lessen the output of their friends' lacrymal glands, if not their own. But those friends need not fear that they will never see the miscreants again, for I have my plans well in hand for several of them to descend to the dungeons too, once a suitable interval has elapsed.

Ah, my cock has not softened in the slightest, but I have distracted myself from thought of Artemisia's arse and no longer feel tempted to descend and give it a second spearing. Where was I? Yes, new milk-slaves to come, and production is already flowing better than I dared hope. Iulia, the Bulgarian teacher I initiated into my schemes last week, has been as willing as I expected – though I almost wish she had refused when I revealed my secret and invited her to collaborate with me in enslaving the pupils of my Academy and exploiting the milk-making potential of their fresh young breasts. Yes, I almost wish she'd refused, had responded with horror to the prospect instead of with delight, for her own tits are very fine and would have yielded in rivers, I am sure, after a few doses of Count Caradul's lactifacient elixir. [Laughter.] I wonder how she has been getting on, spying on her two newly arrived fellow countrywomen from that observation post I have had built between the two dormitories. If I know my Joanna, not so well as she might have hoped! [More laughter.]

Later. It was as I expected: Joanna discovered my Bulgarian slut Iulia's hiding-place before that first encounter with her dorm was over. I am having Iulia suck me now by way of punishment, but though I am fully stiff and her poor mouth is crammed to capacity, I am in no danger of premature discharge. Not after Caliginia has been seen to, as she was but half-an-hour past, and two of the three new milk-slaves before her: it will be some time before my seminal vats are refilled, and even fingering my slut's bum weals – as I am doing now, to my own great satisfaction and her even greater dissatisfaction – will not hasten the process. Yes, Joanna spied her out, or rather *sniffed* her out: Iulia had been masturbating merrily as she observed the goings-on in the dorm and gorged her ears on the thwack of bum-paddle on bum, but I have noted myself that her pussy-juice is copious and heavily musked. Apparently, one of the *moths* in the room began to behave suspiciously near the wall behind which Iulia was hidden.

Noting this, Joanna suspended bum-beating for a minute while she investigated. Her eyes were then assisted by her nostrils – I must remember to flood them thoroughly with semen when I lay hands to her again – which reported the scent of my Iulia's frotted-forth pussy-juice and Joanna soon had the spy-holes-cum-breathing-holes of Iulia's hideaway sniffed out. Next, with the enthusiastic assistance of two of her girls – both anxious, no doubt, to forget the pain of their paddled backsides in the search – she uncovered the catch in the wall that released the door, and poor Iulia was exposed. I can imagine the gush of sex-heated air as the door swung open, and see Iulia blinking with dismay, hand still busy, perhaps, between her splayed thighs, even as Joanna's strong hand closed in her hair and hauled her forth like a snail from its shell.

Aye, for a snail would leave a slime trail too, and now that I investigate – yes, my Bulgarian slut's pussy is heavily crusted, and my fingertips are skilful enough to read and date three separate layers to the juice that has been gushing from it since last I laid hand to it. The first represents her excited anticipatory masturbation when, having received her orders from me, she first climbed into the observation post and waited for Joanna to reach the dorm; the second represents her voyeuristic masturbation as she watched Joanna set to work on the bums of her newly met girls; and the third represents her response to the sexual torture with which Joanna tried to wring the truth of her espionage out of her. But my Iulia did not crack – except down here, *cariad*,* eh? – and Joanna could not get her to confess that it was I who set her to the task of spying on the dorm.

Nevertheless, my respect for Joanna increases even more, for when I began to listen to the tale of what she had done to poor Iulia, I felt my cock, which I had thought ready to slumber for at least an hour after my session with Caliginia, soon raise his head and begin to look around him for relief. Iulia's pussy and bottom being, alas, off-limits for the nonce, for I promised her never to penetrate them when I recruited her to my cause – not a promise I have the slightest intention of keeping, I must inform you, *cariad* – I demanded that she suck me with the same mouth with which, by telling the tale, she had aroused me. And so here we find ourselves: she sucking, I being sucked, as I ponder again Joanna's punishment of her fellow countrywoman.

She claimed that the technique originated in Transmarynia, and even gave it a Transmarynian name, but I confess to strong doubts as to her veracity. *I* have never heard of quim-itch, and I suspect this was a private invention given an exotic veneer to impress her girls more thoroughly. And certainly, from Iulia's

106

account, they took to it even more enthusiastically than one might have expected, given that it was granting them an opportunity both to take their revenge on Iulia, an old enemy of theirs, and to postpone further punishment of their own. First, Iulia says, Joanna had one of the girls piss in a chamber pot. Having come fresh and sweating from vigorous exercise, the girl produced concentrated piss of a dark 'sowl' – yellow, that is – which was then used to daub the most sensitive part of poor Iulia's pussy as she was held down on a bed, thighs wide-splayed, with grinning girls clutching her by ankle and wrist.

Then came the part that began to stiffen me to full erection: one by one, all the girls in the dorm – those holding Iulia down exchanged places with their fellows – filed past the foot of the bed, kneeling at Joanna's command to *blow* gently on Iulia's exposed and piss-painted pussyhorn. The result, of course, was that the piss began to *dry*, setting up a gradually strengthening *itch* on her most sensitive part. Oh, poor Iulia suffers anew as the *thought* of it inflames my brain, for I am clutching her head harder to me and my cockhead has rung the clapper of her uvula. Yes, the thought of poor Iulia splayed on the bed, held down by grinning minxes as other minxes, also grinning, wait in line to kneel and blow softly against her pussy, glistening with its own dried juices and with crystals of the piss with which it has been painted. Such simple tools – piss and breath – and yet Joanna converts them into instruments of the most exquisite torture. Iulia's struggles to free a hand and relieve her clitoris of the itch were soon frantic, she tells me, but Joanna's response was to *worsen* her torment: her clitoris was redaubed with piss and gentle girl-breath was sent puffing across it anew.

Only the thought of my anger kept Iulia from breaking and telling Joanna what she demanded to know in exchange for one of the girls tonguing the drying piss from her pussy and clitoris. This was when I began to eye Iulia's mouth with carnal appetite, and when she told of Joanna's next step – to have piss daubed on selected points of her pussy-lips and on her nipples, before girls began to puff on her simultaneously at pussy and tit – I could no longer hold back and gruffly ordered her to commence sucking me, as a punishment for allowing herself to be discovered and tortured in this fashion. She tried to buy me off and prevent the invasion of her mouth with the news that Joanna had refined the torture still further when the labia-and-nipple daubings and puff-ings proved futile, but I was not to be denied. The images she had set working in my head were enough to be going on with, and I will hear and record the refinement of the torture later.

Mina Harker's Journal, 12 October.

I begin my own journal in my and Joanna's secret shorthand, for my darling's poor wrist is really in no fit state for writing and she is still recovering from what we have witnessed this morning in the Count's office. I too find my hand trembling as I write, and my stomach alternately tightens and loosens with nausea at the memory of the horrors enacted before our hidden eyes; but I find the courage to go on from two things. First is the thought that the Count's crimes must be recorded in detail, as an eternal warning to the future women of Europe; second is the renewed reversal of roles between Joanna and myself, whereby she is the temporarily weaker party and I the stronger. I cannot, and must not, fail her.

To begin, then. Joanna, as her own journal has told, promised to report her Transmarynian dorm-charge Ruth to the Count for disobedience; and though she had the greatest foreboding of what it might entail for the poor girl, she could not evade the promise, which had been made before the entire dorm. The smile that flashed on the Count's face when she made her report confirmed her worst suspicions, and the Count, who is already confident enough to have begun resuming his perverted patterns of wakefulness and sleeping in Romania, ordered that the girl be brought to him some hours past her own bedtime. Hereupon, Joanna resolved to find some means of witnessing what transacted between the Count and the Transmarynian girl. A little later, the two of us found a moment to explore his empty office on the ground floor and confirm the suitability of a place of concealment Joanna had already marked down.

A moment was all we needed to do so: the monster, as though flaunting his true nature to all the world, has *plants* in his office, nourished on the light that falls through his rarely curtained windows, and there was space for us to conceal ourselves later behind a bank of some delicate-leafed 'fern' (as I have learned from Joanna to call it). When we had left the office, the hours that then passed till the concealment proper dragged on leaden feet. Joanna would not tell me what she feared the Count would do to the poor Transmarynian girl, but I needed no spur for my own lurid imaginings; and when at last, slipping from our respective dorms as the hour of the interview approached, we hurried towards the Count's office, I was already in the grip of a sick and deepening apprehension.

We found the office unoccupied and went to earth behind the bank of fern: at this hour, as we have already discovered from subtle questioning of our girls and fellow teachers, the Count is most likely of all to have performed his regular trick of vanishing somehow from the Academy, being found neither in his bedroom nor in his office nor in any other spot – that is to say, in any other spot *above* ground. Joanna was convinced, on first hearing this, that at these times the monster was descending *beneath* the Academy, to underground dungeons that correspond with those of his castle in distant Wales; and the wisdom of her insight was confirmed after we had been in the office no more than five minutes. We both heard ascending footsteps echoing beneath the floor, then a grunt of effort, and saw, peeping through the ferns, a *trapdoor* swing open before the Count's desk.

Then the Count's own head and shoulders were raising through it, and I clutched at Joanna's shoulder, my heart arrested in my breast, as I saw his vace tongue licking obscenely at trickles of white fluid on his lips and chin. Ugh, he had been feeding from milk-slaves chained beneath us, among whom – my left hand, which Joanna holds tight as I pen these words, answers her grip – we both suspect our dear Caliginia and Artemisia to be included. Ugh – then came a second horror as the rest of the Count's body rose through the trapdoor, for his thigh-member was unbuttoned and jutting half-erect through his dress, its full length glistening with a mixture of sexual fluids.

An acrid reek, doubtless derived from the Count's own contribution to the mixture, reached our nostrils the moment after, mixed with the musk of pussy-juice and the homely tang of bum-dung. He had skewered some unfortunate pussy and some perhaps more unfortunate arse within the half-hour – Joanna, who is not suffering from a slight, anxiety-spawned cold as I am, believes she detected the musk of two pussies and perhaps even three in the scent that reached us. But then the Count was out of the trapdoor and letting it thud shut behind him as he strode across the floor straight towards us.

Joanna nearly cried out at this point, not merely in fear of the Count's advance, but also because my clutch at her shoulder tightened convulsively. But he had not seen us, he had another task to pursue: that of seizing hold of his thigh-member and drawing back the curtain of skin on its swollen head to direct a heavy stream of piss onto the ferns behind which we crouched. Splatters of it, obscenely hot and reeking with his monstrous sex odour, fell on my face and lips, and I forced back the vomit that rose in my throat. He seemed to piss for minutes on end; then, with a shake and grunt, he was done, and turned away to a washstand in one corner of his office, where he cleaned his thigh-member – 'cock' is the word, I remember now – in preparation for the interview with Joanna's dorm charge. And how I wish I had had water to cleanse my piss-defiled face, and not been forced to do so with the sleeve of my dress!

We heard the footsteps of an approaching pair of women along the corridor some seconds before he did, with his coarse hearing, but I gasped silently to see the speed with which he reacted: his limbs were a positive blur as he snatched up some object on a shelf and slid behind his desk, setting the object before him on the desktop and jamming himself and his chair tight up against the desk as a knock sounded on his door.

'Enter,' he called, as Joanna and I frowned at what we saw on the desk before him: the object he had snatched up was a narrow cloth-covered *cage* about thirty or forty centimetres in height, as though for some tall bird. But now the door was swinging open and one of the Academy's nightwardens was ushering a yawning girl into the Count's presence: the tall Transmarynian girl Ruth from Joanna's dorm. I was watching the Count's eyes as the pair came in, and felt a sickening lurch in my stomach as I saw a glitter there as of a wolf spying a lamb. He planned to enact some perverted horror before us, but what form it would take I could, as yet, only guess.

The nightwarden pushed the girl forwards to stand in front of the Count's desk, where Joanna and I could not see her face or the front of her body, then left the room at his curt nod. As the door closed, leaving the two quite alone (as they both thought), the girl's back and bottom shivered with involuntary fear and I saw the Count's eyes glitter again as they dropped to her breasts, which had evidently juddered most becomingly with her emotion. His thick tongue swept along his lips again, and then he lifted his eyes to the poor girl's face.

'You are Ruth, are you not?' he said in his deep, rumbling Romanian.

The girl tried to speak, but the thickening cloud of menace and threat in the air was too much for her, and she could only nod.

'You have been reported to me by your dormitory mistress, Madame Ignatieva. For –' and here he reached out and slid an open file towards him '– unauthorised punishment of two of your dormitory mates, Sophia and Julia. Is that so?'

Again the girl could only nod, and another shiver ran through her tall body. The Count, evidently more than satisfied by the fear he read in her face, did not drop his eyes to her breasts this time, but again his thick tongue passed over his lips.

'What did you do to them, Ruth, my dear?' he asked. 'Beat them?'

His tongue and lips caressed the words lasciviously. Another nod from the girl, and now I could see that she was trembling with apprehension. The Count's manner was like that of a great snake coiling to strike, or of an eagle spreading its wings to launch itself downwards on its cowering prey. I heard Joanna's breath quickening beside me, and our hands flew together.

'Then you enjoy beating girls, my dear? Beating girls . . . on their bottoms?'

Another nod, almost undetectable in the shaking that had seized the girl's entire body. The menace radiating from the Count, which beat so powerfully on *our* brains, had her as its focus, and she evidently feared an imminent assault. Our hands tightened on each other, and without a word spoken, we sealed a pact for an attempted rescue when the assault came, tiny though both of us believed our chances of success to be. But what was this? With a visible effort, the Count was taking his eyes from the girl's face and nodding with a slow grunt.

'Quite understandable, my dear,' he said, dropping into Transmarynian as though to reassure her (Joanna has translated it for me). 'Quite understandable.'

He looked up again, and now the glitter was gone from his eyes, replaced, though I could scarce credit it, with a look of compassion and concern.

'You are far from home,' he resumed in Romanian, but with a sprinkling of Transmarynian words and phrases evidently designed to make the poor girl feel more at ease, 'missing the "bottoms" I am sure you ministered to there, and sought merely to assuage your "homesickness", no doubt?'

Another nod from the girl, who managed to clear her throat and stammer out a full reply this time. 'Yes, Count . . . Countess Caradul.'

'Ah. I thought it so. But come, my dear, you are trembling –' oh, the hypocrite! '– and evidently fear this chat more than you should. Indeed, any fear at all would be excessive.'

I heard a drawer in his desk go back and he lifted a bottle onto the desktop, then two small glasses.

'Here, my dear. Please share a little Transmarynian, ah, elixir with me. It is an excellent specific –' he was filling the two glasses, and my nostrils twitched as they caught the reek of the stuff drifting across the room '– against nervousness and irrational fears of all kind, my dear.'

He lifted a glass towards the girl, who took it with evident reluctance. I heard her sniff and sneeze, as though the stuff seared her nostrils. The Count smiled kindly, but I saw the menacing glitter return to his eye for a second.

'It *tastes*, my dear, much pleasanter –' he raised his own glass and sipped '– than it smells. Try a little. For your headmistress's sake, my dear. Pinch your nose shut, like this, and sip.'

He demonstrated, and the girl pinched her own nostrils shut and slowly raised the glass to her face.

'Go on, my dear,' said the Count, and my heart constricted in my chest as I saw how closely he watched his victim. There was more to this than met the eye: this was some powerful drug he was forcing her to take, perhaps to render her unconscious that he might perform his assault at leisure. But now I jerked in fright, almost crying out as the girl sipped for a moment, then dropped the glass on the Count's desk as she burst out in a frantic bout of coughing. Realising after a moment what she had done, and that she had spilled her 'elixir' over the Count's desk and the papers there, she began to stammer out, or rather gasp out, apologies between her coughs. But the Count, still playing the sympathetic headmistress, shook his head and waved his hand deprecatingly.

'It is nothing, my dear. I know how strong it is on first acquaintance. You do not have to lick it from the desktop.' I could tell from the way his voice hardened that his first inclination was to order her to do precisely this. 'No. I will pour you another glass.'

He fitted his actions to his words, retrieving the dropped glass and refilling it, then holding it out to the still-coughing girl, who shook her head, sending glittering tears flying left and right.

'Please, mistress, it is t–'

'No!'

The open palm of the Count's free hand came down flat on the desk with a *crack* that made me jump.

'Drink, my dear,' he said. 'It is for your own good. You tried, a little foolishly, to drink too much at a time before. Sample it more *slowly* this time.'

Barely veiled menace was back in his voice and manner, and the poor girl took the glass he proffered, pinched her nose shut, and raised the glass to her lips again.

'Slowly, my dear. Slowly. Ah, yes. That's it.'

The girl coughed again, but much less than before, and she had evidently successfully drank a little of the 'elixir'.

'Now, some *more*,' said the Count. 'A little at a time.'

He raised his own glass as he spoke, and sipped as he watched the girl sip and cough, sip and cough. For a few minutes, nodding and grunting with satisfaction, he urged the girl to drink until the glass she held was three-quarters empty.

'Just a little more, my dear. But would you not like to know the name of what you are drinking, my dear, hmmm?'

The girl sipped, coughed, and stammered.

'It is elixir, isn't it, mistress?'

'It is *an* elixir, my dear,' the Count replied. 'But a special kind, from your homeland and mine. It was once called *aqua vitae*, "water of life", but those of us who know it well generally call it . . . "whisky".'

I jumped a little again, but this time with surprise, not fright, for the girl had not suddenly begun coughing, but had *giggled*.

' "Whixy",' she said, as though the word amused her, and took another sip from her glass, with scarcely a cough this time.

'Nearly right, my dear,' said the Count, not at all disconcerted by her sudden change of mood. His eyes sought out the glass in the girl's hand and he grunted quietly to himself with satisfaction.

'Here, my dear,' he said. 'Let me "top you up".'

He lifted the bottle forwards and the girl, with more giggles, held out her glass for him to add more, tutting with disappointment when he drew the bottle back.

'No,' he said, 'that is enough, for now. You are already pleasantly relaxed, are you not?'

'Y . . . yesh, mishtresh,' the girl replied in Transmarynian, and I frowned with puzzlement. First trembling, then giggling, now *slurring*. If this elixir – this 'whisky' – was a drug, it had effects like none I had ever encountered before. Save, I should have remembered, in the pages of Joanna's journal, where she described the effects of that throat-searing liquid forced on her by the Count's three evil suns.

'Yes, you are very pleasantly relaxed,' the Count continued, 'and we can resume the interview proper.'

He reached out and slid the file on his desk nearer to him, brushing off drops of 'whisky' with a genial click of his tongue.

'I read here that you are an animal lover, my dear. Yes –' and now, glancing up, he positively smiled, for the girl's eyes had evidently widened with understanding on the cage '– I have something here for you. A special little animal.'

'Lickle animal?' the girl said, speaking Transmarynian again and swaying a little where she stood.

'Yes, my dear. A little animal. Or perhaps –' he began to draw the cover off '– not so little.'

Joanna's hand tightened convulsively on mine in anticipation of what was to come, and I might have cried out in pain had I not been held breathless by the horror of what I now witnessed as the cover was lifted away: *inside the cage stood a long tube of flesh, stiff, swollen, and crawling with veins, and seeming to twitch with venomous – with verminous – pride as the girl cried out softly with astonishment.* For a moment, despite the horror that overwhelmed me, knowledge of what it was I saw refused to enter my consciousness, then I slumped forwards in a half-swoon that might have alerted the Count to our presence, had Joanna, with disregard of her own and more justifiable emotion, not seized and supported me.

Aye, for the first time I had witnessed the Count's enormous 'cock', which he was evidently projecting through a hole in the desktop and into the cage, whose floor was lined with wood shavings. For a moment the full knowledge threatened to deepen my swoon to unconsciousness, but now Joanna was gently pinching my earlobe and my nauseated brain was clearing sufficiently to catch the words now spoken by the Count.

'. . . lind cave-worm, my dear,' the Count was rumbling. 'From the mountain caves of my own dear homeland in Wales. And it too, I believe, experiences a certain homesickness. Come, my dear, stroke it.

Tickle it. It will respond to the touch of your hand, I believe.'

The girl was swaying where she stood, eyes evidently fixed on the 'creature' within the cage. The Count was swinging the top of the cage open, and with a disguised thrust of his hips he pushed the 'cave-worm' higher. I could see the way the 'foreskin' was half-drawn back over the swollen 'cockhead' and caught a glitter of fluid leaking from the 'creature's' 'mouth'.

'Come, my dear. Touch it. It will not bite you. Cave-worms are harmless creatures. Stroke the poor thing, and help it forget its homesickness even as ministering to it helps you to do the same.'

The girl's hand came out, and Joanna's hand tightened on mine again as the Count's 'cock' twitched in anticipation. Urgh, and there it was: that sweet girlish hand, whose beauty and grace spoke of Woman, the highest fruit on the highest branch of the Tree of Life, had touched that foul 'cock', whose ugliness and grossness spoke of 'man', a tumour on that same tree. The girl grunted with disgust, and I remembered Joanna's tale of how unnaturally *warm* the Count's flesh was. But her hand did not leave the cock and she began to stroke and caress that deadly member as the Count had instructed her.

'Yes, m–' The Count had to cough away the lust that had evidently and repulsively seized him. 'Yes, my dear. That is the way. Stroke it. Tickle it. Draw back its hood and puff your breath on it. You will remind the dear little creature of the cool air and breezes in its vanished cave dwelling.'

The girl obeyed his instructions again and began, with deluded murmurs and coos of affection, to puff breath on that foul tube of lust-swollen flesh as she continued to stroke and tickle it. I saw the Count's knuckles whiten as he gripped the desktop, for he was fighting off the urge to launch a sexual assault on the girl, I believe: to slip his disguised cock from its cage and hurl himself across the desk on his tender victim. Oh, and he positively groaned as the girl puffed breath on the bald head of his cock, nauseating me to such an extent that I again had to swallow back vomit that lanced up my throat from my roiling guts.

With an unsteady hand, the Count reached out and lifted his own glass of 'elixir' (whisky) and drained it at a gulp. The girl looked up at him, perhaps reading from the movement of the cock in her hand that there was some connexion between the 'cave-worm' and the Count. But he drove the dawning truth from her whisky-fuddled head with another instruction.

'Your own glass is not empty, my dear. Have another few sips, for it will smell the whisky on your breath as you puff air on it, and be reminded of its faraway home.'

Joanna's hand quivered in mine, and I read her rage as clearly as though she had spoken it aloud. Such nonsense he was speaking, spinning a web of lies and deceit around his poor victim as he encouraged her to perform perversions worse than any all the brothels of Bulgaria could show for the past thousand years.

'Good girl,' he was rumbling, for the poor Transmarynian was sipping again at her whisky with her free hand, while her other hand continued to stroke and caress the cock, as though its fleshy warmth now held some special attraction for her.

'Kiss it, my dear. Kiss the dear little creature. The pressure of your lips will . . . ahh –' he shuddered as he inhaled, for the words had barely left his lips than the girl was pressing her own lips to the bald cockhead '– remind it . . . ah . . . of the smooth rock it . . . ah . . . it brushes as it passes . . . ah . . . passes through its native caves.'

I could see no obvious parallel myself, but the girl was apparently beyond such quibbles, for she kissed the cockhead again, invoking another shuddering inhalation from the Count.

'Thank you, my dear. And perhaps . . . ah . . . you could kiss lower *down* its body. The top of the cage will open further, and you can lift it away entirely from the base if you please, allowing you to come at Vermicula from any angle. No, a little further to the right. That catch. Yes, that's it. And now the others. Yes.'

The girl was fumbling at the cage, snapping back catches so that she could do as the Count had instructed her, and fondle and kiss the cock to the even greater satisfaction of its owner.

'Good girl,' the Count said. 'That's the way.'

The Transmarynian girl was lifting the top of the cage away from its base, and the cock stood proudly forth, the leakage of fluid from its 'mouth' almost a *trickle* now. Joanna has told me now that it is some twisted equivalent of our own pussy-moistening, whereby a cock prepares itself for the discharge of its liquid 'orgasm' (how I hate to apply that sacred term to such a twisted monster as the Count). She tasted such leakage when she sucked the cocks of the Count's three suns in that Welsh castle, before they hosed her poor throat with their 'sperm', and here was the same physiological mechanism at work in the father.

'Yes, my dear. Good. Now kiss Vermicula.'

The girl's head lifted from its deluded gaze on the 'cave-worm' and she slurred out: 'Ver . . . Vermic'la, mistress?'

'Yes, my dear. Vermicula. That is the little creature's name. You can translate it, of course.'

The girl's head dropped back to the Count's cock, and she took hold of it again.

'Yes, mistress.'

She leaned forwards and kissed the cock near its base.

'It means.'

Another kiss, higher up.

'Little.'

And another. She was kissing her way up the length of the cock as the Count had instructed her.

'*Worm.*'

A final kiss on the cockhead, and a grunt of surprise.

'Yes, my dear. "Little worm". But what is wrong?'

The girl was rubbing at her lips with her free hand.

'Shalty,' she said. 'Shalty.'

'Ah,' said the Count. 'It is a *lubricant*, my dear, released from a gland in Vermicula's head. It assists the creature to squeeze its way through tight passages. It is obviously very homesick, to have begun doing this. Perhaps ... perhaps, my dear, out of the kindness of your heart, you could ...'

The girl looked up, head wobbling. The Count gazed at her, his eyebrows lifting in enquiry and dislodging fragments of powder from his forehead. The girl snorted with amusement as they bounced down his face, but I confess that I shivered with unease: there was something *sinister* in the sight of it. Now the Count smiled and nodded, as though confirmed in some decision.

'Yes, my dear. Perhaps out of the kindness of your heart you could supply a simulacrum of the cave crack for which the poor creature is longing?'

I sensed Joanna tense beside me. What did the Count intend? A cock assault on the pussy or bottom of the girl?

121

'To ease its homesickness, my dear. Out of the kindness of your heart. Hmmm? You could do it quite easily. Just take its head in your . . . your *mouth* . . . and . . . and *suck*.'

The girl, who had been watching the Count, perhaps to see further fragments of face powder fall, grunted with surprise at this suggestion. Now her head fell to the cock standing erect before her.

'Shuck?' she said, looking up again.

'Yes, my dear. Suck. Just take the head of the creature of your mouth and . . . suck. The moisture and coolth will remind it of its faraway home. Which it will perhaps never see again. Which it will *probably* never see again. The lifespan of the cave-worm is very short, you know. Very short. Poor creature.'

'But,' the girl said. 'It'sh *shalty*. And *warm*.'

'Poor creature,' the Count repeated, as though he had not heard her words. He lowered his own eyes to his cock, pursing his lips sadly. There was a moment's pause, then the girl grunted again – but no, it was not a grunt, but a *sob*. The Count's lying words had touched her tender heart.

'Shalty,' she repeated. 'And warm.'

Her hand came up again and took hold of the cock, curling around its bulk. But the tips of her fingers did not meet.

'Hot,' she corrected herself. 'Not warm. Hot. And –' her head dropped to the cockhead and she sniffed '– shalty.'

Her head came back and she looked at the Count, who raised his eyebrows again.

'A little service, out of the kindness of your heart,' he said, slurring a little himself, too. 'For a poor creature, far from home. Which is also *your* home, my dear. And mine.'

'Shalty shuck?' the girl said, looking at the cock again.

122

'Yes. For a poor creature.'

'Shalty shuck,' the girl said, and her head dropped back to the cock. Breath hissed into the Count's mouth and I realised her mouth must be opening, ready to take the cockhead in. And then – oh, Goddess, how could it be? – there it was: she was doing it, sucking the Count's 'cock', and I closed my eyes with disgust and horror.

'Good girl,' I heard the Count rumble, straining to keep the pleasure out of his voice. '*Kind* girl. Suck the poor creature. Yes. Like that. I think. He s . . . it seems to be enjoying it.'

The girl's mouth came off his cock with a pop and I opened my eyes.

'Shalty,' she mumbled, and then closed her mouth on his cock again. I shivered with disgust but managed to keep my eyes open this time.

'Yes, my dear,' he was saying. 'Salty. It is leaking hard now. Take it deeper. Deeper, my dear. Move your mouth back and forth. Ow! No, my dear. Do not use your teeth. He is a delicate little fellow. Suck him. And rock your mouth back and forth on him. It. On it.'

The Count – the Beast, rather – had started to sweat, for the face powder was darkening on his forehead as the girl clumsily sucked and rocked on his cock.

'Yes, my dear. Yes. That is the way. He is enjoying it greatly. It is enjoying it. Greatly. I can tell. Harder, my dear. Suck harder. Can you feel it swell? It is –'

But he suddenly reached out and caught hold of the girl by her ears, jamming her head down hard over his cock. What was he doing? His mouth came open and he groaned, eyes half closing, eyelids fluttering. His grip on the girl's ears loosened and her head came off his cock with an indignant jerk. She was choking and spluttering and I realised that Joanna was whispering under her breath, over and over.

'The Fiend. The Fiend. The Fiend.'

Now I realised what he had done: spurted that foul sexual fluid of his into the girl's mouth, searing its delicate tissues with its saltiness and heat.

'There, there, my dear.'

He had reached out and was patting her head as she coughed and retched.

'You have pleased him – pleased it very much, you know. Please accept my apologies – I should have warned you of what might ensue if your simulacrum –' he grunted with hypocritical laughter '– was *too* effective. He – it has released its mating fluid. Its seeding fluid, I mean.'

The girl, apparently shocked out of her elixir-induced befuddlement by the taste, the heat and (ah, my stomach rolls yet again at the thought of it) the *thickness* of the Count's sex-fluid, withdrew from his patting hand and stood staring at him, swaying only slightly now.

'You,' she said, 'you *knew*.'

The Count stared at her a moment, then reached out for her glass. 'Knew what, my dear?' he said over the glug of whisky as he refilled her glass.

'You knew that it would . . . it would *squirt*. That is why you held my head down. So I had to swallow it or choke.'

'Really, my dear? I knew? But of course: I could see him wiggle.'

' "Him"?' the girl said. 'What . . . what izh . . . what *is* "him"?'

'It, my dear. I mean it. Here, have another glass. It will take away the nasty taste.'

A smile touched his lips fleetingly before he could

suppress it, and the girl stared at him, I believe, wondering whether she had seen it there.

'You are laugh–' she began accusingly, but the Count held out her glass again with a gruff, 'Take it. Drink. It will take away the taste.'

His dominance, which he seemed able to turn on and off with the ease of the most skilful butchwife, was heavy in the air of the room again, and the girl took the glass with sudden meekness, sipping from it with dropped eyes.

'Good girl,' the Count said. 'Very good girl.'

Joanna nudged me and I looked towards her to see her mouthing something at me. I could not understand her for a moment, then realised it was: 'Cock.'

When I looked back at the scene before me, I saw what I had overlooked before: that the 'cave-worm' was softening and drooping forwards, apparently exhausted by the discharge of its 'sperm' into the poor Transmarynian girl's mouth. Was her ordeal over then? Had the Count sated himself on her? Alas, it soon transpired that the answer was an emphatic 'No'.

The Count watched the girl sipping from her 'whisky', then his eyes dropped cunningly to his cock and he gasped aloud as though in sudden panic and surprise.

'My dear!' he exclaimed, and the girl, whose head was wobbling in befuddlement again, shook it, trying to clear it and look towards him.

'The poor cave-worm,' the Count continued. 'It has discharged too heavily, and I fear it is on the point of . . . *death*.'

The girl, catching the urgency of the moment from his lying histrionics, gasped in horror, and the glass of whisky fell again from her trembling hand, splashing whisky on the Count's desk. She shook her head and suddenly began weeping.

'I am shorry, mishtresh. Shorry. Pleazh forgive –'
she hiccuped incongruously '– pleazh *forgive* me.'

'No blame attaches to you, my dear,' said the
Count, reaching out and taking hold of his cock. 'But
the remedy rests in your hands. Or rather –' he shook
his cock, making it flop sadly '– between your *cheeks*.'

The girl must have gaped foolishly at him, for he
grunted with exasperation.

'Your cheeks, my dear. The cheeks of your *bottom*.
Quick, quick, get undressed and squat atop the table.'

Such were the urgency and command in his voice
that, though I was not the object of his words myself,
I felt a strong impulse to obey him, and had to fight
it down by strength of will. The poor Transmarynian
girl, befuddled by his whisky, feeling herself alone
and friendless, stood no more chance of resisting his
command than a lone sapling stands chance of
resisting the full force of the autumn gale. As the one
bends, so bent she: the girl was undoing her buttons
and tugging off her clothes in less time than it takes
to write it.

The richness of form and flesh that was revealed
affected me, I confess, at both heart and pussy: her
breasts were of perfect symmetry and of more-than-
perfect size – which is to say, they were just *slightly*
in excess of my fondest taste, satisfying the lustful eye
to the full and then embittering the draught with a
drop of satiety, so as to heighten its sweetness. And I
almost groaned to see them quiver as she climbed
atop the desk: such *firmness* they had, like twin fruit
that approach, but do not achieve, their full ripeness.
Aye, it is a strange metaphor for an insectivore such
as I, but no brain can stand within range of the
blazing sun of the Count's personality and escape
unscorched: I was, and am, corrupted by him, and in
that moment rejoiced to be so, for I saw the girl with

126

both my own eyes and *his*, and feasted on a double serving of lust.

But my lust was soon dashed from me by what succeeded when the girl had climbed atop the table and was swinging her body to place the twin moons of her buttocks, at the Count's direction, above the ailing 'cave-worm'. We could now see her face and from the expression thereon I believe that she had no inkling of what the Count intended her to do, as one would expect in a girl of her age and innocence. No, she was motivated by the purest altruism and philogyny (if the word can apply to a worm), and sought merely to rescue a fellow creature from the grip, as she thought it, of imminent death.

But the Count knew what he intended, and my stomach rolled again as I saw his foul cock twitch and begin to restiffen as the shadow of those pearly buttocks fell upon it and the poor girl's bottomhole lay naked and unsuspecting above his cockhead.

'Lower yourself, my dear,' he ordered, his voice thick with reawoken lust. '*Rub* yourself on him.'

The girl gaped over her shoulder at him, and it was plain that she could not understand his instructions. The delay was too much for the Count, and with a snarl of impatience and lust his heavy hands flashed up and seized the body of his victim. She cried out most piteously as his fingers – burning on her cool flesh, I cannot doubt, like coals – fastened to her breasts and seized control of her, and I heard Joanna supress a sob with horror beside me.

'Rub yourself, my dear,' the Count repeated. 'Like *this*.'

The girl was a chip of wood on a mill-race, a feather in a hurricane: he tugged her down on his re-erecting cock and stroked its swelling head up and down the cleft of her buttocks. She moaned with surprise and fright, and stammered out, 'It burns! It burns!'

At this, Joanna turned her head aside from the sight, burying her face against my neck, as though she were the submissive and I the dominant in our partnership. My heart near tore in two with contending compassions: for the innocent girl atop the desk, whose innocent bottom was about to be sacrificed on the altar of the Count's unholy lust; and for my darling Joanna, whose memory of similar, though lesser, suffering at the Count's hands had proved too much.

'Aye,' said the Count, dropping one hand from a breast to seize his victim by the waist and position her for final – urgh! – *penetration.* 'It burns without, and shall now burn –' he filled his lungs with a rush of air '– *within.*'

It verges on blasphemy to recall it, as it *partook* of blasphemy to experience, but I could not be otherwise reminded, at that moment, than of the words of my favourite theologian, the sainted French Marquise de Sade, whose allegory of rewarded virtue was so often at my bedside in my youth. When his heroine, treading thorns that she might later pluck roses, is imprisoned in that convent of hypocritically cruel nuns, one of her companions, sweet Octavie, is assaulted by a nun in some perverted fashion the Marquise, with her habitual reticence and good taste, does not specify.

But in the moment that the Count's cockhead, driven upwards with merciless force and accuracy, breached the sphincter-guarded portal of poor Ruth's bottom and pistoned within, searing her delicate rectal tissues with its unnatural heat, I knew to what it was Octavie had been subject, for the Marquise's words rang in my brain as Ruth's cry of unwilling surrender rang in my ears: *Un cri touchant de la victime nous annonce enfin sa défaite.**

But in the next moment, as the bestial grunts of the Count and the moans and shrieks of Ruth announced that he had commenced his thrusts in the girl's silk-walled bum-chamber, I had my own victim to contend with: Joanna toppled sideways on me, her overburdened brain, struck by the horror of what it was we witnessed, had given way and pulled a pall of unconsciousness over her seared sensibilities. I had to seize and hold her as the Count grunted his way to orgasm, when his thick, vein-crawled cock, thrusting deep between those velvet bum cheeks into a dark paradise of forbidden sensuality, would spurt the boiling load of his heavy balls. Ah, at the thought of it, I myself almost lost consciousness, and Joanna's lithe body was lead heavy against me, resisting my weakening hands.

I pressed my lips to her ear, kissing it and nibbling it gently, seeking to awake her and relieve me of my burden. I succeeded: with a shiver, she came awake, and I warmed with fright at the groan with which she greeted the tableau before us: the beautiful girl, helpless as a doll in the apelike grip of the Count, being lifted and replaced with quickening rhythm on the Count's fleshy thigh-member. But I believe the Count would have been too engrossed on his anal violation of his soft-fleshed victim to hear the detonation of a cannonade in his office: his eyes, I could see, were blazing with lust, and I would have been unsurprised to hear from his victim that their gaze scorched her naked back.

Then, as though I caught the thought from that monstrous brain, the Count protruded his tongue and leaned forwards to begin licking the poor girl's back and spine, grunting with satisfaction at the taste of

129

her sweat. Even through the sensation of the repeated retreat and reinvasion of her bowels she felt the heat and moisture of that vast tongue, and her futile struggles for freedom pathetically increased. But it was apparent that the licking was a prelude to paroxysm: the Count's grip on her body shifted, both of his vast hands leaping around and forwards to seize her breasts and plunge her firmly down on his cock as he took a final lick of her smooth and delectable skin.

The girl gasped on a new note, and I saw her eyes widen with surprise and her face tighten and loosen to the spurts of boiling 'sperm' being fired from the heavy piece of artillery inserted into the breech in her bottom. So strong and so unfamiliar was the sensation that she seemed oblivious to the merciless grip on her tits, though I guessed [correctly. Edx.] that it would be recorded for days to come in finger-mark bruises. One spurt I counted, two, three, four, five I counted, six, seven, eight; and then the sexual tension that had brooded thundercloud-like in the office since the beginning of the interview had broken with almost an audible thunderclap, and I was aware with disgust of the feral odour of the Count's lust-sweat, nostril-piercing and musky as some great animal's.

When he lifted the girl – with an uncorking *pop* – off his thigh-member, the office was invaded by a new and even fouler odour, salty and marine, and I heard Joanna murmuring a prayer beside me. It was an unneeded clue, though I felt a pang at the thought of what memories must be hammering in her brain: the new odour was that of the Count's 'sperm', glistening on the subsiding length of his cock, and dripping from the bumhole of his whimpering victim.

When the Count spoke again, I positively quivered with surprise: what I had witnessed had been so brutal, so far beyond the boundaries of even the worst dominant's cruellest behaviour, that my brain had reclassified him as wholly beast, with no breath of either compassion or intelligence. To hear him *speak* was a sudden and shocking contradiction of this reclassification, and for a moment I struggled to understand what he was saying.

'Excellent, my dear. Truly excellent. You have a bottom worthy of a nation's homage and worship, and do not fear that I will neglect to mine it again and even more thoroughly before another day has passed.' (At this, the girl, who was slumped forwards on the desk moaning in semi-delirium, made an effort to struggle forwards and off the desk, as though the prospect of another anal penetration had shocked her back to her senses.)

'No, my dear,' the Count continued, withdrawing his cock through the hole in the desk and standing up, 'I cannot see you depart yet.'

He moved swiftly round the desk and caught hold of the girl as she slid to the floor. She struggled in his steely grip, but tall and sturdy as she was, he was taller and sturdier by far and her resistance was as futile as that of a tiny moth caught in a freshly constructed spider's web. A pang of fear shot through me as I watched him jerk her clean off her feet with no more effort than if he lifted a slim folder from his desk.

'Thank you, my dear,' he said, planting a kiss on her moaning mouth as one hand slid down her back to her buttocks, which they fondled and squeezed as he kissed her again. 'Such a sweet morsel you are, and I have hopes that your pussy will prove even tighter and more pleasurable than your bottom.'

The girl cannot have understood what he said, else surely she would have fainted in his arms. Instead, she beat at him with fists no more effective, on his oaklike chest, than falling acorns.

'Come, my dear,' he said, 'cease this, or you shall surely reawaken my concupiscence and I will be forced to bugger it away for a second time.'

He turned where he stood as his second hand dropped to her buttocks, almost as though he deliberately intended to give us a glimpse of her silken bum cheeks full-on, their cleft splayed by his hands so that her bumhole, momentarily gaping from his cock-penetration, flashed and shone in our horrified eyes. Joanna shuddered with disgust and disbelief beside me, and when one of his huge forefingers circled the swollen rim of the girl's bumhole and then slid slowly within, I sensed her head drop to shield her from the sight.

My own disgust was no less deep, but seemed to hold me paralysed, so that I saw the finger disappear almost to its full length, probing for the depths of her hitherto inviolable bum-chamber. The girl cried out with indignation, beating on his chest harder, and her head dropped suddenly to his shoulder. The Count swore in Transmarynian, then laughed as he lifted his other hand and seized her by the neck, dragging her head away from him.

'You minx,' he rumbled, for she had evidently tried to bite him, driven finally to animalism by the perversions he practised on her. 'But what is sauce for the goose, my dear, is sauce for the gander.'

By now both of us were shivering with the fear of our final realisation that any assault on him launched by the two of us would have been as likely of success as the assault of two autumn leaves on the north wind, and so it was that we watched in disgusted and horrified silence as he hoisted her higher into the air, one hand clamped still on her neck, the other still busy directing his probing finger on her bottom, and played the gander to her goose; viz., nibbling and gnawing her breasts in a way that, to judge from her cries and struggles, was intended to set her down the path to premature and wholly unnatural lactation.

When at last the pain of his mammarian attentions was too much to bear and she fainted, he withdrew his finger from her bottom, wiped it on her back with vertical and horizontal strokes that had an air of *proprietorship*, and hoisted her limp body over his shoulder as he stooped and lifted the trapdoor in the floor of his office. Then, beginning to sing a Transmarynian song whose words Joanna has reluctantly agreed to recall and translate for me, he descended with her to his slave-dungeons, his voice drifting up to us where we hugged each other wordlessly for comfort in face of the unspeakable evil we had just witnessed.

'Twelve milkmaids,
Chained underground,
Twelve milkmaids,
Chained underground,
And whatever their friends may do,
They never will be found,
For they're twelve milkmaids,
Chained underground . . .'
                              (To the tune of 'Ten Glart* Bottles'.)

Count Caradul's Diary, 12 October
(Kept in phonograph in Welsh).

I return from chaining up the twelfth of my new milkmaids: a freshly buggered young Transmarynian, her bottom leaking as freely as her eyes. To judge by the taste of her breast skin and nipples, she will be a quick milker: I never bit a girl yet with that freshness and floweriness of flavour who was not yielding at

133

top rate within a fortnight. In fact, she brings my mind back to my future plans: the *breeding* scheme I intend to organise among the women of Europe once my power is consolidated here and I have more sons to assist me. The female body is not yet meeting my exact specifications – or rather, not yet meeting my various sets of specification, for I do not intend to create a uniform model. I wish, for example, to have various sex-models of female: some bred toothless and with warmer mouths, for fellatio; others with tighter and warmer pussies, and with bottoms better adapted to reception of a cock; yet others with extra pairs of breasts, who will both excite us men more in coitus and supply more milk to keep us strong as the centuries of lives stretch to millennia.

Ah, the thought of such multiple breasts, the pleasure they will afford to the ruthless hand and the oceans of milk they will supply, makes me stiffen again, and it is fortunate for Joanna and her dear little femmewife that they have departed my office, else I might be dragging them forth from their hiding place to meet their doom prematurely. I wonder, in fact, that they kept their peace before the spectacle I laid on for them: one of Joanna's own dorm charges tricked into cock-sucking and sperm-swallowing before their very eyes, and then brutally buggered atop my desk. Oh, my cock is raging now, and I will have to call for a maid or return to my milk-dungeons to pacify it. Where is my coin? Right. *Cap** for a maid, *pajura** for the milk-dungeons. And . . . *pajura* it is.

Joanna Harker's Journal, 13(?) October.

[The journal resumes *in medias res* part-way down a burnt page. Editrix.]

[o]r Mina, that I should have brought her to this heart of brightness and home of all that is most evil and corrupt in the world today. But I suspect, as I have often suspected before, that Mina in truth is the stronger of us two, as perhaps the submissive is the stronger half of all butchwife–femmewife pairs, for they are supple and bend to storms that snap the trunks of seemingly sturdier trees, then raise their boughs and laugh when the storm is passed. Certainly, she it was who stood firmer in the face of the Count's perverted abuse of that poor, poor Transmarynian girl, whose fate I shall never cease to reproach myself with, even when she is brought – as I pray she be speedily brought – back from the captivity she presently endures beneath the Academy.

Ah, a bleak and sardonic smile touches my lips as I pen the word, but my *other* lips, tight as I squeeze them between my thighs, respond too. There is little formal education given here, but much 'training by paining', as that Transmarynian saying has it. The pain in my wrist has eased to an occasional twinge now, but I owe that to cold compresses, massage and comfrey tablets supplied by Matron, who is already, so she tells me, an expert in injuries of disciplinary overexertion. My old skill with my left hand, which I have not exercised for years, has been willy-nilly resurrected while I ease the burden on my right an . . .

[More is lost to the burnt section here. Editrix.]

. . . nning our expedition to his dungeons. Mina has already begun to spy out his movements, and believes she has tabulated his 'sunbathing': she has seen his clear-walled-and-lidded container on its iron frame-work atop the Academy's roof. Can I write its true name without vomiting? Aye, perhaps. She has seen his glass coffin (yes, I can) atop the Academy's roof, and I was counting the seconds till she returned from the mission to find it. Great as my fears for her safety were, my own memories of another roof, far off in Wales, were too fresh and strong to allow me to accompany her, and though I sought to dissuade her, her reasoning was impossible to overturn. We *must* have intelligence of his movements if we are to defeat him, and Mina's slighter frame, lighter step, and sharper ear equip her far better for the role of *espionne** than I. She has even suggested – but this I have adamantly opposed – that she spy on him when he retires to his sunbathing at midday. Even if the risk were a hundredth as small and the reward a hundred times as great I could not allow it.

As it is, I suspect her of becoming carried away by her success so far, and would spank the truth out of her if I could spare the energy, and (alas) summon the inclination, after all I am having to perform with the girls of both my dorm and my classes. This is an extra reason to hate the Count: that he has sated me with punishing and rendered me unfit to beat my own femmewife. I never thought I would write this, but at times I almost grow weary of the sight and sound of bare female bottoms under discipline. It is like my childhood dream of owning a sweet shop and gorging all day on caramelised butterfly wings and almond wasps (always my two favourites). If *that* had ever come true, I see now that I should have been heartily sick of sweets before the day was out. My employment here fulfils a similar dream, and almost seems to bring with it a similar satiety.

This is why my mind returns often to the *sealed* section in my dorm's punishment cupboard. I have questioned two of my girls about it now, and though they deny all knowledge of what is concealed therein, from the looks on their faces they know well enough, by repute if not direct experience. My nipples peak and pussy tingles, I confess, and all my old appetite for doling out discipline surges up within me, as I speculate for myself. If I did not know the Count better, I should speculate that the previous dorm mistress was dismissed for employing its contents, but that cannot be. Far likelier that she was dismissed for *refusing* to employ its contents, when the Count, after weighing her in the balance and finding her apparently unwanting, invited her to do so. Yes, I have sensed his eye on me with especial intensity in the past couple of days, and I wonder whether he is reaching a similar decision concerning myself.

And concerning Mina. She has risen to the challenge of her dorm like one born to the task, and had she not confessed to me privately how onerous her duties sometimes prove, I might have begun to fear for our relationship in future. But even if she exaggerates her weariness for my sake, I know that her love of submission is woven too far into her nature to be unplucked by her sojourn in the Academy, unless it is prolonged far, far longer, and I sense no danger of that. Somehow or other a crisis approaches, and approaches fast. It may come today, when we descend to the dungeons in search of Caliginia and Artemisia and Dr Helsingvili. There is something in the atmosphere that reminds me unpleasantly of the Count's castle in Wales and that day when I ascended to his glass coffin on the roof, only to discover that . . .

But I will not write of it. 'Twould be an ill omen, even were my stomach fit to face the description, however brief, of what befell me then. Nor shall I invite Nemesis by vowing to defeat the Count. That is in the lap of the Goddess, and I trust in Her to see

us all safe home to harbour one day, whatever storms
we pass through en route.

Count Caradul's Diary, October 14
(Kept in phonograph in Welsh).

Ah, I come fresh, and full-bellied, from the milk-
dungeons, and it is as I suspected. Joanna and her
femmewife – I still feel that superstitious disinclination to name her till the moment at which I truly
possess her – have visited my little captives today,
who could not disguise their excitement or hope at
the visit, try as they might. It was plain on their faces,
and also in their orifices. Artemisia's cries were *too*
loud and struggles *too* vigorous when I invaded her
bottom, and I know that she is already dreaming of
the revenge she shall take on me. Where before her
rage came naturally, tonight she had to summon it by
force of will, and misjudged its strength. Well, I soon
had her dancing to her old tune, for I had *her*
femmewife Caliginia in to suck her pussy while I saw
to Caliginia's bottom, unplumbed this past few days,
during which I have been servicing her pussy.

The sight of her darling's slender body shuddering
to its foundations under the assault of my cock
brought out the veins in Artemisia's neck and the
muscles in her arms as she struggled to tear herself
loose from her chains – oh, and how magnificently
her breasts shook, swollen with the rage of my assault
on Caliginia and the pleasure of Caliginia's tongue on
her pussy! In fact, they were positively storm-tossed
by her rage, and I distinctly heard strains of Ricarda
Wagner swelling up in my ears as I approached, and
drew back, from orgasm. I have dictated a memo to
Ilona for an order to be placed for one of the latest
'musical phonograms'. I will not play my bugger-and-

suck trick with her and Caliginia again before it arrives; and then I shall play it to the accompaniment of *Die Fliegende Holländerin* or *Der Walkürenritt*. It will be a fitting artistic tribute to Artemisia's breasts, which are works of the finest natural *art*, comparable to the finest mountains of Europe.

Aye, I almost lost my stroke as I gazed upon them, and when I had spurted in Caliginia's bum-chamber you may be sure that I sated my thirst greedily from their nipples, leaving Caliginia, on my orders, to lap up the splatters of milk already forced from them by the violence of Artemisia's emotion. And then, to complete my replacement of Artemisia's factitious rage with its true form, I had Caliginia lick my cock clean of its two anal transits in front of her, then suck it till it was stiff as a spear. But I did not discharge in her mouth, as Artemisia apparently feared. No, something worse was in store for my Wagnerian maiden: she had drunk my sperm, and received it as an enema; now it was time for a *douche*.

Aye, I took the virginity of her pussy tonight, and a tough task to enter the velvet-walled chamber I had too, despite Caliginia's earlier lingual ministrations. In the end, I had Caliginia fist an initial entrance, her face raised pleadingly to her lover's as she pushed her small hand home; and then I eased a way in between the opened pussy-lips. I know that Artemisia would have sacrificed herself thus to save Caliginia from having to receive and swallow a salty mouthful, but she had been offered no such choice: I had refrained from spurting inside Caliginia's mouth at my own pleasure, saving my ball-juice for the initial baptism of Artemisia's womb. I cannot hope yet that she is ready to receive it, for her sperm-training by bum and mouth has not run its full course, but there is always a chance and she will certainly be ready before the month is out. And what a child I will breed from her! If it is a boy, he will have a cock like an oak and a heart cruel as the sun; if a girl, she will surely be willing to stand at my side and assist me in my final subjugation of Europe.

Indeed, I might crown her Vempress of my Vempire. From Artemisia's loins and mine one such female can surely come in time, but perhaps I am premature to expect a girl from Artemisia primigravida* or secundigravida.* There is too much masculine force in her, which will turn male any early foetus. But in time my Vempress shall come, and be Artemisia's daughter.

Mina Harker's Journal, 14 October.

Again I take up pen in Joanna's stead, for though her wrist is better than before, our trip to the dungeons has affected her more deeply than either of us had feared. I do not believe she will ever wholly recover from what she experienced in Transmarynia at the hands (and worse) of the Count and his suns: her mind has suffered blows whose impressions a lifetime will not suffice to erase, and her sensibilities have been sensitised, not hardened. Even now, as I write, she rests her head in my lap and I stroke her hair, feeling her tremble occasionally as memory strikes anew. It is this that gives me the courage to go on: if Joanna were strong, then I might be weak, knowing that she could carry on the fight.

But she cannot by herself and I must support her as a true femmewife should. My hatred for the Count grows brighter in this, even as my love for Joanna grows yet darker and sweeter. He will pay for what he has done to her, and to those poor creatures lying chained even now beneath us. And within 'poor creatures' I include not merely those the spider-like fiend has trapped in his web from the Academy, but our friends, last seen in that clearing in Bucharest, after Joanna and I had ascended with such deep hopes in our balloon. But just as I do not feel that the city I *now* inhabit is Bucharest, while the Count's presence broods here, so when I name our friends I feel I do not capture their present essence. It is only the *bodies* of Caliginia and Artemisia and Dr Helsingvili and Artemisia's friends Căpitana Rosamunda and Locotenent Sara that are chained and at his mercy. Their *souls* are far away and do not suffer the indignities and agonies he heaps upon their flesh.

But is this wishful thinking? On the surface, yes; but something deeper within me insists that it is not. There is a space at the core of each of us that the Count cannot reach, however hard he tries. Even if he establishes his 'empire' and all Europe comes under his thrall, the essence of femininity will remain pure and uncorrupted, and in time will overthrow him. Like the sun he worships, his triumph is but temporary: night always returns, and always lies somewhere beyond the reach of light. He keeps his lamps burning unextinguished in his dungeons, so that the nakedness of his slaves is ever ready for his greedy eyes and greedier hands and – no, I will not say it – but those lamps are even greedier than he. They burn constantly and must be refilled again and again and again with oil to hold back the darkness, which waits with infinite patience to return.

A gentle snore from Joanna has broken the thread of my philosophising and brought a smile to my lips. My stroking left hand has worked its soothing magic and Morphea renews my beloved butchwife's spirit in her obsidian halls. And while Joanna rests, I must work and recall what it is we have witnessed today, while that foulness lay above us in his coffin and absorbed the killing rays of the day-star. Joanna was apprehensive, I remember, for she felt that my espionage had been too successful to be credible.

'He knows what we plan and will pounce when we least expect it,' she said, as we crept into his office, hands shielding our eyes from the glare of the noon sun that streamed through the uncurtained windows. I tried to make light of her comment, which struck me too with a shiver of fear.

'Then he cannot pounce at all,' I said, 'for when we least expect him to pounce, we will know that we must expect him to pounce.'

Joanna struck affectionately at my bottom, and for a moment, so accustomed have I become to the role of dominant in my stay at the Academy, I felt indignant; then the sting of the blow, gentle though it was, reminded me of my true nature, and I cursed the Count anew for the position in which he has placed me. But all thought of this was suddenly driven from my head, for Joanna, who was lifting the trapdoor, suddenly let it fall with a bang and stumbled back with a gasp of horror.

'What is it, my love?' I asked, moving to her, though listening hard to learn whether the noise would bring a curious servant. Joanna was biting the knuckles of her left hand, with which she had lifted the trapdoor, and would not answer for a moment. Then her answer came, and I frowned with puzzlement.

'The *smell*,' she said.

'The smell, my love?'

She seemed to recover herself a little, and stammeringly explained. 'Of milk, Mina. The smell of milk and *sweat*. It rises from below as it did . . . as it did in Wales, and my memories rush on me again. Of horror, Mina. My memories of horror.'

She stepped back further from the trapdoor, closed again though it was, and I nodded with a grunt of sympathy.

'I understand, my love. But look: I have the solution.'

I turned from the light and began to tear a strip of material from my dress. I pretended the cloth was tougher than it was, and asked for Joanna's help. She came to me, and I shivered pleasurably at the ease with which she tore off a strip as I requested.

'What now?' she asked as she handed it to me; and I pursed my lips with a smile, shaking my head as I turned away from her, lifting from my pocket the bottle of perfume I had confiscated from a pupil earlier in the day. A sudden sniff from Joanna behind me as the strip of cloth absorbed its load, followed by a chuckle, told me that she had guessed what I intended, and when I turned back to her, she was smiling broadly as she shielded her eyes from the sun.

'I feel threatened by such ingenuity in my femmewife,' she said as she took the strip from me and tied it around her head, covering her nostrils so that they might be shielded from the smell of the dungeons. 'And I shall punish you severely for it, when we are safe out of here.'

'With my ingenuity I shall evade you,' I returned.

'You will but postpone your doom,' she said, crossing the room to the trapdoor again, 'and your bottom, dear Mina, will curse you for it.'

She was smiling again as she lifted the trap, and her smile faltered but a moment as the air from the dungeons flowed out over her again.

'It works?' I asked.

She nodded without replying, and beckoned me to follow her as she laid the trap flat and began to climb down the steps that were revealed below her. The smell of milk and sweat, underlain with the hot reek of burning lamps, was already in my nostrils, and though it came to me with no underlay of memory, Joanna's fear had given it sinister import and I had to make a positive effort of will to follow her down the steps, so much stronger did it become with each step I descended. Joanna had stopped a little below me, and looked back now.

'Draw the trap closed as you come through it,' she said. 'A servant or –' I sensed rather than saw her throat node and smooth with a bolus of fear '– or the Count himself may come to the office while we are below. We will listen on our return for occupancy.'

'Very well,' I said, and did as she asked. When the trap was closed, the atmosphere, already heavy with *emotion* as much as *odour*, seemed to redouble in thickness, and the sound of Joanna's feet descending the stair ahead of me reached my ears as though from great distance. I hurried after her, and then heard her feet falter and stop as a *moan* reached our ears from the dungeons that awaited us.

As I approached Joanna, I found her murmuring a prayer; and when I took hold of her from behind, I found her whole body trembling. I did not need to be told what ailed her: that moan, I knew, brought back memories of her descent to similar dungeons far away, in the Count's castle in Wales.

'Come, my darling,' I whispered into her ear, not having to raise myself on tiptoes for once, for I was higher up the stair than she. 'We must have courage, for their sake if not for ours.'

Then, daringly, for my taking the initiative thus was almost unknown in our previous relationship, I reached for her breasts and gave them a squeeze, my hands feeling small and delicate against their bulk and firmness. I felt Joanna stiffen with surprise; and then my anxiety broke into relief, for she laughed and turned her head back to nuzzle and kiss me.

'Slut,' she said. 'It should be *I* driving *thee* forwards with words of sound counsel. But do not fear: I am keeping an account of all that passes, and thou shalt pay in full when, *Dea volente*,* the Count is vanquished.'

She was gnawing gently at my lips now, but my hands were still on her tits and with sudden inspiration I squeezed again, harder than before, thrusting my mouth against her and gnawing back, as though we were two dominants contending for supremacy.

'Or *thou* shalt,' I told her, and had to tighten my grip yet more on her tits, for she burst out into louder laughter, which echoed weirdly between the walls of the stair.

'Be *quiet*,' I told her, shaking her tits with mock anger, 'or I shall think you have a head of sawdust, which is no qualification for espionage.'

With another snort of laughter, she kissed me again, then shrugged my hands from her breasts and began to descend the stair again. I followed her, wondering what those below were thinking if they had heard Joanna's laughter, which had been of joy and gladness, not of triumph and cruelty. Well, I would soon know, for I now heard Joanna's feet reach the foot of the stair and pass forwards onto a corridor whose echoes told me, before I was on the level too, of open doorways on left and right.

Then my feet too were on the corridor, and I hurried after Joanna, who had reached the first of the doorways and had stopped to look through it. I heard her gasp with horror, and when I reached her side she was trembling again. The doorway was wide, with more than enough room for the two of us to stand and look within the room beyond it. Would that it had not been so, and that I might have had longer to prepare myself for what lay within! But perhaps my emotion would have been heightened by anticipation, and it was better to see quickly what awaited my eyes since first I set foot within the Academy's precincts.

Oh, yes, as you can see, my dear future reader (I pray that you do await these words in the future, and that you *are* dear; which is to say, that you are female), I am trying to postpone the moment of description, but I cannot postpone it for ever. So what did I see within that first chamber of the Count's dungeons, lit by the harsh and virulent light of lamps burning with perverted brightness from the ceiling and the single long, curving wall? Well, that tells you that the chamber was circular or elliptical, but I must settle the ambiguity (circular) and give you its diameter – ten metres, perhaps. Oh, I can postpone it no longer, I must describe what the chamber contained: thrones like those Joanna had described in her journal from Wales, and sitting atop three of them, the three young women who sat naked and chained and who peered fearfully at us with tear-stained faces as we paused in the doorway.

But if they, and their looks of undoubtedly well-justified fear and apprehension, were bad enough, the greatest horror of that chamber was perhaps not what was present but what was *not*. For these three girls were widely separated each from the other, so as to emphasise the vastness of the chamber. Aye, there were many thrones *un*occupied, their seats pierced by large bum-ready holes, and many sets of chains hanging loose above them. How many young women would be present when the chamber was filled, ready to satisfy the Count's perverted pleasures? And ready (urgh, my stomach rolls at thought of it) for *milking*?

But I did not begin to calculate, for Joanna suddenly cried out softly and moved forwards, running across the chamber to one of the chained and naked girls. For a moment, I could not decipher what she had said, and then I realised it had been 'Ruth!' Now I too recognised one of the girls: it was that Transmarynian we had seen buggered, tit-gnawed and tricked into cock-sucking in the Count's office. But though I had seen her face clearly in the office, I would barely have known her *here*, even had the light of the dungeons been kinder on my eyes: the single day she had spent below had marked her face too heavily with tears and woe. Joanna tells me now that it was less the girl's face that she somehow recognised, having longer acquaintance with it than I, than her *tits*, which, truth to tell, were of exceptional size and beauty even for the girls of the Academy, and no doubt explained why the Count was so eager to get the poor girl below.

I crossed the chamber in Joanna's wake, hearing the girl plead with Joanna to be released – a plea echoed from left and right by the other two girls. Joanna, with a sob in her voice, replied that this was impossible: we were still plotting the Count's downfall, and they might have to stay where they were for some time yet. At this, all three began to weep most piteously, their tits jerking with their emotion and beginning to shine with the tears that rained heavily upon them. Joanna begged their forgiveness in broken tones that quite worried me, for I knew the scene before us was recalling that *earlier* scene to her, with the big-breasted Welsh girl beneath the Count's castle in Transmarynia. To distract my darling, I reminded her that we were on a mission of espionage, and must gather intelligence for use against our common enemy. Then, leaving her to interrogate the Transmarynian girl, I went to one of the other girls, asking her name, her nationality, and her length of stay in the dungeon.

'Yolanda, mistress,' she told me, sniffing back tears, her face still beautiful despite the dark circles beneath her eyes that spoke of sleepless days and much suffering. 'I am of Ispain, and I am here three weeks almost.'

I asked the girl what the Count had done to her, and she began sobbing anew, so that I was forced to murmur soothingly to her, wiping her tears from her face with her own soft raven locks. She stammered out her story, and by now I was aware of a gathering tension in my loins that I could not mistake for other than *arousal*. Aye, perverse as it was, the act of talking to this tormented young woman, chained and abused in a dungeon-chamber of the enemy of all my kind, was awakening my concupiscence. The girl was telling her story between sobs.

''E, 'e b . . . he bite *las tetas*, mistress,' she said, nodding downwards at her twin firm globes, glistening with the brine of her tears, 'my, 'ow you say, my *teeties*, and 'e bring out, 'ow you say, you know, *la leche*.'

'Milk,' I said, feeling my tongue thickened in my mouth and my voice strangely hollow and distant in my ears.

'Meelk, mistress, jes,' said the girl, the thickness of her accent adding to my lust, 'and I yam no mother. Then . . . then 'e drink of me, mistress, every day 'e drink of me, and . . . and other theengs, mistress. Other theengs wheech I . . . I cannot say.'

'Are they . . . sexual things?' I asked gently, and her dark eyes, glistening with tears, flashing with emotion, lifted to mine, then fell as she flushed darkly, rendering her more desirable to me than ever. She murmured something, and I asked the question again. Her eyes lifted to mine for the second time, and my pussy pulsed with lust, releasing a wave of pussy-juice to begin trickling down my thighs.

148

'Jes, mistress,' she said, her eyes falling. 'Seks-oo-al theengs.'

My heart was hammering in my chest, and I had to clench my right hand to keep it from diving beneath my skirt and frotting my clitoris even as I stood there. More questions came crowding to my lips unbidden – aye, unbidden, but not unexpected, not unwanted. I stooped to breathe them in her ear.

'He forces himself upon you? Physically? With . . . with his thigh-member? And . . . spurts?'

She did not understand all my words, I believe, but my meaning was as clear as the scent of lemon, and she shivered with memories of horror and degradation. Again her eyes lifted to mine.

'Jes, mistress,' she began to say; but her shiver and the flash of her lifted eyes had been too much for me, and my open mouth clamped over hers as my eager hands seized her tear-slippery breasts, squeezing and kneading their gorgeous firmness and bulk. She cried out as I kissed her, but something in her understood my assault and responded to it, so that her tongue fenced against mine as I thrust it into her opening mouth. Milk was squirting against my fingers and palms as I continued to manipulate her breasts, and she was trembling with pain and, unmistakably, with lust. I dropped my head from her mouth to her right breast even as I dropped my hand from her right breast to her pussy, and sucked hard at her engorged nipple even as my milk-lubricated fingers slid and tickled at her juicing pussy-lips. Fresh milk gushed into my mouth, cool and sweet, and I choked in my eagerness to gulp it down.

In the next instant, a strong hand had seized my shoulder and was wrenching me backwards, tearing my mouth off that fountaining tit, so that spurting milk struck my face as I relinquished it. A voice that

149

I barely recognised as Joanna's was hissing indignantly, 'Mina, what are you doing?'

She had dragged me backwards so hard that I fell to the floor, landing heavily on my bottom. I looked up at Joanna's anger-bright face, wiping at a trickle of milk on my chin and noting that she had removed her perfume-band.

'Drinking from her,' I said defiantly.

The anger on her on her face was contending with concern and horror, as though she could not understand either what she had seen or the nature of my reply.

'Drinking, Mina? From this poor slave? As th–'

But now came an unexpected interruption: from the lips of the poor slave herself.

'Jes, mistress,' she said quietly, and my pussy bubbled with lust. 'She drink from me, and I *love* eet.'

Joanna's eyes turned to her, and now her face was full of bewilderment too. Then her look cleared, and she shook her head, simultaneously looking upwards and shaking her fist.

'He has perverted you both,' she said. 'I curse him for it.'

I was trying to get to my feet, but with a snort Joanna forestalled me, seizing me by the wrist and tugging upwards.

'Ow,' I said, but she snorted again.

'He has perverted you,' she repeated. 'Perverted you both. Girls, we must leave you.'

She was dragging me from the chamber, and I could only turn my head helplessly and signal farewell with my eyebrows to the Spanish girl, who pouted to see her breast-drinker taken from her so quickly, after so little milk had been sucked from her firm and youthful breast. What delights the third girl might have offered I considered only later, but from the intonation of the words she shouted after us (I did not recognise the language, but believe it might have been Swedish or Dutch) and the glimpse of her face I caught as Joanna dragged me back through the doorway, she too was disappointed to see us go.

Outside, Joanna paused to upbraid me, her own breast working with her emotion as she whispered to me furiously: 'Mina, I am at a loss to understand your behaviour. How could you, how *could* you take advantage of a young girl thus, when she lies chained and helpless?'

I lifted a vertical forefinger to her face, laying it gently on her lips as I whispered in reply. 'Hush, my love. Do not upbraid me so. I am weak and she . . . she aroused me.'

From the flicker in Joanna's eye, I knew that she had shared my arousal and that the roughness with which she had torn me from the Spanish girl, and the vehemence of her condemnation of me, were in part aimed at *herself*. I smiled inwardly, and cunningly continued: 'And why not, my love? What renders the Count's enslavement of them so monstrous is the illegitimacy of his claim to their bodies. But for us, who are no freaks of nature but true womankind, what illegitimacy can there be in exploiting their helplessness for our own pleasure? We have every right to it by the superiority of our class, of our years, and of our breeding. No, my love, I did no wrong and will do no wrong if I do the same in the next chamber we enter. Nor,' I added, seeing acceptance and rejection of my words contend for mastery in her face, 'shalt *thou*, my love. Come, what dost thou say?'

I lifted my finger from her lips and Joanna blinked, then smiled ruefully and laughed.

'Slut,' she said. 'What an avalanche of pain you are heaping up for your poor bottom when we are safe out of this. I cannot have my femmewife instructing me in the ways of dominance, or I will be the laughing stock of Bucharest.'

'But whether Bucharest learn of it or not, thou *hast* had her instructing thee thus,' I said. 'And she wishes to know thy answer.'

She seized my hand and pulled me further along the corridor to the next doorway, saying nothing till she had peered around the jamb and seen what was within. I saw her eyes widen, and she licked her lips after her old familiar fashion, sending a shiver of apprehension down my spine. Now she looked back at me.

'Come,' she said, 'I will *show* you my answer.'

She walked into the chamber that awaited us, pulling me with her. Now it was my eyes that widened, for the two stripped girls in this chamber were not chained to thrones along the single sloping wall but strapped on the middle of the floor into frameworks of gleaming steel, slender ankles manacled far apart, that their pussies might lie naked and defenceless between their wide-splayed thighs. How they had managed to fall asleep I do not know, but asleep they were and perhaps the frameworks were not so uncomfortable as they looked. Joanna pulled me right up to them, stepping lightly, I realised, so as not to wake them, then released my wrist and motioned me to her side.

I came forwards, ready to feast my eyes on the pussies splayed before me, then grunted with unease. What had the Count been doing to the girls? Their almost-identical pussies seemed to have been shaved or (I shivered deliciously at the thought of it) plucked quite bare of hairs, and though they looked in the prime of health, I could see white bubbles of pus up each pussy-lip. Had he *infected* them with some sexual disease, to satisfy some perverted lust even more contorted and blasphemous than those he had already flaunted?

I moved forwards a little, sniffing, and now my puzzlement grew, for the pussies smelt as healthy as they looked: prime firm-fleshed pudenda on two eighteen- or nineteen-year-old girls. Was it pus after all? But then Joanna, with a clatter, both solved the mystery and woke the two girls: she had tried to pick up an instrument from a tray set into one of the frameworks, lost her grip on it and let it fall back to the tray, which was heaped with similar instruments and with *pearls*. The Count was . . .

But I had no time for speculating, for the two girls' eyes had flown open at the sound and they had cried out with surprise soon succeeded by delight, for they thought, poor things, like the trio we had just left, that we were there to rescue them from their captivity. It was now that I realised, giving their faces the same attention that I had previously given their pussies, that they were *twins*. Joanna broke into their excited and ungrammatical babble, asking them their names, nationalities, and length of stay below ground, and they were telling us that they were indeed twins, Maria and Magdalena of Poland, both with a year's scholarship to the Academy and both having now spent a fortday bitterly ruing the cruel deception by which they were imprisoned underground.

Joanna broke into their babble again (I sensed that the two girls were naturally loquacious and gregarious, and had long grown bored of talking only to each other), asking them how they pissed and dunged, strapped as they were, and what precisely the Count was doing to them in the frameworks. One of them (whether Maria or Magdalena I could not tell, so call her Magdia) burst out indignantly: 'Ve may piss bot vonce a day, mistresses, and dung also, into pots she hold beneass uss. Ozzervice' – and she accurately imitated the sound of a whip meeting plump buttock flesh, taking a naïve pleasure and pride in her own imitative skill.

'Yuss!' said the other (call her Marlena) over the final *viip-thwup*, 'she punish uss, mistresses. Viz vhips ond also, how do you say –' she said something in Polish to Magdia, who supplied the Romanian word required '– yuss, viz *kines*, mistresses. In most cruel vey, on ours bare bottoms.'

I distinctly heard Joanna swallow hard in the silence that followed, and smiled inwardly, sensing her surge of lust match my own.

'And why,' Joanna said, trying to appear nonchalant, 'why does he, does *she*, have you strapped into these *frameworks*, with your –' she swallowed again '– your poor pussies on open display.

'*Perla!*' the twins cried together. 'She put perlss for ours pussies, mistresses,' Marlena added, succeeded by Magdia's: 'Yuss, perlss, mistresses, on ze lips, and also . . . also *inside*.'

'Inside?' Joanna asked, and I saw that her hands were clenched to stop them trembling.

'Yuss,' said Marlena, and the change in her tone made us look harder at her and see that both she and her sister were blushing. 'She is a beast, mistresses. She have strange –' she spoke again in Polish to Magdia, who shook her head '– strange *flesh* between hers legs. Like octopus arm, you know, bot *stiff*, like branch of tree.'

'Ah,' Joanna said, shaking her head gravely. 'We know of this. It is her *tentacle*. Her octopus arm, that is to say.'

'Yuss,' said Marlena. 'Ten-ta-cle. Her ten-ta-cle. She say, oh –' the poor girl rattled off what sounded like a prayer in Polish '– she say she vant to put octopus arm, to put ten-ta-cle, in ours pussies, bot she say she get more pleasure, more tickling, if *perlss* in pussies before she do zis.'

Joanna gasped with a horror in which I could detect more than a hint of pretence.

'This is horrifying,' she said. 'Girls, we must examine you at once. Your pussies must be probed for signs of – no, girls,' she went on, raising an authoritative hand, for the two girls had burst out in protest 'we are both medically trained and Dr Kra –' she stopped herself just in time, remembering that I had played the role of a *Polish* doctor in Bulgaria, and could not hope to carry the same deception off successfully with a pair of native speakers '– Dr Krawitz here is an exceptionally well-qualified gynaecologist. She and I, who hold senior positions in the City Hospital here in Bucharest, are assisting the Romanian authorities in getting to the, ah, *bottom* of the evil under way at the Academy. But we must gather evidence before we can act against the monster who has been tormenting you. You must, I am afraid, sacrifice your modesty and allow your pussies to be examined minutely by the two of us. Dr Krawitz, if you would.'

She nodded forwards at Marlena's pussy, and now I too swallowed with sudden lust. Joanna herself had stepped forwards and bowed her head between Magdia's legs, and a faint cry from the Polish girl told me that Joanna's eager fingers were already at work on that soft young pussy flesh. The thought of it had me moving forwards too, head bowing and hands reaching for the soft young pussy flesh of my own 'patient'. Oh, and there, as my fingers touched and stroked, came her soft cry.

I looked up at her, strapped helpless into her framework, nipples pointing ceilingward, so firm and unfallen were her youthful breasts.

'Are you Magdalena?' I asked.

'No, mistress,' she said, whimpering a little as I ran my fingers up and down her pussy-lips, squeezing very gently at the implanted pearls, 'I am Maria.'

'Then your sister is Magdalena,' I said foolishly, too distracted by the sweetness of my task to pay sufficient attention to what I was saying.

'Yuss, mistress. Oh!'

I was tugging gently at one of the pearls, trying to determine how it had been fixed to her pussy flesh. Like an earring, I supposed. I swallowed again, for I was about to break that great taboo of all pure women: to insert an object – namely, a finger – into a girl's pussy. I looked up at her.

'My dear,' I said, hoping she had never received such attentions from a doctor before, lest I offend against some formula followed on these occasions, 'I am about to, about to *probe* you. Do you understand?'

She nodded, looking very scared and very serious, and I gently scratched and tugged the fold of pussy-lip still between my fingers, smiling at her, then smiling harder to see her answering smile. Joanna's young Pole, Magdalena, cried out again, louder, and I knew that one of Joanna's fingers was gently sliding between her pussy-lips and feeling its way up her silken pussy-walls, searching for the pearls inserted there to provide greater pleasure for the Count's 'tentacle'.

'Good girl,' I said. 'But we must be careful. If you would, my dear, please moisten the finger I intend to insert. Will you?'

She nodded again, and I reached forwards, holding out my index finger for her to suck and lick. She sniffed it gently first, and her fading blush reawoke in a way that tugged at my heartstrings. She had smelt her own pussy on my finger, and her eyes swung shyly

156

but mischievously towards me as she opened her mouth and drew the finger in.

'Moisten it well, my darling,' I said. 'For your own sake, for I must push it *deep*.'

Oh, as I spoke the words a forbidden desire flamed up like Erebus-fire within me: to have *another* finger, a greater finger, with a great, bald, blunt tip and no nail, set between my thighs, that I might insert *that* into the firm young body of the girl instead, and thrust repeatedly till I spurted thick and long inside her. Aye, as I watched the girl suck my forefinger I longed to be a second Count, with a great cock between my thighs. Forgive me, Joanna, when you read this, for the perversion of my desire, but I can keep nothing from you, my love, and feel reassured in my submissive normality as I make my confession: my pussy moistens at the thought of how you will punish me for it.

But now I could restrain myself no longer: I pulled my forefinger from the girl's mouth, bringing it free with a pop, and lifted it quickly back between her thighs. Joanna's girl cried out again, but the note of pleasure I detected in it banished my momentary apprehension – what if I injured my Pole with my clumsiness? – and I rubbed my fingertip between her pussy-lips, up, down, up, down, then began slowly to push it inside. The girl shuddered and gave a little cry, and, looking up at her face, I saw that she was biting her lip.

'Please do not tense yourself, my darling,' I said. 'Or you might be injured. Here, I will help you.'

I bent my head and planted a kiss on her soft pubic hair, then another, and another, trickling the kisses downwards till I reached her clitoris, which I kissed three times before beginning to lick and suck gently upon it as I continued to tickle at her pussy-lips with my finger. What the girl thought of my 'bedside manner', I cannot guess, but my lips and tongue soon had their desired effect and, with a tremor of departing tension, she released a sigh of pleasure.

I began to push my finger inside her now, revelling in the silky texture of her pussy flesh; and there, my fingertip had brushed the first of the pearls that studded her pussy-walls. I kissed her clitoris and lifted my head for a moment, hearing Joanna's Magdalena moan and cry out something in her mother tongue.

'How has he inserted the pearls, my darling?' I asked my Maria, gently rubbing my finger on the pearl. Her eyes had closed with the pleasure of my clitty-licking; now they opened, wandering unfocusedly till they fastened on my face.

'Pliss?' she said.

'Wake up, sleepy-head,' I said, and put my face back on her pussy, gently nibbling at one of her pussy-lips. I looked up again, repeating my question.

'Ve do not know, mistress. She . . . she *sleep* us, and vhen ve vake up, ours pussies, zey are . . .'

She looked across at Magdalena, opening her mouth to ask her sister something in Polish, then closed with a pout when she saw that Magdalena was too deeply preoccupied with Joanna's finger up her pussy, and Joanna's mouth on her clitoris. She looked back at me.

'Ours pussies, zey . . . zey are *hurting* a little. And zere are perlss inside. But zen ze hurting, it go avay.'

'Your pussies are aching?' I suggested.

'Yuss, yuss, a-ching. Zat is ze vord. A-ching. Ours pussies, zey are a-ching. But zen ze aching, it go avay.'

'I see,' I said, pushing my finger a little deeper into her pussy and feeling a second pearl, and a third. They seemed to be arranged in *patterns* in the walls of her pussy – I moved my finger, trying to trace the pattern, and Maria moaned and shuddered a little.

'I'm sorry, my darling,' I said, and put my mouth back on her clitoris. I tongued it, then lifted my head again.

'Come, my darling, you should –' I lowered my head and tongued, then raised it '– you should be l . . . oh, you are! Clever girl!'

Yes, she had begun to leak: the flower-throat of her pussy was releasing its nectar, and my finger would glide now, not crawl as it penetrated her to the core. Oh, that the Mina of five days ago could see me now, writing those forbidden words! Five days only, and I am steeped in sin. To penetrate a woman thus, and to revel in the penetration. But worse than to be a penetratrix was my crime of teaching a young girl to revel in the role of penetratee. Had I digitally invaded her with no compensatory clitoris-licking, she would have reacted naturally and healthily: with disgust and anger. But the pleasure of my tongue and lips smoothed the stony path for her delicate feet, strewing it thick with rose petals and scented herbs, so that she could follow it to the end.

Beside me, I heard the moans of Joanna's Magdalena reach their highest pitch, and break into a wail of unmistakable orgasm. Where once the sound – let alone the sight – of a young girl brought to orgasm with a finger buried deep in her tender pussy would have sickened and horrified me, now it only challenged and stimulated me. I too desired to have a beautiful Polish girl moaning her way thus to orgasm under my attentions, with my finger buried in her tender pussy, that I might feel it squeeze and clench on me, gnawing me with its pearly teeth.

So I set to work, licking, sucking, pushing my finger deeper, filling my lungs on the rich scent of her now fast-flowing pussy-juice, till a seemingly identical series of moans broke into a seemingly identical wail of orgasm, and I felt the walls of her pussy clenching and writhing on my finger, which was buried to the first knuckle. But even in that sweet moment, even as I lapped up some of her pussy-juice, bitterness was mixed into my joy, for I was envying the Count his cock again. How did it feel to slide a living and sensitive sex-organ – not a finger substituting for a sex-organ – into a pussy equipped thus with pearl-studded walls? Would the pleasure of it be heightened even beyond his normal transports, to bring his 'sperm' boiling up even faster in his hairy balls, spewing forth in its living pussy-chamber?

I slid my finger out of her, rotating it gently as I did so, to allow her to ride the outfoam of paroxysm a little longer, and she murmured her thanks in between the dying gasps of her orgasm. When it came free with a succulent pop, I surprised myself with the gesture I performed: making the sign of the cross on the rippling, velvet-skinned muscles of her flat and perfect belly. She felt her own juice marking her skin and opened her eyes, lifting her head to look down her body, past the firm mounds of her breasts, topped by stiffened nipples that cried out for my tongue and nibbling teeth, to the mark that glistened on her belly.

She smiled when she saw what it was, and her head fell back with a sigh of contentment.

'Sank you, mistress,' I heard her murmur. 'Now, I feel safe, if she –' no need to particularise her to whom the 'she' referred '– do very bad sings, ze most vorst that she like.'

Joanna told me later that she saw the gesture and heard the girl's words, and was prompted to coat her own pussy-probing finger in pussy-juice and, tonguing the girl's clitoris again to reawaken the surge of orgasm, make the same cross on what seemed the same flat, velvet-skinned belly. And Joanna's girl spoke almost the same words of thanks: I heard them and looked across in surprise. Then I caught Joanna's eye, and she nodded, evidently thinking the same as I. Silently, with a last kiss on the pussies we had pleasured and penetrated, we rose from where we knelt between those slender young thighs and tiptoed from the chamber.

One of them farted as we left, and the innocence and *domesticity* of the sound struck us both, I now know, with a sense that we had done great things in the chamber. Where two innocent girls had hitherto waited in dread and doubt for the next piece of abuse at the hands of a monster, now they faced his evil with courage and confidence, certain that it would soon end and that he would receive his just deserts. All this we had done, and merely by fingering their pussies and tonguing them to orgasm. When we were back on the floor of the corridor, Joanna turned to me and lifted her pussy-probing finger towards my face.

'Lick it,' she said, 'and I will lick yours. Let us see if their pussies are as similar as their faces.'

I nodded assent, and lifted my own pussy-probe towards her lips as she slid hers between mine. We sucked and licked, watching each other's faces as we sampled the pussy-juice wet or encrusted there. Joanna took my hand by the wrist and drew my finger from her mouth.

'Perhaps a little *sweeter* than Magdalena's,' she said. I tugged her finger from my mouth after the same wise.

'Perhaps a little *muskier* than Maria's,' I returned. 'But otherwise one c–'

'Could tell they were twins,' Joanna finished for me, and I laughed.

'Yuss. Von could.'

But in the next moment, even as we jested, rejoicing in the memory of what we had done, realisation of our position was brought back to us: the creak of an opening hinge echoed down the corridor from the stair, and a moment after that heavy feet were on that stair, descending towards us. We were in the Count's slave-dungeons, and here was the dungeon-master himself, returning to his domain. Joanna, as she frankly admits, panicked in that moment, overwhelmed by her memories of the Count's castle in Wales, and it was I who saved us both. Seizing Joanna by the hand, I tugged her along the corridor to the furthest chamber on that stretch, reasoning that it was also the least likely to be entered by the Count.

Imagine our emotion to discover, as we slipped panting through the doorway, that this was the chamber in which our two dear friends were chained: Caliginia and Artemisia. Caliginia, always a light sleeper, was woken by our entrance and gaped at us in incredulous joy, recognising us in spite of our disguise. Her mouth opened to greet us, but we motioned frantically for silence, and Joanna pointed in the direction of the Count's oncoming footsteps. My choice of the furthest chamber did not seem so intelligent now, for from the state of the poor pair chained to their thrones before us, it was evident that the Count had been paying them regular attentions: Caliginia's beautiful breasts were rounder and firmer than ever, evidently swollen with milk produced therein by his bites, while Artemisia's, which I had never had the privilege of viewing unclothed, were truly awe-inspiring, rising and falling gently as she slept but dominating the chamber like twin full moons with their size and majesty.

And the simile was apter than I, or she, might have wished, for just as the true full moon is mottled with seas and craters, so were Artemisia's poor breasts mottled with a mosaic of bruises at all stages of ripeness, from day-old to a fortday-old. Someone had been handling those gorgeous globes with roughness and cruelty, leaving the mark of her fingers thereon to record the wickedness of her heart. And yet, of course, it was not *her* fingers, nor *her* heart, but *his*: this was the Count's literal handiwork we saw before us, and my heart, like Joanna's (as she now tells me), pounded with horror at the thought that his heavy steps were carrying him down the corridor to renew his assault on Artemisia's mammary frontage.

We both gasped with relief as we heard him turn off sooner, into the poor Polish girls' chamber, and perhaps it was our gasp that woke Artemisia. Her face too was filled with confusion, then with incredulous joy, but again we motioned for silence, swiftly tiptoeing across the chamber to our two dear friends, where we could converse with them in whispers. We asked whether the Count was likely to be entering the chamber next, and Artemisia shook her head with relief, telling us that he kept to a strict routine and had visited them once already that day, to 'bugger' Caliginia and – she swallowed as though on bitter cud – to penetrate her, Artemisia, *per vaginam*.* Tears sparkled in her eyes, and she shook her head angrily, suppressing them by force of will.

'I defy the monster,' she whispered, 'but I fear lest he "impregnate" me. This is his vile term, meaning to induce an unnatural pregnancy with this unspeakable "sperm" of his.'

Joanna, with quick sympathy, seized her hand and squeezed it, invoking a rattle from the chain that bound her wrist.

'Nay,' Joanna said in a choked voice that spoke to her own horror, 'do not fear, my brave Artemisia.

From what the monster told me in Transmarynia, a woman must be "sperm-trained" – foul term for a fouler thing! – much longer than the relatively few days he has had thee in his clutches. I . . . I remember his exact words.'

And in a strangely altered voice in which, to my increased horror, I recognised the accents of the Count himself, she recited: ' "The woman must first swallow it and receive it in her arse, so that her body grows used to its presence and does not reject it when finally the cock is inserted in the cunt and sperm squirts home into the womb." '

The chain rattled again as Artemisia, in a sudden reversal of roles, squeezed Joanna's hand, recognising the fugue of involuntary recall into which her plight had sent Joanna.

'Then do not fear for me,' she said, 'for I have swallowed little of his sexual fluid, and absorbed less of it through my bottom than he hopes. Whenever he has –' she swallowed again, overwhelmed by the horror of her memories for a moment '– *buggered* me and squirted his orgasm into my rectum, I have striven to pump the fluid out by muscular contractions as quickly as I might, till I can fart it from my bottomhole, like the refuse it is.'

The sound of the soft laughter with which Joanna greeted this revelation was strange in that evil place. Artemisia smiled grimly in reply, and nodded.

'I will resist him till the end, my sisters,' she said, 'and the heaviest burden I bear is the presence of mine own darling Caliginia here with me. I would let a dozen Counts bugger me hourly, if only she were safe from harm at his hands . . . and worse than his hands.'

'Bless thee, my lady and liege,' Caliginia said, stretching out her own chained hand to her butchwife, though Artemisia's hand, lifting in response, fell short of hers by a finger's length: the Count, with his habitual cruelty to the mind as well as the body, had chained them with a throne between them, that they might strain to touch and comfort each other, and never succeed. But now Artemisia had turned her eyes back on us, and was whispering urgent advice.

'But 'tis better for both of you that you go now whence you came. He will be some time in the chamber he now occupies, heaping sexual abuse on whatever poor girls he keeps chained there –' my eyes and Joanna's met in sorrowful flash, for the 'poor girls' of the chamber were more than a phrase to us '– and you will have time to return up the stair and through the trapdoor in that room of his. Go, while you still have time. He will not abuse us again at this time, but he will certainly pause in that doorway to feast his eyes on our helpless nakedness, before passing on to other chambers which now are occupied deeper in his dungeons.'

Joanna needed no second telling, having seen all that she wished of the dungeons, but I paused a moment to ask after Dr Helsingvili. Artemisia shook her head.

'We do not know, but we believe she is chained with my military friends, deeper in the dungeons. Caliginia tells me that she had heard their voices crying out as ours do, when the Count grants us his attentions, and I sometimes think I have heard the same. But they must be far off, perhaps on a lower level with another trapdoor to pass. Do not seek them out, I beg you. Go now, and keep the moon of hope full in our hearts, for we will know that you are near us and still free to plot a way of defeating this monster.'

But I paused a further moment, to kiss both her poor bruised breasts, then Caliginia's, before rushing to Joanna where she stood waiting in the doorway. Then, with a wave and a whispered farewell, we passed from their sight, slipping silently back up the corridor to the stair and the trapdoor. We could hear grunts and moans from the chamber in which the Polish twins were imprisoned, but I did not glance to one side as we passed the doorway, irrationally convincing myself that if I did not look in, no one would look out. Poor Joanna, however, compelled by some 'imp of the perverse', as Edwina Allan Poe has so aptly christened it, could not resist, as I learned from the choking cry that reached my ears a moment later. I turned and saw, to my horror, that she was frozen at the doorway, staring with bulging eyes at some horror being enacted within the chamber amid the grunts and moans.

I reached her in a heartbeat, seized hold of her hand, and tugged her away, breathing a prayer of thanksgiving to the Goddess that her cry had not been heard by the Count. After a moment's resistance, she came, but some shield of will that had sustained her in the Count's dungeons till that point had plainly broken within her, and she was near fainting with her emotion. What she saw within the chamber she will not tell, though I believe she cannot be cleansed of her sickness of soul until she does so, and I can guess, of course. It was the Count, sheathing and resheathing his foul cock as deep as its equally foul balls in one of the girls' tender orifices.

She gripped my hand tight as I drew her to the stair, but she had not wholly lost her will, for it was she who recalled me to the need to *listen* before we raised the trapdoor at the end of the climb. It was as well that we did so, for through the apparent silence that first met our probing ears came the soft susurrus of *breath* and an occasional faint rustle of *paper*.

Someone was evidently sitting at the Count's desk, leafing through documents. For a moment, Joanna's fears directed her hearing, for she whispered the suspicion that it was one of the Count's suns, but I shook my head. The breathing was that of a young woman, and the occasional ill-bred sniff and scratching told me that the young woman was one of the Count's hirelings, a vulgar Romanian or more vulgar Bulgarian.

Indeed, I guessed what was going on before we raised the trapdoor and pounced: that a Count's spy was spying on the Count, relying on her sharp ears to catch the heavy tread of his returning footsteps well before he reached the top of the stair. But she had not expected *women* to be returning up the stair, and would have been lucky to hear our feet even had she had her ear pressed to the wood of the trapdoor. I whispered my suspicions to Joanna and suggested that we wait no longer, but emerge now and kidnap the miscreant; and after a moment's consideration she agreed. We could not wait indefinitely at the head of the stair, for the Count, despite Artemisia's predictions, might return to the upper level of the Academy very soon.

Of course, we would hear him coming, but we would have to rush through the trapdoor then, and if the girl were still there at his desk, we might not be able to overpower her before he were upon us. No, better by far to emerge now. Accordingly, I lifted the trapdoor a fraction, peering through the crack, and was rewarded with the sight of a very pretty pair of bare feet swinging beneath the Count's desk as the girl continued her reading with her shoes off for greater comfort. Joanna pinched my bottom from behind, and I wriggled it. It was the signal for me to count to three and then burst forth. One . . . two . . . three . . .

The girl at the desk, I hope and believe, had the shock of her young life to see two women bursting forth from the trapdoor. While I stayed behind to lower the trapdoor carefully again, Joanna rushed upon her and she barely had time to squeak before her dress was over her head and Joanna was expertly womanhandling her from the room. I paused to tidy away the papers she had been illicitly reading, dropping them back in the cabinet from which they had plainly come, and grabbed up the pair of smoked spectacles, fallen to the desk, that the girl had been using against the glare of the Count's uncurtained windows. Then I followed Joanna.

It was just as I was leaving the office and about to heave a sigh of relief that I remembered the girl's shoes. It might have ruined everything if they had been left where they were, under the Count's desk, for he would have guessed that she had been sitting in his chair and almost certainly wrung the truth out of her. That the disordered papers in the cabinet – I had dropped them back and closed the cabinet in haste – would alert him I intended to guard against by ordering the girl to rearrange them as they should be when we released her. I was confident that by then we would have imposed a healthy fear of our retribution in the girl; and the thought of it made me smile as I hurried after Joanna through the sleeping Academy, the girl's spectacles in one hand and her shoes in the other.

We had decided to take her somewhere both safe from interruption and rich in resources of persuasion for our session of interrogation, and had settled on one of the physics laboratories. The electrical equipment there, so one of our newest colleagues had proudly told us, was second to none, and puzzlingly so when she compared it to some of the other scientific equipment provided by the Academy. She did not understand the innuendoes with which Joanna and I greeted her remark, easily though they were read by some of the other teachers in the staffroom at the time (our 'fellow' Bulgarians in particular). No, she actually still takes the Academy at face value, and does her best to teach her subject, foolishly believing that the Count will approve. Well, she will learn better when he inspects her classes and rates her for discipline; and when she fails to meet his standards, she will be lucky if he does not demonstrate the potential of her 'electrical equipment' on her own person.

Certainly, Joanna and I have done so on the person of that girl captured in the Count's office, and I believe that if we had not gagged her with her own knickers, her shrieks would have informed the whole Academy of our experimental rigor. That physics tutoress was right: even I, who am quite the opposite of an expert, could see that the devices I was lifting from their plainly marked cupboard – as Joanna stripped the girl and lashed her to a bench top – were of excellent and very recent manufacture. I carried them over to Joanna one by one with several pairs of asbestos gloves, and she thanked me, seeming to forget her recent emotions below ground in the joy of having her hands on a fresh victim. Those emotions would return later, alas, but Joanna's instincts as a dominant are too strong to ever be wholly submerged by fear or grief, and were sustaining her now as I watched, my nipples peaking both at Joanna's words and tone and at what they portended for our poor plucked girl-fowl.

'What *we* were doing is no concern of yours, slut,' Joanna was saying, trying on the asbestos gloves until she found the pair that fitted her best, for the girl (a

Romanian) had made a feeble attempt to justify her own conduct by turning the interrogation back on the two of us. 'It is *you* who are under sentence, not we, for it was *you* who were reading private papers in your employer's office. So, are you going to inform on us to the Countess?'

The girl paused, chewing her lip anxiously, then nodded with evident reluctance.

'Oh, mistress, I must, I must,' she said. 'It is what she will expect of me, and if I disobey – oh, she is too cruel, too strong, and I do not wish that I too –'

She broke off, and Joanna snorted with suspicion. 'What is it that you do not wish? Do you speak of her *dungeons*? Have you seen them as we have? Then in the name of all that is holy, girl, why do you not join us in the struggle against this monster?'

The girl shook her head. 'No, no, mistress, I cannot. She is too strong, too cruel, too clever. It will be hopeless, and she has promised that I –'

'Silence,' Joanna hissed. She snatched up the girl's discarded knickers and tied them firmly around the girl's mouth. 'It is plain that you are one of her bought women, prepared to betray your sisters for silver and for a share of the power the Countess hopes to win. Indeed, the two of us suspect that you servant-sluts sell your *bodies* to her too, in a way that even the most depraved and abandoned of whores would abominate and abhor. Words are of no use against your type; we must employ the rhetoric you can understand: the argument, my darling little slut, of –' she leaned close to the girl, whose eyes were widening fearfully above her gag, and hissed in her ear '– *pain*. Weigh the following two thoughts as you contemplate informing on us to the Countess.

'First, we caught you sowl-handed reading her private papers. If we are captured, we will certainly bring that up against you, and will tell her that you are part of the resistance being waged against her. Can you imagine the vengeance she will wreak upon you if she believes our tale?'

From the rolling of the girl's eyes and the squeaks of protest that escaped the gag, it was plain that she could.

'But that is not all,' Joanna continued, 'and here is the second thought you must consider. If you inform on us, we and our friends will not rest till we are avenged on you. A little of what *that* will entail we are about to teach you now. We are cruel and ruthless women, my little slut, and you are a pawn in our game. So: think well, slutlet. Are you prepared to make a promise in the Goddess's name to remain silent? Yea or nay?'

The two of us leaned close to the girl's face with instinctual cruelty, drinking in the struggle of contending fears that was apparent on her face. Whatever she did, her poor bottom and titties – to say nothing of her delicate orifices – might pay a very heavy price.

'Well?' Joanna demanded. '*Da sau nu?*'*

The girl blinked and her throat noded and smoothed; then slowly, with tears beginning to glisten in her eyes, she shook her head. Joanna hissed with involuntary excitement.

'One last chance, slutlet. Yea or nay?'

The shake of the head came more quickly this time, as though the girl's previous decision had strengthened her resolve.

'Very well then,' said Joanna. 'On your head, or rather –' she paused lasciviously '– *elsewhere* be it, foolish one. I think *this* will be suitable for an initial exploration of her capacity for pain, Lidiya,' she said to me, slipping off the gloves and tapping one of the

171

devices I had set ready on the bench top. 'So if you will prepare to attach the electrodes and crank the handle, I will moisten the points of contact.'

. I thought at first that she meant me to attach the electrodes of the thing to the girl's pussy, for her fingers immediately dove there, sliding up and down her pussy-lips; but she was merely heightening the humiliation of her next order by coating her fingers in the girl's own pussy-flavour.

'Now, slut,' she said to our helpless victim, lowering the gag. 'Lick my fingers. We must have your –' she did not speak the word, but plucked at first one, then the other of the girl's nervously stiffening nipples '– well-moistened for attachment of the electrodes, must we not?'

And she thrust her left hand at the girl's mouth.

'Lick. Or when we begin cranking we will continue far longer than we presently plan.'

The girl's mouth opened, but only the tip of her tongue emerged.

'*Lick!*' Joanna ordered fiercely, and the girl began to lick her tormentor's fingers, her face wrinkling with distaste at the pussy-flavour that clung to them.

'Continue,' Joanna said, replacing her left hand with her right as she lowered her left to the girl's right nipple and began to massage the spittle in. The girl licked the fingers of Joanna's right hand, but it was plain that something was amiss.

'Your tongue is too dry,' Joanna told her, lifting the gag back into place. 'Make it moister or I will conclude that you are withholding your spittle out of dumb insolence. What's that? Moister, girl. Make it moister.'

The girl was shaking her head and squeaking again through her gag.

'Lidiya,' Joanna told me, her left hand still strumming on the girl's right nipple, which was stiffer than ever, 'lower her gag a moment.'

I obeyed, and the girl gasped out that her mouth was dry out of nervousness, not inso–

'Silence her,' Joanna ordered, and I tugged the gag back into place.

'Your mouth,' she told the girl, 'is dry out of insolence. Nothing else. Your attempted excuse merely compounds your crime, but luckily I believe a substitute spittle has appeared. Lidiya, her right nipple is ready for its electrode. Pray attach it while I moisten her left nipple with . . . *this*.'

And her fingers dove triumphantly at the girl's pussy, which I now noticed was leaking freely. Joanna sniffed appreciatively as she moistened her fingers anew.

'Fresh as the matrix makes it,' she said.

I shook my head, resuming my attachment of the electrode, which I had suspended as I watched Joanna at work. 'I don't agree,' I said, rubbing the electrode on the girl's stiff right nipple, then opening the clip and preparing to attach it.

'Hmmm?' said Joanna, glancing up at me for a moment as she worked her fingers deeper in the girl's pussy.

'I don't agree.'

The girl, already trembling and squeaking in protest at what Joanna was doing, squeaked louder as I let the clip close on her nipple.

'Pussy-juice is not generated by the matrix,' I continued, 'but by cells in the walls of the pussy.'

'Under the direction of the womb,' Joanna said, lifting her fingers from the shining slit in which she had been working them and smiling as the pussy-juice stretched in shining lines. 'See its quality, Mina!'

I coughed to cover her slip and, realising what she

had done, Joanna quickly lifted her moistened fingers to the girl's left nipple and began rubbing the juice in.

'No,' I said, 'the pussy-walls are not directed by the womb but by nerves running to sexual regions of the brain.'

'That is not the tradition, Lidiya,' Joanna said, tugging at the nipple to lengthen it, so she could massage the pussy-juice in even more thoroughly.

'But it is the best medical opinion, my dear Vasilka, and I would remind you of my own medical expertise. In Bulgaria.'

Joanna suppressed a smile, and nodded as though finally convinced. 'You are right, Dr Lidiya. I bow to your superior wisdom. It is not the girl's womb but her sluttish brain that has directed the flow of the pussy-juice with which I have now prepared her nipple for your electrode. There.'

'I thank you,' I said, and unceremoniously attached the second electrode to the accompaniment of a second loud squeak from the girl. 'And now, we are ready.'

'Not quite, doctor,' said Joanna maliciously. 'We may be ready but is . . . the patient?'

'You mean . . .?'

'Yes. Our sluttish little servant girl. Captured *spying* on her own mistress, and now rightly readied for punishment. But that punishment will be severe and long-lasting. Is she in a fit state to receive it? What, my dear Dr Lidiya, is your . . . *professional* opinion?'

I took a long look at the girl, feasting my eyes on her naked body: her dark and shining hair, the smoothness of her pale and quivering flesh, its plains and hollows, peaks and gullies, the discrete copse of her pubic hair above the glistening valley of her pussy. Then I smiled and motioned Joanna back as I stooped over the girl, pinching the flesh of her breasts, running a fingertip down her flanks, probing her belly button, prodding and squeezing her thighs, rocking and tugging at her kneecaps, tickling her toes and the soles of her feet, then returning to run a finger down her pussy-lips, coating it with pussy-juice. I stepped back, allowing a thread of pussy-juice to stretch till it snapped, then lifting the laden finger to my lips and sucking on it slowly and meditatively.

'She is young,' I said. 'Firm-fleshed and in the peak of condition. Her pussy-juice is a trifle strongly flavoured, perhaps –' I reached out and re-coated my finger to taste it again '– mmmm, yes, just a *trifle* strongly flavoured, but this too speaks to her vitality and power to withstand what we have in mind for her. I judge her fit.'

'Are you sure?' Joanna asked.

'Yes. I would stake my professional reputation on it.'

'But has your examination been as thorough as it might be?'

'Breasts, flanks, belly, thighs, knees, feet, pussy. I have checked them all.'

'Externally,' Joanna said. 'But what of ... *internally*? We are moving into uncharted waters here, doctor. We intend to subject her to sensations of a kind, and of a strength, the like of which are previously unknown to her. Electrical torture.' She rolled the words on her tongue, then repeated them with relish. 'Electrical torture. That is what she is about to endure. And we must be more than certain that she is fit to endure it. Examine her internally, doctor.'

The girl's widened eyes, fearfully fixed on Joanna's face as she delivered her dialogue, now rolled to me as Joanna waited for an answer. I thrust out my lower lip, pondering, popped my lips, and slowly nodded.

'You are right, my dear Vasilka. These are uncharted waters, as you rightly say. We must be triply sure that our little barque is fit to sail them and return safe to harbour. I will examine her internally.'

I stepped back to the girl, and watched her eyes above her gag as I rubbed my forefingers slowly up and down her pussy, beginning to prise her pussy-lips apart to make the internal examination. How delicious it was to see her distress, her baffled outrage and disgust, as I not so much *assaulted* as *sapped* the defences of her pussy. And there, my fingers were sliding into those juice-slicked silken depths, invading the most intimate part of her being – save, perhaps, for the tight-sealed little bumhole she concealed between her tender bum cheeks.

Her eyes rolled back in her head with a mixture of horror and, struggle though she might to conceal it, *pleasure*. I utter heresy now, perhaps, but is it true what the Count said to Joanna in Transmarynia? Namely, that invasion of the pussy was once natural for women? And even perhaps – revolting though the thought be – *desired* by us? For see how this slut began to writhe involuntarily as I slid my fingers deep and then partly withdrew them ... then slid them deep, and withdrew them ... slid them deep and withdrew them ... slid them and withdrew them ...

She was positively gushing within seconds, soaking the bench between her thighs and beneath her buttocks, and when I fully withdrew my fingers with slurps and pops and stood back, breathing heavily, my hands were soaked and dripping with pussy-juice.

'Well?' Joanna said. 'Have you completed your internal examination?'

I raised my hands to my face and sniffed them, licked them, then began to massage the juice into my cheeks and forehead.

'The fresh juice of a young pussy,' I said in response to the look of amusement on Joanna's face. 'It is a sovereign specific against wrinkles and ageing, as they have always taught in the town where I was born.'

'I may try some myself, a little later then,' Joanna said. 'But what of your internal examination. Have you finished it?'

'Yes,' I said, massaging the juice into my eyebrows and scalp too. 'I have completed it and my previous judgment stands. She is fit for pain. For electrical torture.'

Joanna shook her head, and it was plain that she was in one of her 'specific' moods, when she left no leaf unturned in the humiliation and softening of a victim – no doubt because she forgot, in her victimising, the memories of her victimisation by the Count.

'But you said "triply sure",' she reminded me. 'As yet, you are only *doubly* sure. You must also investigate her internally in the *second* of her secret orifices. With *this*.'

I had completed my juice-massage now, and lowered my hands to see Joanna holding aloft, to a squeak of protest from the girl, an unusually large *thermometer*, of the type, I vaguely recalled from my own schooldays, designed for taking the temperature of boiling fluids during experiments. I remembered now that I had heard Joanna opening cupboard doors as I probed the girl's pussy, and realised she had been searching for such a thermometer to complete our pre-tormentual humiliation and softening of our tender victim.

'Hmmm,' I said, nodding and glancing at the girl's face with a cruel and slowly expanding smile.

'You are right, my dear Vasilka,' I continued, ' "Triply sure" were my words, and as yet I am but *doubly* sure of my diagnosis. I must insert this fine instrument in her *bottom* and discover her temperature. It will be excellent practice for me, for rectal examinations were but a small part of the curriculum at the rather *conservative* medical school I attended for my training, and live subjects were understandably reluctant to make themselves available for the clumsy attentions of us students.

'In fact,' I went on, walking forwards to take the thermometer from Joanna, 'this will be the *first* rectal thermometer I have ever inserted. And the standard medical variety is, of course, *far* smaller.'

It was hard to restrain my laughter as I saw the distress into which my lying words had thrown the girl – though I was not lying when I said that this would be the first rectal thermometer I had ever inserted. That was perfectly true: what was not true was that I had any medical training at all. If she had known *that*, her struggles to break free would have been even more vigorous.

'Grant me your assistance, please, my dear Vasilka,' I said, as I rubbed the end of the thermometer between the girl's thighs, working it in the still thickly oozing juice of her pussy. 'You must lift her buttocks clear of the bench, and open her buttock cheeks, exposing her rectal portal to my invasion.'

Heightened squeaks of protest from the girl at this, which I heightened yet further with a deft flick of my wrist that sent the thermometer sliding between her pussy-lips. I rotated it clockwise, then anti-clockwise, then withdrew it, thoroughly lubricated for insertion into her bottom.

'Thank you,' I said, for Joanna had taken hold of the girl's hips and, with a slight grunt, lifted her bottom clear of the bench. 'But I have been thinking, Vasi. "Invasion" is an unfortunate turn of phrase for

178

what I am about to undertake. This is a serious medical procedure and I betray a most unprofessional attitude in speaking of it in such terms. I am not *invading* the poor girl – yes, swing them open – quite the reverse, in fact. I am *protecting* – a little wider – her. I am making triply sure that – and just a little more – she is fit to endure a flood of electricity through her tender nipples. And perhaps – ah, the little minx is resisting – through her pussy-lips also. But there, *that's* a good girl.'

I had rotated the bulb of the thermometer, pushing hard as it coated the girl's sphincter with her own pussy-juice, and I grunted a little with surprise as, with a sudden jerk, it slid through and was lodged in the vestibule of her rectum.

'That was a good girl,' I said. 'To yield so quickly. I wonder how often . . . But Mummy wants to go just a *leetle* deeper.'

I rotated and pushed again, and the thermometer slid a little deeper to the accompaniment of more squeaks of protest from the girl.

'Oh, it's getting a little more difficult now. So how does that saying go?' With my free hand I reached for her pussy and began to moisten my fingers with pussy-juice. ' "A spoonful of sugar helps the medicine go down." Or a handful of pussy-juice –' I lifted my hand to her face and rubbed her lips with pussy-juice '– helps the thermometer . . . go . . . *up.'*

The poor girl's body shuddered as half of the thick length of the thermometer slid smoothly between her bum cheeks, invading what I had now decided was indeed the most intimate part of her body. The average woman would faint at the prospect of being vaginally invaded; at the prospect of being *anally* invaded she might be at a complete loss and unable, for some moments, to understand what threatened her, for the concept would be so alien. The anus as avenue of assault? The rectum as route of gratification? And doubtless the breast of our little victim, the Romanian servant girl lashed to that bench, was the scene as much of puzzlement and disbelief as of indignation and anger.

And indeed, I could read those conflicting emotions in her face. That her pussy should be invaded by my eager fingers was shocking but not entirely incomprehensible; that her *bottom* should be was outside all her experience. I began to rock the thermometer back and forth, 'buggering' her, and noticed that her pussy was shining with fresh pussy-juice.

'Vasilka,' I said, my voice unsteady with the pleasure of dominating and humiliating our victim thus, 'look at the slut. I am performing a standard medical procedure, entirely in her own interests, and look: she responds to a large firm object up her small tight bottom with –'

'*Pleasure!*' Joanna completed for me, her voice dripping expertly with disgust. As I continued to pump the thermometer in the girl's bottom, Joanna released a hand from the now mostly redundant task of holding her body up for my assault and stuck a finger in her leaking pussy, twirling it to collect some of her juice. Then she lifted it slowly clear, and the two of us watched the thread stretch and stretch.

'Pleasure,' she repeated. 'The girl is an anal pervert, my dear Lidiya, an anal pervert of the worst and, well, most perverted kind. Listen to her!'

Little gasps of ecstasy were escaping around the girl's gag and, scarce though I could believe it, she was positively rocking her bottom at the instrument invading it. The thread of pussy-juice Joanna was stretching snapped at last and I felt a drop of it hit my face.

'Do you know,' Joanna mused, twirling her finger in the girl's pussy-juice once again, 'I believe she is approaching ... no, I cannot say it, it is too disgusting.'

'Tell me,' I said, a little out of breath. My wrist was starting to ache a little now from the effort of pumping the thermometer in the girl's bottom, which was now accepting almost three-quarters of its length.

'No,' said Joanna, stretching another thread of pussy-juice from the girl's pussy. 'It truly is too disgusting.'

'I am a doctor,' I reminded her. 'Nothing could shock me. What is it you believe she is approaching as I perform this unpleasant but necessary medical procedure on her?'

The second thread of pussy-juice snapped, and I felt three drops hit my face this time, one just near my lips. I licked for it, hearing the girl's gasps become louder and feeling her bottom rock even more greedily for the firm shaft of the thermometer.

'I believe ...' said Joanna. 'Oh, it really is disgusting, but I believe that she is approaching ... *orgasm*. And if I just ...'

Her finger returned to the girl's pussy, but not to gather pussy-juice this time, rather, to stroke and tweak the girl's clitoris. A second's worth of clitoral masturbation was sufficient: I felt the thermometer jerk and quiver in my hand as the girl's sphincter tightened on it with her final ecstasy, and her whole body shuddered and spasmed as shining droplets of sweat sprung out suddenly on her smooth skin.

'See?' Joanna said, still rubbing the girl's clitoris gently, to prolong her orgasm.

'Yes,' I said. 'And you were right. It *was* truly disgusting. Even for me, with my medical training. But she will be the one to suffer, if the tightening of her bottom on my thermometer has distorted its reading and causes me to diagnose her fit for the electrical torture when in fact she is not.'

I was trying to pull the thermometer out, but it was as though it had been glued in place. The girl's sphincter was still spasmed shut with the pleasure of being simultaneously buggered and clitorally stimulated. Then, slowly, her muscles began to relax, and I could pull the thermometer free. She moaned beneath her gag as it came out, retreating from her bowels and, as it came finally free with a loud *pupp*, her body shuddered again with an aftershock of her orgasmic bliss.

'Well?' Joanna asked, her finger leaving the girl's clitoris at last.

I lifted the thermometer, trying to read the measurement through the mixture of rectal mucus and pussy-juice with which it was coated. 'Thirty-two degrees of the Celsius,' I said. 'Or however one says it.'

'Yes? Thirty-two degrees?'

'Yes. Thirty-two on the button.'

'And is that good or bad?'

'D'you know, I was off sick on the day we did body temperature at med school. But it looks fine to me.'

'And to me,' said Joanna briskly. 'The electrical torture will commence fortw . . .

A bell is ringing to signal that one of the girls has escaped from the punishment block, and all teachers must turn out to assist in the hunt. I will resume my narrative of the electrical torture on my return. M.

Count Caradul's Diary, 14 October
(Kept in phonograph in Welsh).

The plot thickens – aye, thickens, I am happy to say,
like my first batch of Romanian-made girl-yoghurt.
And it thickens most around my pair of *spies*: my
dearest Joanna and her beautiful femmewife, whose
name, as I noted before, I decline to utter until I
possess her in the only true sense, which is to say,
sexually. Well, the two of them have indeed entered
my dungeons. More than that, they have played
there with my prisoners! The excitement that overwhelmed me as, from afar, I smelt proof of their
dalliance with my Polish twins was something I have
not felt since the first days of my assuming control of
the Academy; and when I entered the twins' chamber,
their glowing faces and glistening pussies caused me
almost to lose control of my sperm and splatter the
interior of my 'knickers' before I had even lowered
them.

Yes, that occasional affliction of my youth, sponta-
neous ejaculation under sudden excitement, which I
thought long ago departed for ever, was almost upon
me again. I paused to recollect myself a few moments,
forcing the lids back on the boiling vats of semen in
my balls; *then* it was down with my 'knickers' and up
with my cock in the nearest of the orifices that
beckoned: Magdalena's freshly lubricated pussy,
whose tender lips and silken, pearl-studded throat I
had denied myself too long. Oh, but I am glad I did
so: the pleasure I had anticipated in fucking it was
heightened almost to the point of delirium by my
delay. Those pearls I have carefully inserted in the
pair of them are positioned with scientific exactitude
and skill to provide the maximum of sensation to the
invading glans – that, at least, has been my boast to

my sons, and more than pleasure was at stake as I put my boast to the test.

For my pride was at stake also: was I as expert in pussies as I avowed myself to be? Has my fucking of so many hundreds of them over the centuries been more than animalistic, more than the crude satisfaction of an ancestral instinct, the scratching of a recurrent sexual itch? In short, am I no barbarian but rather a *scientist*? I am delighted to report that the answer to all these questions is a loud and definite '*Ïe!*'* Only a true expert in pussies, a true scientist, could have 'empearled' a pussy and doubled the pleasure it afforded while causing only the minimum pain and inconvenience to the owner of the aforesaid pussy.

Not that avoiding pain or inconvenience to a woman is, of course, the most important consideration when one is employing her as a vessel for one's pleasure, but an empearled pussy must be healthy too, I believe, or the pearls may begin to fall out. Ah, my cock is granite hard again at the mere thought of it, or rather, at the mere thought of *them*, for it was not Magdalena's pussy alone that I come fresh from poking, but Maria's too. And there, if extra proof were needed (which it was not), I confirmed my expertise: I had arranged the pearls along her pussy-walls after a radically different fashion, but the pleasure they afforded was quite as great as that afforded by Magdalena's pearls.

Indeed, when I began to 'spiral' my cock into Maria, with a rotation of my hips, I fancy that the pleasure was, relatively speaking, somewhat higher. After all, I had spurted most copiously in Magdalena's pearl-chamber barely minutes before, and the sensitivity of my glans was correspondingly reduced. Next time – and that next time will not be long delayed, I promise – I will penetrate Maria's pussy first, having allowed my seminal vats to refill for at least two hours beforehand, then see how well Magdalena pleases me when I penetrate her without delay. Not so well, I predict, though I recognise that the test, to be truly scientific, would have to be performed blindfold and with nostrils sealed with gum, lest one is informed by scent – there are subtle but definite differences between the two – which of these delightful Polish twins one's cock has been sheathed in.

Arglwydd!,* I have provoked myself too much with my descriptions and must ring for a servant to deal with my raging erection. But this time I will try that experiment I have been planning for some time. She can suck me but she must not swallow my ejaculate. Rather, she will catch and hold it in her mouth, then dribble it forth (as I watch and direct operations) into a *syringe*, which she will then carry below into the dungeons for injection into the mouth or bumhole of a selected slave. In this way, I will be able to continue my sperm-training of that slave at long range, so to speak, and yet do so without greatly reducing the pleasure I would have experienced had I been there in person to inject her with my own fleshy 'syringe'. Yes, this 'telesperming' commends itself more and more to me the more I ponder on it. I do not intend to impregnate any of my servants above ground *per vaginam*, and yet several of them have been swallowing my sperm almost since I arrived in Romania. This waste must stop, and will stop today.

Mina Harker's Journal, 14 October (continued).

I am back from the hunt for the girl escaped from the punishment block, and it is a positive effort to push away the vivid memories of the capture and return to the electrical torture Joanna and I conducted in that physics laboratory. But I have begun the narrative of that episode, and Joanna insists that I finish it, while she sketches the capture of the escapee beside me. That sore wrist of hers, which afflicted her so at the beginning of our stay here, has turned out a blessing in disguise, for she has become quite proficient at writing with her *left* hand, which means that the two of us can sit side by side and attend to each other's pussies with a tickling finger, she writing with her left hand and devoting a finger of her right hand to the task, I doing the reverse. See? I have just pressed a pussy-juice-laden fingertip to the paper and left a memorial of her arousal. I will have to blow on the spot before I begin writing overleaf, lest the pages stick together.

So, to return to the young Romanian servant girl we had lashed to that bench in the laboratory. That large thermometer had just been withdrawn from her bumhole, having been thrust almost to its limits in her tight bum-chamber, and I had finally pronounced her fit to endure the torture whereby we planned to convince her to say nothing to the Count of seeing us emerge from his slave-dungeons.

'Recheck the electrodes,' Joanna ordered me. 'Ensure that the perverted excitement with which she welcomed that thermometer into the utmost depths of her bum has not shaken them loose.'

I moved down the bench to the girl's breasts and rechecked the electrodes I had attached to her luscious nipples. She was still a little dazed with the orgasm Joanna had fingered out of her as I 'buggered' her with the thermometer, but the sensation of my fingers tugging on her tits brought her out of it, and she murmured in protest through her gag.

'Silence,' said Joanna. 'Save your breath for when you need it – which will, you little slut, be very soon, I promise you. Are they well attached, Dr Lidiya?'

'Yes,' I said, giving a final tug and prod at the girl's tits, then moving back down the bench to stand ready at the crank of the electrical generator by which the electrodes would be supplied.

'Excellent,' said Joanna, 'and you anticipate my next order admirably. Now, slut, a final chance is offered you before you experience something that will be, I hazard, unique in your brief life. That is to say, electricity through your nipples. Will you promise to say nothing of what you saw to the Countess? Nod your head for "yes", shake it for "no".'

We both watched, eyes gleaming cruelly, for her response, and I confess I was praying hard to the Goddess that her response be 'No'. It was not only our slut who came fresh to the experience of electricity through nipples – so did Joanna and I, albeit from an entirely different perspective. Our slut had never felt such electricity flow through her nipples, and we had never watched anyone feeling such electricity flow through her nipples.

(My tickling finger, which I have perhaps plied a little more vigorously in hope of just such an outcome, has assisted Joanna to orgasm beside me, and while she waits for her writing hand to stop shaking I can ask her what she thought as she watched and waited for the girl's response. Ah, it appears that she too was praying to the Goddess that the slut continued to refuse; and with two such prayers of such strength and sincerity arrowing earthwards, what other outcome could there be?)

Yes, picture the two of us standing over our naked prey as it lay lashed to that bench, our eyes gloating on the clash of emotions in that clear-skinned, smooth-planed young face. And imagine Joanna's breath, temporarily suspended with anticipation and excitement, hissing from her mouth as our prey reaches its agonised decision and slowly . . . reluctantly . . . with tears beginning to trickle from its dear sweet eyes . . . shakes its *insolent*, its *disobedient*, its *sluttish* head '*No*'.

' "No" it is,' said Joanna, and her right hand lifted into the air like a blade held vertical. 'When I *chop*, Dr Lidiya, count three seconds and begin cranking. That will give me time to position my hands on her body and hold her down, lest she shake the electrodes loose from her titties with the violence of her reaction. Very well?'

'Very well,' I said. 'But you have forgotten your gloves.'

'Ah, yes. In my ex . . ., that is to say, in my *zeal* I have. Thank you.'

She picked up the pair of asbestos gloves that fitted her best and slipped them on, tugging them firmly into place before she lifted her right hand as before.

'When I chop, Dr Lidiya, wait three seconds and crank. Very well?'

'Very well.'

The poor servant girl, her nerves stretched almost to snapping by these delays and diversions, had begun to tremble all over, and the electrodes attached to her nipples were jingling faintly, like sleigh bells heard very far off on a clear, cold winter's night. I noticed Joanna's hand was trembling too as she held it ready to chop, then, with a start, realised that *my* hand was trembling on the crank of the generator. We were a ménage à trois, united psychically by a single thought: that within seconds electricity would pour down two copper wires and into two tender tit-mounds via two even tenderer nipples. But for

Joanna and me that thought was the source of *pleasurable* excitement; for our poor victim, strapped to her bench, it was a source of *painful* excitement.

But pain, for a masochist, is pleasure, as the girl proved even as our shared excitement mounted to almost unbearable pitch; for she broke it with a sudden long, loud fart of incongruous depth and resonance for a girl of such delicate frame and features. Evidently, the buggery with the thermometer had expanded her bum-chamber, and the walls had not yet begun to close. In a single glance, Joanna and I exchanged ideas for the dialogue that followed, nodded slightly, and began.

'Filthy slut,' I said.

'Indeed,' said Joanna, allowing her gloved hand to drop. 'We cannot have her interrupting the solemnity of our chastisement in that disgusting fashion.'

'No. But what is the solution?'

'It is obvious. Her upper mouth is gagged, but her *lower* mouth is not and is able to speak in that disgusting and insolent fashion.

'Therefore . . .?'

'Yes. Therefore, her bottom must be plugged too.'

'Indeed. With the thermometer, perhaps?'

Joanna pondered a second, then shook her head. 'No. The force of the punishment that awaits her may cause her bottom to tighten so hard that it snaps. And we cannot have her breaking a valuable piece of the Academy's equipment like that.'

'No, you are right. We cannot. Then what shall we use instead?'

'Open a few cupboards. See what you can come up with for *going* up with.'

'At once.'

Eyes wide again, the poor servant girl, lashed to the bench, tried to lift her head and see what I was

189

removing from cupboard after cupboard and setting atop the bench for Joanna's decision.

'You, slut,' said Joanna, noticing her movement, 'mind your own business. You will know soon enough what we have selected to gag your bottom-hole with, when you feel it sliding into you. Ah, *that* would be suitable, I feel, my dear Dr Lidiya.'

'It is rather large,' I said. 'Some lubricant is required, surely?'

'No. Force it up as it is. Screw it home millimetre by millimetre. Let the slut squirm, struggle and sweat: she has brought this on herself.'

'No,' I said. 'That would be too cruel. Far too cruel. Now that I have picked it up, I realise it is even bigger than it first looked. The poor girl will think she is having a *house* forced up her bottom. Even if it is lubricated. *Without* lubrication it will be like . . .'

'Bucharest Cathedral?' Joanna suggested.

'At least. Or perhaps . . .'

'Mont Blanc?'

'Quite possibly. It will certainly bring tears to her eyes.'

'If it does, use them for lubrication.'

'But it could be halfway up by then. I will have to slide it out, soak it in her tears, and slide it up again. Doubling her trouble. And think: the salt in her tears will sting her stretched sphincter very badly.'

'Then double her trouble. Sting her sphincter. The slut has brought it on herself. Force it up her now. I am impatient to begin the electrical torture and do not wish to have her interrupt it with one of her disgusting farts. Force it up her. Now.'

What the poor girl thought I was about to force up her I have no idea, but plainly Joanna and I had planted some most distressing ideas in her head, for when I placed the head of the pestle on her bottomhole she quivered and squeaked like a frightened mouse, her eyes rolling fearfully.

'Stop that, slut,' said Joanna. 'We were only teasing. There will be a moooooment of strain . . . and there, it is up.'

With a gasp and a shiver of relief, the girl accepted the pestle into her bottom, and I turned it one way, then the other back, before pronouncing myself satisfied.

'Gagged fore and aft,' I said. 'We can begin.'

'Yes,' said Joanna. But she tugged one of her asbestos gloves off first and ran a bare finger down between the girl's breasts, over her belly, dipping in and out of her belly button, and to the upper fringes of her silky black pubic hair.

'Look,' Joanna said, lifting her finger, which glistened with fresh sweat. 'We made her more anxious than even we hoped with our little game.'

I moved close to her, opening my mouth and pleading with my eyebrows. Joanna popped her sweat-moistened fingertip into it and I sucked, savouring the taste of the girl's fresh and fearful flesh. Joanna drew the finger out with a pop, and chuckled cruelly.

'Yes,' she said, 'more anxious than even we hoped. And now, doubtless, having anticipated much pain and received almost nothing, she thinks the ordeal that awaits her with the electrodes will not prove so fearsome after all. Doesn't she?'

She ran the finger down the girl's body again, and this time popped the sweat-moistened tip into her own mouth, pulling it forth with a louder pop that made the girl jump a little.

'Doesn't she?' she repeated, beginning to slide her asbestos glove on again. 'Well, I am afraid, very much afraid, her hopes will have been raised only to be cruelly dashed. Are you ready, Dr Lidiya?'

'Yes,' I said, and I was, with my hand waiting on the crank of the generator.

'Good. Then I will chop, and on the silent count of three, after I have seized her succulent body and held it firm against the storm of agony that is about to blast it, you will begin cranking.'

Her hand rose into the air, ready to chop, and I stopped breathing. Our shared excitement was back, building in the air, and perhaps the girl would have farted involuntarily again, breaking the tension as she had before. But now her bottomhole, like her mouth, was firmly gagged, and only her eyes could speak, rolling in her sweat-shiny face. I remember that I was watching a fat drop roll down her shapely nose when Joanna, with a hiss of anticipation, chopped her hand down and I began counting off silently, mouthing the words.

One. Joanna's asbestos-gloved hands had flashed out and seized the girl's body, groping it for Joanna's pleasure and also to select the firm and fleshiest spots. *Two*. Her hands were fixed now, tightening on the girl, her fingertips sinking into her flesh. *Three*. Smiling ruthlessly, Joanna turned her head and locked gazes with me, her mouth moving in a silent echo of mine.

I began cranking, and felt the joy of domination surge over me in a wave as the highest pitched yet of the girl's squeaks escaped her gag and Joanna cursed with the effort of holding down her slender, electrified body.

'Crank!' Joanna ordered, her voice full with a greater joy of domination. 'Crank!'

I cranked, generating electricity for the torture of the girl's nipples and breasts. Ah, what blessings Science has placed in the hands of us *bourgeoisie*! The bottoms of the lower orders have always been ours to beat and bruise, for they are designed by Mother Nature to absorb punishment and recover, time after time, but their nipples and breasts have been beyond the pale of most punishment, being too delicate for harsh treatment. We might squeeze and twist a little, perhaps bite gently, certainly flick and pinch, but no more, even in Bulgaria. Then Science plucks the very lightning shaft from Heaven and adapts it not only to the mundane tasks of illumination and powering machinery but also to the sublime: titty torture.

At last we can pain our lower orders powerfully through their breasts, and when we cease to pain them, no marks are left. This was brought home most strongly to me – though most strongly of all to our poor victim, of course – when Joanna, with a second chop of her asbestos-gloved hand, signalled me to stop cranking. I did so, and when Joanna released the girl fully, her body continued to tremble with exquisite echoes of the pain I had poured into her, while tears poured in liquid tribute to the efficacy of our torture. And she *hummed* in protest. I was about to ask the tune she hummed when Joanna sniffed and hissed again.

'Look at the slut,' she said, almost tearing off her glove in her eagerness to push her fingers between the girl's thighs, and I saw that a second liquid tribute to the torture was flowing from the girl's pussy. Joanna dabbled there and then raised her fingers, strings of pussy-juice stretching from them like the strings of a marionette. Indeed, the conceit occurred to Joanna too, for she looked at me with a smile and twiddled her fingers, saying, 'Our little puppet dances to our tune of pleasure and pain!'

I laughed, but then stopped as the name of the tune the girl was humming came to me and its *significance* struck me.

'Listen!' I said to Joanna, who was dabbling in the girl's pussy-juice again.

'To what?'

I cursed in frustration: Joanna's tin ear has often prevented the two of us from sharing one of my greatest passions, though it was instrumental in bringing us together, when she was leaving a concert of baroque music with ten minutes but elapsed and I was hurrying in, having been delayed en route. We collided in a doorway, and Joanna soon had me dragged to one of the lavatories for a spanking, though I insisted that she chose the cubicle nearest the stage, wherein I could listen to the music as she set to work on my bum cheeks. To this day a snatch of Tomasina Albinoni never fails to set my bottom tingling and my pussy pouting, though for Joanna it might as well be the music of an Italian ice-cream salesgirl – another sound that for me never f . . .

But I have waxed nostalgic, and dangerously so, considering our situation. We will never know such happy days again unless we defeat the monstrous evil of the Count, and the more we know of his psychology and tactics the better able we will be to wage our war. This is why I must record the tune the girl was humming, and her reason for humming it. The tune was the '*Internationale*', and her reason for humming it was revealed when Joanna, convinced finally that the information would be of importance, untied her gag and asked her. Such was her anger and humiliation at the strength of the torture and its effect on her now far-from-private parts, that she concealed nothing but spat her reason into our faces.

'It is the song of liberation for us oppressed women you lackeys of the ruling classes have trodden into the mire for too long! But a day would be too long, an hour, a minute, though it was paid in a century of sim–'

194

Joanna balled the gag – the girl's knickers, as I have remarked above – and thrust it back in her open mouth.

'Shut up with your subversive socialist drivelling, you slut,' she said. 'Dr Lidiya, if you would – but what?'

'No, Vasilka,' I said. 'Let the slut continue. These drivellings of hers, as you most aptly term them, are of the greatest interest. Do you not see?'

'Ah,' Joanna said. 'Yes. How foolish of me. Very foolish.'

She plucked the knickers from the girl's mouth and dropped them with a click of disgust, for they were soaked with her spittle.

'Slut,' she said. 'Let us hear what you were saying again. But this time, tell us also where you have *learned* this subversion. Has the Countess taught it you? Has she convinced you that she means to spearhead the revolution preached by that madwoman Karla Marx?'

The girl, realising her emotions had carried her tongue too far, was silent now, but it was plain to read in her face that Joanna's shrewd questions had struck home.

'You fool,' Joanna said. 'We call you our puppet and do so openly; she too could call you her puppet, and with far greater truth, but instead she turns a smiling face to you and pours lies into your foolish ears. Understand this, girl: she promises you freedom while preparing for you and your sisters a slavery worse than any you have experienced hitherto. Do you not see? Do you not *smell* it, girl, in her dungeons, where your sisters sit chained and she exploits their poor breasts to *profit* – mark the word well – to *profit* from their stolen milk?'

The girl still said nothing, but shook her head in response, as though she struggled against the impulse to defend the hideous Count from the accusations Joanna rightly heaped upon him, while knowing that she must keep silent to keep from doing further harm to her mistress's plan to benefit the lower orders (as she foolishly thought it).

'Well, girl?' Joanna said. 'Reconcile, if you can, her milk profits with her profession of anti-capitalist principles. And reconcile the monstrous thigh-member, I guess – aye, and rightly, I see in your face – you have seen in . . . in operation with her claims to high moral purpose. She is a monster, girl, not fully human, and her only loyalties are to herself, to her own monstrous kind and to their never-ending greed for pleasure at the expense of women. *All* women, you deluded socialists included.

'Bah! I see words are of no use,' she went on, stooping to pick up the girl's spittle-soaked knickers and opening them to gag her. 'Lidiya, prepare to crank again. Ha, yes, prepare to crank again while I demonstrate on the very flesh of our captive the unbridgeable gulf that yawns between us "lackeys of the ruling classes" and the Countess and her unspeakable "suns". Have you heard her use that word of them, slut? Then ponder its significance well as we continue. Lidiya, crank while I tickle our little slut's not-so-little clitoris. Ungloved, so that my fingertips too are tickled with the electricity that flows through her body. And let her ponder the significance of this also: that we pleasure her as we pain her, after the eternal reciprocity that has existed between ruler and ruled, for we are all, in the words of Johanna Goethe, cells in the body of *Das Ewig-Weibliche*.*

'But this reciprocity does not exist between the Countess and the women she cruelly exploits or tricks and manipulates with the intention of cruelly exploiting later. Ponder that girl, as we pain and pleasure thee. Dr Lidiya, if you will begin.'

I watched her place her ungloved fingers again to the girl's pussy, and begin gently stroking and teasing her clitoris as she placed the gloved palm of her other hand on the girl's flat belly and pressed down hard, preparing to hold her down as before. I swallowed, knowing that I would pain the woman I loved when I started cranking, and wondering whether some permanent strain of submission had entered my darling as a result of her experiences in the Count's castle in Wales.

'Dr Lidiya, if you please,' Joanna said, and I smiled at the anger in her voice occasioned by my slight delay. No, she did not sound as though she were turned submissive, and I realised her willingness to be pained was the true sacrifice it appeared: it was to convince the girl of the truth of what Joanna had said, not to scratch some perverse itch in Joanna's Count-corrupted psyche. I cranked, and heard Joanna hiss as trickles of electricity that had flowed down the wires, into the girl's nipples, then her breasts, then her slender young body, reached the girl's pussy and the ungloved fingers that tickled there.

I looked up from the generator, and saw that the girl's eyes were rolling with the conflicting sensations the two of us were setting up in her body: the pain of electricity, and the pleasure of masturbation.

'Faster,' Joanna ordered, and through the savoury reek of the girl's pain-moistened flesh I caught the acrid whiff of Joanna's own sweat and the musk of her leaking pussy. She was performing a sex-act not merely *on* the girl but *with* her, though the only skin-to-skin contact she maintained with the slut was via her fingers. I obeyed, cranking harder, and heard

Joanna hiss louder. She would tell me later that what she experienced as she pleasured the girl in this way was like nothing before in her experience: the slut seemed to have stings in her pussy, which pricked at her fingers as she plucked and tweaked at her clitoris, or stroked and strummed her swelling pussy-lips. Her fingers were growing numb, and yet losing none of their sensitivity, as though the stings could strike through a thickening outer layer of horn to the nerve-rich pulp beneath.

'Faster,' she ordered again and, as I obeyed, my hand whirling in a complete circle almost sixty times to the minute, I smelt my own sweat, mingling in a rich bouquet with Joanna's and the girl's. Joanna tells me now that the girl was flopping and bouncing under the single palm placed on her belly like a stranded salmon, and she barely had the strength to hold her down as she tickled that sting-filled pussy and its clitoris. How long the two of us kept up that final gallop – I on the handle of the generator, Joanna on the pussy of the girl – I do not know, but it ended when Joanna, with a wail of breaking will, tore her hand from the girl's pussy and flashed it down between her own thighs, where, too eager to burrow, it seized a great handful of cloth and began rubbing through it at Joanna's own and too-long-neglected clitoris.

But Joanna did not cease to pleasure the girl when she tore her hand from her pussy: no, with insane devotion to duty, *she plunged her head between her thighs and, reckless of the stings of electricity that stabbed at her lips and tongue, cunnilingued her furiously to final orgasm, which arrived simultaneous with her own.* And simultaneous with mine, I confess: even as I cranked at the generator with one hand, the other was busy beneath my skirt, frotting in a drizzle of pussy-juice at a pleasure-famished clitoris. I collapsed to the floor when orgasm came, ramming my fingers up inside myself to feel my own pussy-walls clench and writhe on me, and moaning with ecstasy into the moans of Joanna and the girl.

Slowly, the sound of Joanna sucking the girl's pussy clean of juice brought me to my senses, and I pulled my fingers clear of my own pussy and got unsteadily to my feet. The handle of the generator had stopped turning as soon as my hand left it, but the girl was trembling with minute shocks under Joanna's tongue and lips as though electricity had never ceased to flow. I walked past Joanna's head, bowed firmly to the chalice of the girl's pussy, tugged down the girl's gag, and presented my dripping fingers (in which I could still feel the pressure of my own clamping pussy-walls) to her mouth. She sucked at them with instinctual greed, and when they were sucked clean I dragged them forth and kissed her, fencing my swollen tongue against hers as Joanna's juice-swallowing brought her to a second orgasm.

Her mouth was as sweet and fresh as her pussy, and I prayed to the Goddess that the Count's vile cock had never invaded either of these two sanctuaries, let alone the girl's tight bottomhole. But who knew what he might have persuaded her to, dangling the bait of revolution and of personal power for the girl in the socialist paradise that followed? But perhaps now she was persuaded that the old dispensation was not so rotten after all. It would be up to Joanna to question her concerning this, but Joanna, I could hear, was still greedily cunnilinguing the girl. This was too much of a good thing: we had intended to *persuade* the girl, not pleasure her to delirium. I broke the kiss, moved behind Joanna and knelt, lifting up the hem of her skirt and peering up between her thighs.

They were drenched with pussy-juice and as I thrust my head up between them I felt it smear my cheeks and flatten my hair. Joanna hardly felt the invasion, she tells me now, and paid no attention to it till my tongue began to lap at her pussy and I began to drink the brine-musky liquor that she had been distilling there as she had been drinking the girl's. This brought her finally back to her senses, and my lips curved in a smile against the moist and fleshy folds of her pussy as I heard her slurping and sucking stop and felt her thighs quiver against my clamped-flat ears.

She had lifted her head from the girl's pussy and I knew that she would be wiping her mouth clean as she surveyed the girl's face. Yes, and now came her voice, muffled but clear through the thigh-cage in which my head was held.

'Well, girl, have we brought you to your senses? Do you recognise now the goodness of the social arrangement whereby we exercise power and you submit to it? For we sow pleasure even as we reap pain in the bodies of sluts such as yourself, and you were born to service as a hundred generations of your spit-mothers* were before you.'

(I interject here the observation that this cannot, if the Count's words are accepted, be true: a hundred generations of your spit-mothers would carry us back well past the point at which, according to him, the Goddessly pattern of spit-mother bearing twaughter came into the world. Before then, we women were born by the fusion of Woman and such creatures as the Count – mans, that is the word. Joanna has argued to me that the Count was lying when he told of this, seeking to aggrandise himself with typical arrogance and egocentricity, but I remember that Dr

200

Helsingvili betrayed no scepticism when she echoed his words; and despite my disgust and horror I cannot but accept it myself. Indeed, does not Joanna contradict herself in denying it, for is she not fighting precisely to avert the threat of the Count *re*-establishing the ancient Evil over which he gloated in his Welsh castle?)

I could not see the girl's response, of course, but Joanna tells me now that she watched violent emotion contend in her face as she racked her poor pain-stung, ecstasy-sweetened brain to decide who spoke truth to her. Was it the 'Countess', a known abuser and exploiter, with 'her' grandiose tales of liberation for the oppressed working girls of Europe? Or was it Joanna, cruel but kind, telling her that the dreams of liberation implanted in her breast by the 'Countess' were a chimera and she would, metaphorically speaking, pursue them over a precipice to not only her own destruction but also the destruction of those she held dear?

The girl's decision, when it came, was unspoken: tears sprang unbidden into her eyes and she looked up at her tormentress (who was struggling, she now tells me, to concentrate on the girl, such was the power of the sensations my tongue was arousing between her thighs), blinked, smiled, and slowly nodded. Joanna smiled and nodded in return and then, slipping the glove off her left hand, used that to diddle the girl's pussy again while her right stretched sideways to the handle of the generator and gently began to crank it. The girl shivered with pleasure as the electricity began to flow through her nipples again, and I, with head inserted between Joanna's thighs and tongue busily lapping, experienced the electricity for the first time: passing through the girl's body, it rushed up Joanna's diddling fingers, into her arm and shoulder, then down, down, through her glorious chest and strong loins to her pussy, where it met my eager tongue and lips with tickles of strange sensation.

Count Caradul's Diary, 15 October
(Kept in phonograph in Welsh).

I come fresh to my diary from my second 'telesperming' of the day: sucked by a servant girl, I have spurted heavily into her mouth and she has, under pain of my immediate and heavy-handed displeasure, caught the full load of my salty discharge there and not suffered a drop to spill down her throat. Then, under my close supervision, she has dribbled my sperm out into a syringe before taking it below into my milk-dungeons. I oscillate, I note, in what I call them, between milk-dungeons and slave-dungeons, depending on my mood and what aspect of them excites me most. Where was I? Ah, yes, before taking it below into my dungeons to be injected up the bumhole of that big-titted Danish slut whose name – unlike her nipples – I can never get my tongue around. Avida? Alvira? No matter.

And my servant girl can be sure that I will be inspecting the said bumhole minutely before sunset, and wish to find clear evidence that the syringe has been inserted fully into the luscious depths of her tight Scandinavian bottom and emptied to the last drop. I have a theory that a virgin bottom – as this Dane's very nearly is, give or take a buggering or possibly, my stiffening cock seems to be hinting, two on the first day of her imprisonment – should respond to sperm alone, without the accompaniment of buggery, by inflaming to some extent, and I should be able to detect the heat of this by inserting a finger. If I do not detect it, that servant girl's own bottom will shortly glow with heat, though not on the inside. If my theory is wrong and sperm in a virgin or near-virgin bum does not invariably have this effect, well, I will discover the truth in time and no one will have suffered but the servant slut.

The difficulty, of course, is that all previous intra-anal sperm-injections have taken place while a large cock – my own, or that of one of my sons – has been inserted to the balls in the said bottom. And perhaps the inflammation is owed to this alone. Much further research is evidently called for, and I and my sons are the men to do it. But my servant slut is opening the trapdoor and I find that my narrative has re-erected me to such stiffness that she can perform a further 'telesperming' immediately. [In Romanian:] Come here, girl. Your mistress's tentacle and milk-sacks are in need of service again. Suck it and allow your mouth to be filled by them. [Resuming in Welsh after a few seconds of rustling and a sigh of pleasure from the Count:] Ah, she is sucking me again, the foolish slut. She is another of my 'socialist' *révolutionnaires*, too blinded by her hatred of the bourgeoisie ever to question the tales I tell her or to piece together the evidence of my true nature that lies – and I speak quite literally in regard of *one* piece – right under her nose. [Laughter, and end of diary entry.]

Count Caradul's Diary, 15 October (continued).

Fresh from the milk-dungeons, and I feel as though my balls will be empty for a week or more. But I know I will be spurting again within the hour, and already have an orifice and a student in mind. The orifice will be the mouth – the most soothing to my cockhead, which feels somewhat battered after my session below – and the student will be that blonde Transmarynian in Joanna's femmewife's dorm, whose marks in applied botany and other subjects, as I see from the file on the desk before me, have been dropping unacceptably in the past week. Little wonder, for I have been lowering them myself. I will have her in shortly and inform her that her scholarship is on the verge of being revoked, but dangle the prospect of her headmistress being open to bribery.

But of a special kind, of course.

'Your standing in languages is not so uniformly bad as in other subjects,' I will tell her, reflecting the while on my own *standing*. 'Which is to say –' here raising my eyes and fixing them on her significantly '– you are skilled in tongues. And *with* your tongue.'

If I know the girl – and my spies have been busy spinning their webs around her pretty blonde head – she will leap at the offer of gratifying me with her mouth, though I doubt that she will be *quite* so eager when I produce that which I wish her to suck. There may be an attempt to flee at that point, but I will have two sturdy servant sluts in position just outside my door, and she will not get very far. Hmmm, despite my just-concluded session below, I am beginning to stir and stiffen a fraction at the mere thought of it. Yes, she will be dragged back in, with a palm firmly across her mouth, and will be stripped bare as I watch and strum my cock a little. Then she will be whisked off her feet and held horizontal, breasts swinging beneath her, as I advance on her, following the rod of my cock.

If she refuses to raise her head and accept my cockhead into her inexperienced young mouth, one of the servant girls will hook her hand into those soft blonde locks and drag her head up. Poor dear! For I will then prod and rub my cock over her face, while finding some argument to persuade her to open up and let me in. In these circumstances – and I have encountered enough of them to know, let me assure you, dear Diary – I generally drop hints that, if denied entry even a little longer, I will be seeking out some other means of entry to the luscious body before me. Imagination often fails my victims for some moments here, for they fail to realise my full meaning, but once the hints – renewed and clarified if necessary – have been deciphered, they find themselves placed on the horns or horn [laughter] of a *most* uncomfortable dilemma.

If they do not open their mouths, they finally realise, the large, excited and very solid organ prodding their delicate faces will shift its scene of operation and begin knocking for entry on their bottoms or pussies. Some have fainted with sheer horror when this realisation sinks in, and have found themselves brought round, spluttering and coughing, with a mouthful, and throatful, of *sal vitale.** Those who do not faint stammer out their acceptance of my terms sooner or later, and open their mouths for entry. After all, they will all have lapped and sucked pussies and pussy-thorns many times before, and the leap to a cock is not so very vast. Or at least, it is not when set against the leap of accepting a cock into one or another or both of their lower orifices. And this Transmarynian slut will be no different, I suggest. The meaning of my hints, or my direct statement, if I am too impatient for play, will begin work in her exquisite little head, and if she does not faint – I have bet a brave servant slut a brisk bum-warming that she will not, against the buttocks of a student who was insolent to that servant last week – she will open her mouth and suck me, and I will soon be discharging

205

despite my pessimistic forecast at the beginning of this diary entry.

And the time has come, now that I have gathered my thoughts – and, indeed, my breath! – to explain *why* I made that forecast; namely, to describe what it is I have been doing in my milk-dungeons for the past two hours. Richard is back from the expedition I sent him on across the Black Sea to Georgia, where he saw to the disposal of some of the records whose location that pernicious Dr Helsingvili has finally surrendered, tough little bitch that she is. Well, now that he is back, I have been able to begin certain projects that I could not begin alone, and today it was the turn of the milk churn. I wish I could say the name in capital letters, for it requires some mark of distinction. Dismiss from your mind, my dear future transcriber – perhaps you, Gwynnedd, especial favourite among my buggerees, sitting there with a freshly sore bottom, or you, Rhiannon, sweetest-breasted of my Transmarynian milk-slaves – well, dismiss from your mind the humble milk churns you have seen and used in Transmarynia.

This was conceived, and constructed, on a *much* grander scale. Even so, my ambitions have been swelling daily since I arrived in Romania, and this milk churn barely seems to match them now. I will build larger still in future, when my milk-slaves are numbered not in dozens, as they are in Transmarynia and will shortly be at the Academy, but in hundreds. Nay, in thousands. And that will be in Bucharest alone. Rivers of milk will flow daily from the breasts of my slaves, to be churned into fresh butter or fermented into fresh yoghurt, or, in time, to cram warehouse after warehouse with aromatic girl-cheese of all varieties. Then silver will flood into my coffers even as milk floods from the breasts of my slaves, and as the women of Europe flock to buy my products, so they will enable me to buy and bribe my way to greater and greater security, in preparation for the final day of reckoning, on which I will overthrow the old order and usher in the new. Aye, my new order, when all female Europe will lie beneath my heel and no orifice shall be denied me. [Sound of heavy breathing for several seconds, then a cough.]

But I grow carried away with my dreams of the future. From tiny breast-buds mighty mammaries grow, aye, but I must not count my pussies before they are thatched. So, to return to my milk churn, my mighty milk churn, which stands higher than you do, Gwynedd or Rhiannon, and which is built of sturdy Romanian oak with six chambers, each of which can be detached from the central drum for cleaning or replacement. Why six chambers, perhaps you ask? Well, my dears, or rather, my dear, I will tell you. Perhaps you will not know, sluttish peasant that you remain despite the education I have generously granted you, of that winter game the Russian nobles play with their peasant girls, whereby one chamber of a six-chambered pistol is loaded and the chambers spun for a one-in-six chance of firing. Yes, a naked girl – one of six stripped for the game – has to fire it at a large and freshly filled pot of girl-piss stationed above her head. If she wins the spin and the pistol does not discharge, the chambers are spun again and the pistol passes to the next naked girl who comes reluctantly forwards to stand beneath the piss-pot.

And round the circle it goes until the pistol goes off with a bang and some poor peasant girl is drenched in piss, whereupon she is taken, still dripping, to be chained outside in the bitter cold. When the piss has frozen on her body, she is brought back in and the five remaining girls have to lick it off her body. It is said that the shivering waif is often brought to several intense orgasms by the tongues working with vigour, to the encouragement of beaten bottoms, on her piss-ice-sheened body but that is her pleasure, not that of the observers, and it is difficult to understand, perhaps, why the Russian nobles participate in the game with such enthusiasm. After all, it is easy to imagine more interesting uses that could be found for the bodies of six naked peasant girls, but I believe this game tends to take place towards the end of their proverbially intense drinking sessions, when their drunkenness lends it a glamour lost in more sober moods.

Be that as it may, the game is known as 'Russian roulette', and is often used as a metaphor or symbol among literary folk for some risky task in which one partakes willy-nilly – which is to say, not willy, but nilly. Well, I have invented a variant on it in which young girls partake with even greater reluctance. My variant is known as 'Bulgarian roulette', and from the rechristening you will already begin to guess something of its nature. I have played it today five times, and three bottoms, not to mention my cock, will pay testimony to the demands it places on its participants. How is it played? Cast your mind back to the milk churn, you slut, and its six detachable milk-chambers. I mentioned that the milk churn stands higher than either of you, and add now that that it is almost as high as myself.

This means that I can fit myself into one of those six chambers, where one day soon milk will slosh and churn, freshly drawn from the aching breasts of Bucharest's milk-slaves. And there lies the basis of Bulgarian roulette. The milk churn is to be powered by the very girls whose breasts will supply it: there are ankle-chained treadles for them to work with puffs and pants of exertion as, facing away from the milk churn, with heavy breasts swinging to their every movement, they support themselves on the wooden bar to which their wrists are chained. There is an adjustable crotch-bar too, you will be pleased to hear, fixed just a little too high between their thighs, so that their pussies are crushed against it as they treadle. Ah, it will be a sight to see, when all six treadles are occupied and six naked milk-slaves are churning a full load of milk. Today, only one treadle was occupied at a time, for this was Bulgarian roulette, and the single treadler was not churning a full load of milk. That would have been beyond her powers, however much her bum was warmed with palm or paddle: only one chamber was full and not with milk, rather with a lustful Count Caradul, sporting an erection of stiffness and size exceptional even by the standards of his first days at an Academy of girls hand selected for beauty and perfection of breast.

But I wanted the milk-slave players in my little game to work up a sweat when they spun me, sick with the dread that my battering ram would soon be knocking for entrance at the gate of their bum-castles, and so each of the other chambers in the milk-churn contained a heavy keg of salted caterpillar. I also had no wish to emerge and find myself quite unable to stand from the vigour with which my chamber spun and tumbled, and so Richard un-coupled part of the mechanism controlling the milk churn. Accordingly, the churn would spin as a whole but the chambers would not move individually. Richard had also seen, for I have had this game in mind for many months, to the installation of hand-holds in each chamber, and of spyholes suitable both for peering in, to check on the progress of a churning, and for peering out. These were plugged from the

209

outside with little disks of walnut-wood on copper chains, and as soon as I was installed in my chamber I unplugged mine with a jab of my forefinger and peered out to watch the first player being chained by wrist and ankle to her treadle and hand-bar, while the crotch-bar was adjusted to her discomfort between her heavy thighs. It was big-buttocked, big-breasted Bella, a gorgeously hairy and fragrant Italian slut of some nineteen years whose school marks had been among the first to dip unacceptably low.

Cue an interview with her headmistress from which she emerged with semen drying in her delicate but definite moustache of dark, silky hair – which I would not have her shave off for worlds – as, struggling furiously, she was carried below to my dungeons to be readied for milk-slavery. Oh, would hers be the bum I would first penetrate? I strummed my cock impatiently as I peered out, watching the play of muscles in her fine, velvet-skinned buttocks as she shifted, chains clinking, ready to begin her treadling. Then Richard closed my spyhole – I, like the girls against whom I played, would have no idea whether the game were won or lost till the moment at which the milk churn stopped moving and I opened the spyhole again – and I heard the buttock-stinging crack of the whip with which he signalled the girl to begin treadling.

For a moment, two moments, three, nothing happened, and it was evident that the milk churn, even for well-fleshed Bella, was proving difficult to set into motion. But then, with a jerk, the churn began to move, its wood creaking in protest, and I released my cock and seized the hand-holds. The whip cracked again across those velvety buttocks and I heard Richard shout, 'More effort, you slut!' I smiled with pleasure, for if Bella was struggling to turn the thing

210

on her own, just think of what the lighter-boned girls would face. That whip of Richard's would have cracked many times on bum flesh before the session was over. The thought made me groan with lust and my cock throbbed down its full length, eager to be sheathed to its full length in girl flesh. Again the whip cracked and I sniffed deeply, fantasising that I could already smell the sweat that was surely beginning to trickle in the thickly forested dells of Bella's armpits, crotch and bumhole. The milk churn was turning at a little above walking pace now, accelerating slowly but steadily, and perhaps it was not so much of an effort after all, once it was set in motion.

Well, another keg of salted caterpillar in each of the other five chambers would see off that little problem, though on second thoughts that might be excessive. I wanted my girls to sweat, not to incapacitate themselves, and Yolanda, a slender Portuguese girl who was fifth in line to play Bulgarian roulette, already had little enough energy to spare from the task of carrying her large breasts, which had grown larger – and noticeably more tender – since I converted her to milk-slavery. By now my chamber was starting to rock a little, so fast was the milk churn turning, and I sniffed again, trying to catch the rich scent of Bella's sweat through the solid oak of the chamber wall. Then the whip cracked for the third time and I heard Richard order my milk-slave to cease treadling. It was at this moment that the game began in earnest and Bella's firm buttocks and virgin bumhole were at stake in earnest: the churn would continue to turn under its own inertia, but slowing, slowing, slowing, till at last it came to a halt and I would see who had won: I or my milkmaid.

Oh, my cock throbbed again, for above the diminishing squeaks and rattles of the churn I could hear

Bella positively *praying* that she would escape unscathed. Richard, knowing his father's mind as well as I know his, my son's, allowed her to amuse and arouse me for a few seconds longer and then cracked his whip across her arse with an order for silence. The churn was back at walking pace now and I could barely contain my impatience: once every rotation those gorgeous Italian buttocks were passing directly in front of my cock, but would the milk churn come to a rest where *its* prayers – and mine – were answered or *hers* were? Two lines had been chalked on the floor, marking out the sixth of it in which the treadle girl was stationed, and if the spyhole opened on this sixth of floor her arse was mine for the buggering. Creak, creak, went the churn, slowing, slowing, slowing, and I felt as though my lustful gaze would scorch a hole through the oak.

And then, with a sudden jerk, the churn was at rest. My heavy forefinger, assailer of a thousand bumholes and pussies, but rarely more eager for an orifice than today, jabbed out at the plugged spyhole. I missed on the first attempt, for I was still dizzy from the rotation, but the next forced the plug out and I crushed the end of my nose against the oak in my rush to see through the spyhole. Alas, my failure to win was immediately apparent in the empty treadle and dangling set of treadle-chains that met my eye. Richard's whip cracked again, but on air this time, ordering Bella to be unchained and the next girl put in her place, and I had to exercise all my will to keep my hand off my disappointed cock, which, brought to near boiling by my anticipation of success, was throbbing mindlessly for attention and would undoubtedly spurt copiously within two or three strokes of masturbation. But its disappointment was disappearing swiftly, I could feel, for I had conjured up the image of the girl who was being set in Bella's place, and my cockhead was sniffing eagerly for her bumhole and the silken depths of her arse beyond.

Aye, Belgian Eugenie would be an adequate substitute – indeed, my rapidly remounting lust was soon telling me, a *more* than adequate substitute. She was a long-haired dryad of the Ardennes with exquisitely smooth and unmarked skin that sank and curved over breasts and buttocks smaller than Bella's but no less shapely and firm. And how they would glisten with her sweat! And sweat she would, I was sure, for what Bella had found a heavy task – setting the churn into motion – she would find a heavier. I heard the chains rattle as they were fastened to her slender wrists and ankles and my cock throbbed again at the thought of her waiting there helpless for me, her bottom utterly unprotected from my assault – if I won the one-in-six throw of Bulgarian roulette.

Ah, there was Richard replugging the spyhole, and I seized the hand-holds again, waiting for the crack of the whip that would order Eugenie to start work on the treadles. There it came, kissing that Belgian bottom with lips of fire, and the churn creaked almost at once, jerked, jerked again, and then, to my surprise, began slowly but definitely to move. There was hidden power in Eugenie's slender thighs and calves, it was apparent, if she could get the churn turning so swiftly, and I filed away the thought for later: it would be amusing to match her against Bella on the treadles, each of which could be individually adjusted to turn the churn either clockwise or anticlockwise.

I had been turning anti-clockwise before; this time, to counter-act the dizziness Richard and I had anticipated, I was turning clockwise. The whip cracked again, but it was more by way of gesture than out of need, for Eugenie had already got a respectable speed up, a little below walking pace but increasing quickly. The discovery of her athleticism excited me, for I had never guessed it from her appearance, as though the pussy or arsehole of a plain woman, speared more from force of habit than from lust, proved tighter, hotter and more pleasurable than that of a more superficially attractive woman. But in this case I was uncovering an unexpected treasure in a woman I had already judged attractive, and my hopes of what her arsehole might offer – and the hopes of my cock – were raised accordingly. The churn was above walking pace now, creaking and rocking, and Richard's whip had cracked in earnest only once.

Oh, I could see the play of muscles in Eugenie's buttocks and thighs as she worked hard on that treadle, breasts swinging, silk-fringed pussy-lips flashing in her crotch-gap against that too-high crotch-bar, but her pink and unpenetrated bumhole squeezed firmly out of sight between her bum cheeks. Well, that would avail her nothing if she lost the game: she would feel my cockhead burn like an ember against her cool, sweat-moistened skin as I rubbed it in her bum crack, then lodged it firmly for the sure-to-be-successful assault on her anal virginity. But a thought struck me: *was* it sure to be successful? I was so excited that the struggle to get in might trigger my sperm-flood before I *was* actually in. And if I failed to win this round, the frustration of my cock and balls would only increase, making premature ejaculation all the more likely on the next – which I might again fail to win.

This game held hidden perils, I was now realising, and I wondered whether to have myself first sucked to thorough orgasm when I played it again, ensuring that my first victory in the game proper would not prove pyrrhic. But that was for later: Richard's whip was cracking again and his voice ordering Eugenie to stop treadling, and I would soon know whether my cock or her bum had been victorious. As though responding to my heightened lust, the churn seemed to be slowing more strongly this time, and I could catch no prayer to the Goddess through its diminishing creaks and rattles. Perhaps Eugenie was praying silently or had simply resigned herself to fate. I was at walking pace again, slowing rapidly, and in a few seconds more my index finger could stab out and knock the plug in the spyhole free, so I could thrust my face against the wood of the chamber and see if I had won.

There: I was stopped, and my finger stabbed out. Again I missed for reason of dizziness, though not by as much, for I had anticipated it this time. But now the plug was out, and I was pressing my eye eagerly to the spyhole. Would I see blank wall and empty treadle again, or the gleaming curves of female buttocks, glistening with the sweat of heavy exertions? Oh, it was the latter, the latter, for Eugenie's bowed head, sleek back, swelling buttocks and slender legs were plainly in view. My cock jerked an extra few degrees upright, its sperm-slit oozing freely in anticipation of the feast of bum flesh that awaited it. I heard Richard walking across the floor to the array of handles that controlled the mechanism of the milk churn, ready to seize the handle that tipped my chamber forwards and allowed me to climb out (I would have to be careful not to bang my cock against the wood as I did so, for fear of triggering the orgasm that was already coiled and quivering in my balls).

There: the milk churn shook and rattled and my chamber began to tip forwards. If it had been full of freshly churned girl-butter, a barrel would have been waiting to receive its load when its lid was uncapped; as it was, it was full of lustful Count, not butter, and, when the trembling hands of Eugenie's companions began to undo the catches of the lid and tug it off, I snorted with impatience and struck the underside of the lid a blow with my fist, jerking it half-open to squeaks of surprise. Another blow and it was fully off and I began to crawl forth, carefully holding my cock up against my belly by its root, my eyes fixed on the treasure that awaited it and me: Eugenie's sweat-shining buttocks. So transfixed was I on the prize of her buttocks that I spared the other girls scarcely a glance, naked though they were, merely growling to them, 'Bring her butter' as I rose to my feet. I swayed for a moment, shaking my head to fight off the dizziness of the spin in the milk churn, but my lust was an effective counter and within moments I was striding the two paces that brought me up behind my chained and trembling victim.

A cough from Richard discretely reminded me of his presence, and I turned my head impatiently to see him squeezing a large erection through the cloth of his dress.

'Papa,' he said in Transmarynian, 'if I could leave you for a few minutes, to see to girls in another chamber?'

'Of course, my son,' I replied in Romanian. 'Get yourself a blow job and some mouthfuls of milk. I intend to linger a while over the preparation for this first buggery, but you will know by the screams when it has begun and my ejaculation will not be long delayed after that.'

'Thank you, Papa,' Richard said, now also speaking in Romanian. 'I will hurry back when I hear them to supervise the next session of roulette.'

'Good,' I replied absently, turning back to Eugenie and half-hearing Richard stride from the chamber en route, I did not doubt, for the Polish twins Maria and Magdalena. My index finger jabbed out again, finding the knobbles of Eugenie's spine beneath the silken skin of her neck, which was trembling in fright from our just-ended conversation. I put my mouth to one of her ears and whispered to her as my finger slid down, down, pushing a wave of sweat ahead of it till it entered the valley that led to her bum-canyon, where sweat was more heavily collected still.

'Do not worry, my darling,' I whispered to her. 'We were teasing thee, he and I. Thou wilt certainly experience *moderate* discomfort when I enter thee, but it will not rise to excess and bring thee to screaming.'

Now my fingertip had arrived at her bumhole, squeezed in futile protection, as I had anticipated, between her powerful bum cheeks, and I began to rub her sweat into it, lubricating her for entry with a product of her own body. Ah, I could feel the quivering *tension* in the orifice, the energy she was pouring into it to hold it shut against the assault that would shortly be launched against it. Her sweat alone would not be sufficient to smooth the way for my cock, which itself was quivering on the brink of orgasm, but fortunately her sweat alone was not all my sapping finger had to employ.

A voice murmured diffidently beside me, and I glanced sideways to see a naked Bella holding up a tray for me. It contained six packets of girl-butter, the first of the millions that would soon be produced by my dairies in Europe, each of which, besides the label of my company (Caradul Milk Products in a specially chosen Transmarynian script), was stamped with the name of one of the girls taking part in this first game of Bulgarian roulette. Milk from each had been turned into butter on my specific orders for the game, for I was going to bugger them using their own butter for lubrication.

'Open Eugenie's packet,' I said, testing Eugenie's bumhole for tightness again with my finger. She would not have the strength to keep me out for long, particularly if I had a firm hold on her tits and squeezed in punishment of her resistance, but I was impatient for entry and the butter was a necessary accelerant. Ah, and that reminded me: I had to do something to obviate the risk of premature ejaculation. Once I was in and had forced my cock up her narrow arse-chamber until my pubic hair was rasping against her tight-stretched bumhole – well, at that point I had no objection to spurting, for it would allow me to withdraw and begin the next session of the roulette immediately; but I refused to spurt before I was in at all, or before I was fully in. Accordingly, as Bella began to open the packet of Eugenie's breast-butter, I glanced back over my shoulder and grunted a command to one of the other girls, the dark-eyed Juana.

'You, you Spanish slut, what is your name?'

'Juana, Contessa,' she stammered, obviously afraid that a new rule was about to be introduced and Eugenie would not be the girl to be buggered first after all.

'Aye, Juana,' I said. 'Come and kneel behind me. Lick my balls and then blow on them. You other three, whatever your names are, you can kneel with her and assist her at the blowing, when she has licked my balls thoroughly. And remember: if you make me spurt, your bottoms will regret it, even as my cock is compensated for your clumsiness by the pleasure it takes in your misfortune.'

This was a trick I have employed before when in danger of premature emission. It is not so great a disaster when one has the ability, as I have, to re-erect swiftly and spurt with barely diminished force into the next orifice that offers itself, but I compare it to the spilling of the day's first wine after only a sip or two. It is true enough that one can easily refill the glass and drink again, but something has been lost nevertheless and a refilled glass is precisely that: refilled. So it is, to reduce the risk of *ejaculatio praecox,* that I sometimes have a girl lick my balls and then blow on them, cooling them and lowering the pressure of the sperm that has pooled there in too eager anticipation of release.

'*Sí,* Contessa,' the Spanish slut said, nervously dropping a curtsey with her two equally nervous companions, and I grunted indifferently, turning my attention back to the bottom I intended to invade and to the now-open packet of breast-butter with which I intended to ease my passage. Air stirred between my thighs as Juana, having crawled to me, raised her head there, mouth opening for the heavily hanging sac of my balls; and I grunted again as I felt her tongue, soft and soothing as moistened velvet, begin to lick them. Poor girl: her mouth would not be rid of the taste of my ball-sweat for hours, as I have learned from questioning of my girl-slaves over the years, and she would already be struggling to master her impulse to retch. Yet still she had called me 'Countess', as though refusing to accept the evidence of my true non-female nature: the enormous cock she had already sucked a dozen times or more and might soon be accepting up her own *via posterior,** and the heavy balls she was now attempting to moisten.

'More spittle, you lazy slut,' I instructed her, poking a finger into the block of Eugenie's girl-butter and gouging up a large dollop. As I lifted it carefully to the bumhole of the girl who had produced it, I

219

heard Juana trying to work up more spittle in her mouth. Ah, it would take forever. I pushed the butter home between Eugenie's bum cheeks and began to rub it in, half-turning to look behind me.

'Sluts,' I said in Transmarynian, which was already a language of dread in my dungeons, 'your Spanish companion is suffering from a dry mouth. You must all chip in and assist her, or rather, you must all *spit* in and assist her. While she lies on her back with her mouth open, I wish to see the other four of you fill her mouth with your spittle, of which she is not to swallow a single drop.'

I grunted, for my rubbing finger had had its effect: the butter was melting and I could feel Eugenie's bumhole absorbing it. Soon I would have my finger up her, rubbing more butter in; and soon after that, she would be ready for buggery.

'Do you understand?' I continued, for Juana was still licking at my balls and only one of the young and beautiful faces that gazed up at me showed any comprehension of my instructions.

'Well? Answer me: do you not understand?'

The only nod was from Greta, a Norwegian blonde whose firm and curiously spherical, gravity-defying tits had responded exceptionally well to my milk-bites; all the others shook their heads and I heard Bella murmur, 'No, mistress' from beside me. I swore, half in exasperation at the obtuseness of my slaves, half in satisfaction at the progress of my buttering, for my fingertip had slid into Eugenie's bumhole a little for the first time.

'You, you cod-eating slut,' I said to Greta, 'translate into Romanian.'

I gouged up another fingerload of butter and set to work on Eugenie's bottom again. This time, as though blood was rushing to the region in anticipation of the assault to be launched on it, the butter melted almost at once and I managed to force a goodly amount inside. Behind me, Greta was translating my instructions into Romanian, and I felt Juana's tongue, which was drier than ever, finally desert my balls. It was a pity that, with a fresh arse to prepare for buggery, I would not be able to watch the other girls spittling into her open mouth, but – well, no, I *could* do so, if I stood to one side and worked at Eugenie's bum from the flank, as it were.

'You,' I said to Bella, seizing the block of Eugenie's girl-butter from the tray she held, 'get rid of that –' I nodded at the tray '– and help moisten Juana's mouth.'

So it was that I *did* watch the spittling, standing to one side of my intended victim of buggery and feeding fingerload after fingerload of her own fresh butter up her arse, as a young Spanish girl lay naked on the floor with mouth open and was supplied with the spittle of four other young and naked girls of varying nationality. It was partly in hope of such sights that I abandoned my natal land and transferred to Europe, for though Transmarynia offers a great variety of girl-flesh too, it is stamped mostly with a common origin, for the races intermingled there in the days of male mastery, confined as they were to the ambit of an island. But here, in Europe, there are greater spaces and greater distances between the bodies and mentalities of the girls I have gathered for my Academy.

And I believe the flavours of the spittle Juana received into her mouth, dribbled and spat there by her four companions one by one, must have differed too. It was not quite a pan-European mouthful she accepted, till it was flowing in thin lines over the corners of her lips, for no Slav had been included in my little party, but if she had swallowed she would have been swallowing most of Europe. But she did not swallow, of course, for she was under strict orders to retain the mouthload and deposit it on my balls.

'Enough,' I ordered the four spittlers with another grunt of satisfaction, for Eugenie's bumhole, while losing none of its virginal tightness, was now accepting *two* of my fingers up it, and a quarter of the block of her girl-butter had vanished into the velvety depths of her bum-chamber. 'Juana,' I continued, speaking in Romanian so as not to cause further delay, 'close your mouth now and crawl back to me. You will have to lift my balls up between my thighs and tug them out a little so that you can hold them as you dribble the mouthload over them. Quick. Two more of you – yes, Yolanda and Monique – can catch the overflow in your hands and massage it in. But *gently*. Then all five of you must find a position from which to direct your breath over my balls. I want them thoroughly *cooled*, do you understand, for I do not intend to ejaculate till I have sampled this delightful Belgian arse to its core.'

I laughed then, for I had seen puzzlement flicker on one or two faces as I said 'ejaculate'.

'The denotation of "ejaculate", if not the verb itself, you are all already familiar with,' I said, moving back to stand behind Eugenie as I managed to fit *three* fingers through her sphincter, and heard her groan with both the strain of it and the involuntary pleasure. 'And some amongst you, Eugenie at the head, or rather the rear, will soon be re-familiarised.'

Juana, Yolanda, Greta, Monique and Bella were crawling back across the floor behind me, I could hear, and I pictured Juana's delicate face bloated with the load of spittle she was carrying in her mouth. As

I gouged up a final fingerload of girl-butter to force up Eugenie's now thoroughly lubricated backside, the five girls were in position, their breath faintly tickling the hair on my thighs, and I felt Juana's small hands, trembling with emotion, take hold of my balls and timidly begin to tug them backwards. My cock twitched and I growled a warning.

'Careful with them, slut. If you provoke premature orgasm you will lick up and swallow every drop, and then receive a second dose in the more delicate of your nether mouths.'

The trembling in her hands increased, and she moved my balls with extreme caution now, lifting them backwards, up between my thighs, and slowly tugging them backwards and apart. A moment's sadness struck me at the thought of my coming triumph, for within two or three generations I will no longer strike my young female victims as the monster that, from their point of view, I am. I will have many more sons by then, and cock-and-balls will be familiar objects to the young women we enslave. But there must be a way around this: perhaps villages where girls are brought up in ignorance of the conquest of Europe by men, so that they are brought to us with minds fresh and unsullied, like blank virgin pages on which I and my sons will scrawl with our strong masculine scripts. Yes, that is what we will do.

Juana, having finally positioned my balls right, slowly released her mouthload of spittle over them, moving her head up and down, left and right. The spittle was strangely cool, coming as it did from mouths, and the mouth, of this nocturnal race, and I was reminded of my scheme to breed up hotter girls in future, and indeed *cooler*. Imagine penetrating one's way along a row of alternately hot and cool pussies, granting each three cock strokes, before ordering their owners to turn over and then penetrating their bottoms. Would it be possible to breed a girl whose pussy is hot and bottom is cool, or vice versa? I imagine not, but one could of course achieve the same effect by temporary means: a hot vaginal douche and a stick of ice up the backside. The thought makes me smile now as it made me smile then, as I completed my buttering of Eugenie's magnificent arse. A few moments later, Juana's mouthload of spittle was emptied fully onto my balls.

'Now rub it carefully in, you two other sluts,' I ordered. 'Before all of you *blow* on them.'

A moment's murmuring among the three naked milk-slaves crouched at my rear, concentrating on the heavy balls one of them was holding in her trembling hands, then Yolanda and Monique tipped the handfuls of spittle they had caught over my balls once again, and began to rub it in. My cock twitched again, and my balls were aching dangerously at the attention they were receiving.

'Careful!' I growled. I wiped my buttery fingers on Eugenie's bum cheeks and back, then sucked them finally clean, savouring the flavour of it. It was so pleasant, indeed, that I coated my fingers in it again, reaching down to rub them up and down her back and inner thighs, where sheets of melting butter were creeping floorwards, overflowing from her arsehole. Well born? She was well stuffed now too. I licked my fingers again, then reached down and took hold of my cock, gently rubbing its swollen and straining head in the butter covering the lower part of her bum.

'Careful,' I murmured, addressing myself this time, for I knew that a moment's carelessness would see me spurting frantically over the bum feast I had lovingly prepared for myself. The small cool hands nervously massaging spittle into my balls were bad enough, but now my cock was sliding on smooth bum skin and even nudging at the entrance of her well-lubricated hole. I coughed, lifting my cock away by sheer force of will, and ordered, 'That's enough, sluts. Blow on them. All of you, blow on them. But not too hard at first. I want first zephyrs, then breezes, and only then winds.'

They obeyed admirably, I must say, for I hardly felt the first puffs of breath they directed at what must have been a heavily glistening pair of lust-swollen and heated balls, held up and apart in those small Spanish hands. But gradually they increased the strength of their puffs and I sighed with relief as my scheme began to bear fruit: my balls were cooling and I felt my balls stir in Juana's hands, trying to relax and hang lower.

'Let them find their level, you silly slut,' I said. 'And the rest of you, blow harder. Harder.'

Oh, the relief of it was overwhelming: I would no longer fear spurting as I lodged my cock in Eugenie's well-lubricated bumhole and prepared to thrust, or spurting as first I slid in; and my body celebrated for me, brewing a long, loud fart that I released with a grunt into the faces of the five sluts who had toiled to cool my balls with their own breath and spittle. Disobediently, they abandoned their task as the hot gale of my gaseous discharge blasted their faces, stinging their delicate lips and eyelids and making them cough and splutter with nausea and disbelief as they crawled backwards over the floor. I did not care, and no visions of chastising their smooth, firm bottoms flashed in on me, for my concentration was focused entirely on buggering the bottom already before me, well buttered and ready for entry as its owner, the delectable Belgian slut Eugenie, stood on her treadle chained helpless at ankle and wrist.

I tried to slide her bum cheeks apart with one hand, but my fingers slipped on the butter that coated them and I had to seize hold of each cheek firmly in a single hand – provoking murmurs of apprehension and distaste – before I could swing them open and present my cockhead to her bumhole with a thrust of my hips. But I was not adjusted right, and glanced back over my shoulder at the huddle of naked young women, staring at the tableau of about-to-bugger and about-to-be-buggered with a rapidly shifting mixture of fascination, horror and disgust on their faces – or as much of their faces as I could see, for they were all still pinching their nostrils shut against the reek of my fart.

'You, Greta, come here,' I said in Transmarynian. 'You will have the privilege of presenting my cock to your fellow slut's arsehole. I must have the angle exactly right before I make my first thrust and skewer her like the marshmallow she is. Now translate my instructions for your fellow sluts.'

And as the poor girl crawled to me, she had to translate what I had said into Romanian.

'Very good,' I announced loudly in Transmarynian when she had finished, continuing in Romanian: 'I intend to skewer her like a marshmallow, and melt her in the fire of my bestial lust. Present my cock to the Gate of Paradise, you Norwegian slut. You others, come and kneel here and watch my *introitus**
– and if I catch any of you closing your eyes, they will be opened later by an application of birch or nettle to your bottoms.'

More sounds of crawling from behind me as Greta reluctantly took hold of my cock and moved its head towards the glistening bumhole of her Russian con-slave.

'Draw the foreskin fully back, you silly slut,' I said in Transmarynian. 'And hold it back as you present the head to her entrance. The foreskin! Yes, that is it.

Fully back. Now, hold it in place with one hand while you present the head to her entrance. Good. But press it firmly into place. Hey!' I continued, for Eugenie was moving her buttocks forwards and to left and right, trying to escape my pleasure-greedy cockhead. 'You other girls, seize your disobedient companion and hold her in place.'

The other four had arrived now, their heads clustering around my hips like flowers and their breath coming faster as they witnessed the preparations for Eugenie's buggery. After a moment's pause, they obeyed my instructions, seizing Eugenie's hips and locking her in place for Greta to present my cockhead finally to the Belgian girl's nether mouth.

'At last,' I murmured, then took two, slow, deep breaths, readying myself for the first thrust.

'Hold her,' I said gruffly, feeling a pulse begin to throb and flutter in my throat. It is a solemn thing, is it not, to pluck the flower of a young girl's maidenhood, whether by bottom or pussy, and however many times she may already have swallowed thy sperm? Aye, 'tis so, and I paused to shatter the stillness with another crashing fart before, with a grunt of triumph over the disgusted sniffing and gagging of the girls, I thrust with all the power of my hips. Greta's positioning of my cockhead and my own lubrication of Eugenie's bumhole and rectal antechamber had been judged to perfection, for my cock shouldered aside her sphincter and surged deeper in half a heartbeat – so swiftly, indeed, that the surprise of it overtook the girl's own senses, and a third of my cock had vanished up her before she responded to the invasion with a moan of horror and attempted to jerk her buttocks forwards.

But she was held too firmly by the hands of her fellow slaves, and the straw-clutching energy with which she tried to clench her sphincter on the shaft of my cock, slowing its entrance into the depths of her arse-chamber, was bootless against the butter with which I had lubricated her. Nevertheless, I teased her, gasping with surprise as though her sphincter-clenching had been successful and pausing my thrust for a moment. Then, with a malicious chuckle, I released my hold on her bum cheeks and reached forwards and around her, seizing her breasts with brutal force as I thrust again, inserting my cock to half its length – and with such speed that one of Greta's fingers, with which she still clutched my cockshaft, was carried partly through Eugenie's sphincter too. I took another deep breath and glanced down, revelling in the sight of my cock half-buried between the firm and fleshy curves of a female bottom, and examining the faces of my victim's companions. My threat had been mostly unavailing, it was evident, for three of the sluts had closed their eyes and turned their faces away in horror and disgust, Greta amongst them.

'Greta,' I said, with a further thrust that buried my cock to three-quarters of its length in Eugenie's bum, before sliding it partly out, 'Yolanda –' with another forwards thrust to three-quarters depth '– Monique –' and another '– you have disobeyed me. Ah! And your bottoms will . . . ah . . . pay . . . ah . . . the . . . ah . . . *price*!'

It was too much: despite the spittling and breath-cooling of my balls, the pleasure of thrusting in Eugenie's well-lubricated but deliciously tight and cool bottom, even as I issued a threat of bum-warming to three more girls whose own bottoms would shortly be rouletted, overwhelmed my resolve to delay ejaculation until I was buried in Eugenie to the balls, with my pubic hair tickling and scratching the taut-stretched rim of her sphincter, and my first emission came as I was actually *withdrawing*. On the cry of 'Price!', though I do not recall whether I issued it in Romanian, Transmarynian, or Welsh – or Nepalese, for that matter – I frantically reversed the thrust and stuffed my heavily spurting cock to its limits in the bottom that had delighted it so.

Eugenie, whose groans and grunts had pleasured my ears even as her bottom pleasured my cock and her firmly quivering breasts my fingers and palms, accepted my hot and salty shafts of seed with gratifying sensitivity, for she positively *fainted* as I unloaded the brimming seminal vats of my balls into her. I had the presence of mind to order 'Release her!' and my cock slid an extra quarter-inch deeper as her limp body slumped back against me, her ankle and wrist chains rattling as though in applause of my completed triumph. I have questioned my sluts closely many times on what it is they experience as my cock fires its shafts into their bums, and with rare exceptions they are agreed that the sensation surpasses the merely physical and lifts them sunwards into a realm of piercing clarity and heat. And one has to remember that among the nocturnal, insectivorous sluts of Europe and Transmarynia, this is no positive thing: they shun the sun, grow near blind in bright light, and become enervated and near immobile in great heat.

It is not alone the *heat* of my sperm that does this to a slut, I believe, spurting into a bottom quite unprepared to be assaulted in such wise, but also the *rhythm* with which I spurt, for this speaks in some atavistic fashion to the *nerves* of the bottom and the pussy that neighbours it, and thence to the brain. Heat and rhythm – it is like the strokes of a liquid whip, lashing the slut in her most intimate region after the thrusts and ramming of my cock itself have

229

broken down all other defences. Some have told me that the spurts seem to fill their entire bodies and splatter against the underside of their skulls, as though my initial buggering has rendered them hollow – empty vessels waiting to be filled. And yes, some also admit, and with a sincerity not born of the titty-tweaking or bum-paddling that loosens their tongues, that they *welcomed* my ejaculation as the necessary and true conclusion to my conquest of their bottoms.

I believe this is so: that in the act of buggery, by a primal alchemy of cock-pestle in bum-mortar, I transport my victims back through time, stripping them of their recently acquired habits and beliefs, and reawakening them to their ancient female instincts – which flood forth in their brains with final and irresistible force in response to the spurting of sperm in their bottoms. Yes, and I intend to question my victims in the session of Bulgarian roulette concerning these matters too, as I begin to place my speculations on a firmer footing. A deeper understanding of female psychology and its atavistic underpinnings will be highly useful to me and my sons as we build my empire. Eugenie's faint is already proof against any possible denial of the *power* possessed by my seminal spurts in her bum, and there can be little doubt that, with suitable persuasion, she will soon surrender further details of what she felt as I began to spurt within her.

But I near the end of this phonographic cylinder and a servant girl has brought me some fresh papers to sign in connexion with the purchase of a country house outside Bucharest, where I intend to establish an open-air milking-station. The girl can suck my cock while I sign them, for I have fully re-erected myself with my narrative of the Bulgarian roulette, which I will conclude on a fresh cylinder later in the day.

Count Caradul's Diary, 15 October
(Continued on a wax cylinder partly unplayable by reason of heat damage).

So, I broke off my narrative at the point at which I had just concluded ejaculating in Eugenie's bum, to the roots of which she had assisted me by fainting and slumping back against me. Now it was time to withdraw, have my cock licked clean, and return to the milk churn for a third spin and third chance at a tight and virginal bottom – which I had already decided would be Juana's. Her tongue on my balls had inflamed my lust for her.

'Assist me forth,' I ordered my girls, 'then unchain her.'

My cock was softening slightly in its fleshy socket, unsurprisingly in face of the heaviness of my ejaculation and the slackness of my ball-strings; but now, as five pairs of soft, small hands fastened on my body and began to tug me loose, my balls rehoisted themselves to the fork of my thighs and my cock swelled again in Eugenie's bum, and even twitched as, evidently re-awoken by the sensation, she quivered and lifted her head with a moan. And the moan was repeated as she felt the shaft of my cock sliding back through her sphincter, which is often, I have learned, even more uncomfortable, after its fashion, than the cockhead and -shaft sliding in. Nor do I wonder that this should be so: by the end of a buggering, the sphincter has been tugged and tautened severely by a series of cock thrusts, and though Eugenie had been subject to far fewer than it was my wont to deliver to a fresh bum, I surmised that her anal nerves either were of particular sensitivity or had been tightened to an exceptional pitch by the *circumstances* of her buggery, or, more probably, both.

To be confronted with a certain buggery is doubtless bad enough for my poor victims, but it is like being dragged to a precipice and flung over without ceremony. To dangle above a precipice with strong hope of safety and *then* plunge, with a twang of parting rope, into its depths must be far worse; and that, in effect, was what poor Eugenie had done. She had played my roulette with a five-in-six chance of escaping unscathed, and had lost. These facts of psychology doubtless lay behind the moans with which she greeted the withdrawal of my cock, the final of which almost drowned the uncorking *thuuuk-thwop* with which my cockhead emerged from the delicious depths it had so thoroughly plumbed and so thoroughly inundated. I felt dizzy again for a moment, as though the strength of my re-erection had drained the blood from my brain, and reasserted myself by shrugging off the hands of the girls who had tugged me forth.

'Enough of that, sluts,' I said. 'Bella and Yolanda, lick me clean, while the rest of you unchain little Eugenie and set her on her way to fetch your Mistress Ricarda.'

With evident reluctance – and I cannot blame them, for the twitching shaft and head of my cock was stained with all manner of unmentionables, and positively *steamed* in the coolness of the dungeon air – Bella and Yolanda set to work licking me clean while Eugenie was unchained and assisted, groaning and clutching at her poor bottom, from the treadle.

'Hold,' I said. 'Display my handiwork to me. Her bottomhole, you foolish sluts. Quick. Fold open her bum cheeks and display it to me.'

My cock jerked under the tongues of my cleaning maids as I stooped forwards and inspected the orifice shining between Eugenie's held-open bum cheeks, which quivered and twitched with the discomfort of the inspection. Ah, though the satisfactions of the deed itself are unsurpassable, the satisfactions of *contemplation* of the deed have their place too: the manly bosom swells and the breath gusts with sighs of self-congratulation as one surveys the freshly plucked flower of a bottom's maidenhead. Eugenie's bumhole was swollen and gaping, inflamed from the violence of the cock thrusts it had absorbed and leaking semen heavily, but so great was her youth and the muscular resilience of her nether orifice that already the sphincter was beginning to close. When next I penetrated her – and this will not, I vow, be long delayed – it will be as though I take her anal virginity again. Perhaps, indeed, I have another Artemisia on my hands – or rather, on the end of my cock.

But there were five other bottoms in the room, any one of which might offer equally fine delights, or even finer, and I spared Eugenie's bumhole no more than a minute's scrutiny before ordering her to fetch Mistress Ricarda. Her bum cheeks were released, to her audible relief, and I slapped at her to set her on her way, landing a heavy palm on her firm buttock flesh. But the cry of surprise and pain, and the whimpers of self-pity this provoked, did not lessen as she began to walk, after a fashion, from the chamber, but rather increased; and I slapped the heads of my cock-lickers away as I turned to investigate this phenomenon.

'What ails thee, my plump-buttocked Belgian slut? Thou shouldst be walking with head held high, to think that thy mistress has favoured thee with a bum-poking fit for the Goddess Herself.'

Gasps of horror greeted this blasphemy, and Eugenie's face was bleak as she turned and began to reply to my question.

'My bottom is –'

'I guess it already, slut,' I roared. 'Sore, is it not? And it pains thee as thou walkst! Then crawl, thou numbskull slut. Crawl!'

And crawl she did, going down on her hands and knees and departing from the chamber at the end of a lengthening line of shining sperm-drops, which rained from her bumhole as though eager to escape before her sphincter resealed itself. Turning back to the remainder of my sluts, I ordered Juana chained into the treadle and decided to butter up her bum before the third round of the roulette was played. It would pass the time well before Richard's return and teach the . . .

[The cylinder here becomes distorted from heat and only disconnected phrases are decipherable for two or three minutes.]

. . . wriggled with dis[com]fort . . . answered sullenly that [sh]e was . . . [c]ould not reply for a few mo[ments] . . . [ins]erted my fingers aga[in, str]etch[ing] the rim of . . .

[The cylinder becomes decipherable again here.]

. . . [r]oared with laughter as Richard's words recalled Joseph's letter of yesterday to me. I will set down the details to clarify them in my own mind and assist me when I reply. Joseph remains in Transmarynia supervising my dairy business there and he wrote that the *smell* of food served to a newly stocked milking-chamber, which had been fasted to cleanse its coming production of foreign flavours, had caused three of the girls to drip spittle disobediently on their own breasts. As they were not yet producing milk, he had indulged himself with nipple-tweaking, pinching and stretching; and then thought no more of it. But a week later, when he was serving the girls of that chamber again, he had occasion to repunish one of the three with nipple-tweaks, and noticed that her mouth overfilled momentarily with spittle and dripped again onto her breasts.

If Richard or Paul had been serving the chamber, the incident would undoubtedly have passed them by, but Joseph is as diligent in fathoming the psychological mechanisms of the female as he is in manipulating her physical mechanisms for pleasure and profit, and he immediately surmised that the phenomenon would replay further study. On the following day he nipple-tweaked the girl again, and noted an increased flow of saliva in her mouth, albeit less than that of the day before. By now he had his theory in place: that a psychic conjunction had been adventitiously fashioned in the girl's nervous system between increased flow of *saliva*, as caused directly by the scent of food after her fast, and stimulation of her *nipples*. Accordingly, when her nipples were tweaked her mouth filled. The conjunction, he surmised, was now weakening with time; and this was confirmed when a nipple-tweaking on the third day produced a reduced flow of spittle.

But what has been done adventitiously may be repeated with purpose, and he set about 'conjunctioning' (as he has christened it) the entire chamber: first fasting the chamber again – I may have something to say about this, for he must surely be reducing the girls' value as milking-stock – then inducing an increased flow of saliva by serving them an odorous dish of fern-moths, then nipple-tweaking the entire chamber. When I read the letter for the first time, I pictured him standing midway between a pair of milk-slaves, his long arms stretched to the breasts of each, fingers working busily on fresh young nipples; and it was not long before I had loaded a servant girl's mouth for another 'telesperming'. But to return to Joseph's experiment: he repeated the procedure on two further days, and then tested the strength of the 'conjunctions' he had formed by nipple-tweaking the girls in the absence of food. Two, he wrote, responded very strongly, leaking spittle freely onto their breasts – one of them being the girl in whom he had first noted the phenomenon – and almost all the remainder responded strongly or fairly strongly, with only two to show barely any response at all.

Since then, he wrote, he had been experimenting with other chambers and with other senses, trying to establish 'conjunctions' between the reaction to sounds and sights in addition to smells and tastes, on the one hand, and nipple-tweaking, on the other, and his results have been both fascinating and copious, and will be despatched shortly, when he has drawn them up in clearer fashion and subjected them to statistical analysis. Richard has pointed out that he is almost certainly skewing his data by relying on nipple-tweaking as one half of his 'conjunctioning', and should have tried stimulation of the pussy and bottom in addition. This is no doubt true, but Joseph has long been devoted to the torment of our slaves' breasts, and will find any excuse to indulge in his preference. This excuse, unlike some he has produced in the past, has been an excellent one, and may produce highly valuable techniques in future. Joseph did not write of an obvious speculation, but I know he was not unaware that it would occur to me: if increased flow of saliva can be induced by such stimulation, why not increased flow of other female fluids, such as breast milk?

We have long known that there are herbs and drugs to increase milk flow, but of course they taint or pollute the milk and I have used them very sparingly in the past. With Joseph's techniques fully developed, we might be able to employ these drugs simultaneously with other forms of stimulation; and when we cease to employ the drugs and allow them to be washed from our milk-sluts' bodies, the 'conjunctions' we will have established will allow us to increase milk flow by repeating the 'conjuncted' stimulation. From what I have seen so far in my Academy, I can expect to make excellent milkers of some of the southern races, such as the Spanish and Greeks, but quantity is not always quality and the prospect of increasing production in some of my less heavily flowing but more lacteally valuable girls is, I confess, an extremely enticing one. Imagine if that Copenhagen slut, whose creamy milk is fit to produce yoghurts and cheeses for any royal family in Europe, were able to be milked like one of those three sluts from Seville! Yes, Joseph has uncovered a possible cornucopia here, and I wonder whether if, in ten years' time, it will be habitual for a milking-chamber to be fitted with pussy and earlobe electrodes, with which to trickle shocks into its milking-sluts before they are pumped dry for that day?

A delightful prospect on several levels and I will certainly outline it to Joseph when I reply to him. There is no doubt that he will devote him[self] . . .

[The remainder of the cylinder is indecipherable through heat distortion.]

Mina Harker's Journal, 17 October

I return to my journal at midday, no less, after some twenfers' pause, quite limp with exhaustion and spent emotion. Joanna, on whom the burden of the new arrivals has fallen even heavier than on myself, is deeply asleep across from me, snoring softly as she does only when bone tired or unable to lie on her back. At present it is both, for she sleeps in an armchair in the staffroom of the 'Academy' – ah, disgust at the Count's imposture has overwhelmed me too much and too often for me ever to refer to it without the ironising cage of quotation marks.

But I see that I run ahead of myself, and must try to gather my scattered thoughts. It is difficult, like trying to catch autumn leaves in a whirlwind, and I know that I am running a great risk writing my journal in the staffroom, for the Count's spies are everywhere among the staff and the practice of private writing would be a tasty morsel for them to convey to their 'master', as I believe he denominates himself. But the two of us have had the privilege of being asked to do 'day duty' while staff and students sleep, and it seems as safe as it could ever be. Whether it be so or not, I *must* write now, for we do not know when we will have a quarter-hour of time to ourselves again in the week that lies ahead and I wish to record our impressions of the past several hours. Concentrate, Mina, concentrate.

Yes, the new arrivals. That is the first point. The 'Academy' was already overcrowded when we arrived, though we soon found that the number of pupils was dwindling by the day, as the Count found excuses to 'expel' delinquent girls – which meant, of course, to kidnap them into his dungeons as slaves for 'milk-training'. Well, the number of pupils has doubled since then, and done so literally overday.* All over Europe, it appears, his agents have been continuing to interview and accept fresh candidates for entry to his 'Academy for Underprivileged Young Women of the Lower Classes', and last day the dam burst: we had dozens of young women arriving at half-hourly intervals from the station. The confusion was universal, and I believe that the Count was enabled to siphon some of them off almost at once into his dungeons: Joanna's discerning eye caught three faces in particular among the newcomers that she swears had vanished later, and my heart is struck through with a pang of sympathy as I think of the poor dears, arriving with such great hopes of their coming education, only to be bundled into captivity by a monster whose likeness they can never have glimpsed even in their foulest nightmares.

But he could not imprison *all* of his new arrivals at once, despite the arrogance and certainty of success evidenced in his actions, and so we teachers were left with the task of registering new names and sorting out luggage and finding places in dormitories and soothing homesickness – and, oh, a hundred other things. Then, on top of all this, came our classes, which are now crammed to overflowing and in which we now operate under even stricter instructions from the Count. 'Discipline I demand, and discipline I will have' – I can hear his words now, and see his eyes flash ironically between Joanna and me, as though he were singling us out amongst the rest of the staff. Joanna refuses to believe that this was so, but I think what she really refuses is to face the prospect that our true identities have been uncovered by the monster.

And it is true, as she urges, that the Count was casting many ironic glances at this assembly of staff, as he issued his new orders with an ill-concealed glee of secret knowledge and power. 'Discipline I demand, and discipline I will have.' Ah, the monster, the monster! How can he walk the fair face of the moonlit earth unstruck by a thunderbolt of the Goddess's wrath? I – we – must trust that is only because a worse fate lies in store for him, during which he will expiate a hundred times over the crimes he has committed against the womankind of Europe and Transmarynia. 'Discipline I demand, and discipline I will have.' I cannot drive the words from my head, nor silence what they recall: the surflike patter of bottoms being beaten all over the 'Academy' as classes later proceeded. We are also under instruction to send girls to him for infractions previously ruled too minor for his notice, and I am in no doubt that expulsions, already running very high, will climb yet higher in the weeks ahead, as he works to reduce the student body of the 'Academy' again – or rather, to transfer his 'underprivileged girls of the lower classes' from above ground to below.

I have paused for a moment to massage my aching brows with my hand, and the heat of the spankings I have administered is still glowing perceptibly in my fingers and palm. Joanna's wrist, which she had thought recovered and stronger than ever, is wrapped in a bandage again, and I have no doubt that teachers who work here, if their employment is much prolonged, will pay in their later years for the punishment they are required to perform here daily. Wrists and fingers will ache with arthritis, and we will pay with pain for the pleasure we derived from the pain of the girls who have been tricked into attending the 'Academy'.

My thoughts grow morbid, I see, and my wrist too is aching from the spankings I have performed, so I will conclude here, before slipping back to my room

240

to hide my journal. It is already past the hour at which Joanna asked me to wake her, but I will let her sleep a little longer when I return. I will shield her as much as I can of this 'day duty' imposed by our considerate employer, who expressed concern that some of 'my new girls' – and to hear the way his tongue caressed the words tightened the stomach with nausea – would begin sleepwalking after the strains of their journey and excitement and anxiety of beginning their 'new lives' – with further tongue-caressing and an eye-flash of double meaning – at 'my Academy'. Oh, the beast, the beast! May the Goddess, if it be Her will, strike him surely; if not swiftly, then surely.

Letter of Doratea Susanasdottir, Icelandic student at the Academy, to her mother, 18 October.

Academy for Underprivileged Young Women
of the Lower Classes,
68 Strada Şelari,
Bucharest,
Queendom of Romania.

Dear Mama,

My head is still whirling from my journey and my arrival at the Academy, but I promised to write you, and herewith despatch you my first impressions of the Academy. Well – and I beg of you, do not distress yourself at what you are about to read – they are 'mixed'. That is to say, they are in part good, in part bad, and in part – I cannot avoid the word – *sinister*. To have the smallest part out of the way: it is, alas, the *good* things that I have seen here. The decency and piety of many of my fellow new arrivals, and *some* of those longer-established

241

students, are equalled, from what I can gather, only by their beauty. To walk about the Academy is like some dream of Heaven, Mama, for almost all the faces one encounters are those of young angels, with frames and grace of movement to match. Such *breasts* I have seen in my dormitory as we girls undressed and knelt by our beds to pray: ah, well, you have often rebuked me for the pride I take in my own, dear Mama, but I have received my comeuppance here. Though I need not hang my head in shame, one can see half-a-dozen pairs to match mine in a single glance and one or two to surpass them, by some criteria, in the next glance.

Nor are beautiful breasts and faces the only delights for the eye in my dormitory: beautiful bottoms too are unveiled in profusion when we retire for the day. But here I move to the *bad*, Mama, for those bottoms are often mottled or blushing with the marks of the severe handling they have received during the schoolnight. Aye, the handing, which is to say the *spanking*, and the *paddling*, and the *tawsing*, and the *nettling*, and the *thistling* – a great patch of land bordering the sports fields is given over to the cultivation of those cruel plants, and the sports mistresses are ever ready with heavy bunches of one or the other, or both. I have escaped *that* thus far, but I have been spanked thrice and paddled once, and know that a tawsing within a day or two is as inevitable as moonrise.

And please, Mama, do not think me oversensitive in this. Perhaps you smile and say to yourself that your coddled child encounters true discipline for the first time in her life, and 'kicks against the pricks' as a less sheltered lass from the true lower classes would not. It is not so, I swear by the Black Madonna of Reykjavik. Discipline I expected and could accept, but the usage of bottoms here – aye, and breasts too, if some whispers are to be believed – surpasses the boundary of true loving discipline and pushes far into a sun-seared upland of – can I use the word with sincerity?, I ask myself, and answer truly that I can – a sun-seared upland of *perversion*. Yes, Mama: perversion. I wrote above that here 'almost all the faces one encounters are those of young angels'. Well, in the residuum one finds the faces not of angels but of *devils*. No, there I have allowed myself to be carried away. Not all the teachers – for it is of the teachers' faces that I write – seem devils from their appearance. Two in particular have struck me as good and decent women, despite the heaviness with which they punish, and oddly enough they are Bulgarian, Mistress Lidiya and Mistress Vasilka.

I say 'oddly' because the other Bulgarians on the staff both *look* like devils and *behave* like devils. Their faces, however superficially attractive, are full of ill-suppressed cruelty and lust, and their hands twitch with greed for punishment of their overcrowded classes. I speak literally, Mama: I have seen one, in what purported to be a French class, drop her chalk in her eagerness at the plump curves of an Austrian girl's bottom. And for what? For questioning that teacher's command of her avowed subject, which the least Francophone amongst us could see was far from perfect. Indeed, far from even *adequate*. And yet next door a native speaker of French, no less, was teaching mathematics with similar ineptitude, and punishing bottoms as freely as her Bulgarian colleague, who was, but a few days before, teaching the subject for which, if older students are to be believed, she is well-enough qualified: namely, *mathematics*.

I would call it 'Alice in Wonderland' stuff, Mama, but it is not so. There was deliberate intent in the overturning of the curriculum that took place on the arrival of us new girls, whereby teachers abandoned their usual subjects and took up those for which they were least well suited. It is deliberately designed to grant teachers the excuse for harsher and more frequent punishment of their classes, who are naturally in a state of alternate bewilderment and resentment. And with more punishment – and here I approach the 'sinister' aspect of the Academy, Mama, and my homesickness seems somehow to melt away in the face of deeper-rooted and deadlier emotion – with more punishment, I say, go more interviews with the headmistress of the Academy, the Countess Caradul. When I think how that name reassured you, Mama, when you first expressed doubts at my application for a scholarship here, I am caught between tears and laughter. Your instincts for your twaughter's* safety were correct, and that which coaxed them to sleep – an aristocratic name – was in fact the surest vindication of them.

My pen trembles as I come to write of her now, and I glance behind me, fearful least somehow I am observed. Aye, Mama, in this 'high-minded' school of which both of us had such hopes I have had to find a hideaway to compose a truthful letter to you, for our 'official' correspondence with our families and friends is confined to a meagre postcard, whose scribbled lines all pass under the eyes of our dormitory monitors and mistress. To facilitate this we are under strict orders to write only in Romanian – one poor Ukrainian girl in my dormitory had her bottom stripped and paddled on the spot, with some quite gratuitous breast-squeezing, for protesting that her Mama could not understand Romanian. All these measures have only one source, I am certain: the Countess herself. Hers is the presence that broods throughout the Academy, hers the anger that all of us, from the humblest student to the deputy headmistress, go in constant fear of, and hers the step all ears listen for.

And hear often, Mama, for it falls heavy and indeed can sometimes be *felt* in the floor sooner than it is heard. And it speaks truly of her whom it precedes: the Countess is a veritable giantess, with shoulders broader than any I have seen before and a blunt chin that might have been modelled on the ice-defying prow of an Icelandic fisher-boat. A homely touch, you might feel, but to see that chin jut and tilt as she delivers one of her lectures is to see the primeval force of the woman's personality. And her voice, Mama! It rumbles and growls almost like that of a *bear*, and I swear I found myself murmuring lines from the Eddas in the assembly hall where she welcomed us newcomers. She sometimes seems more akin to an ogre or troll than to a woman, and some girls whisper that *hair* sprouts on her face which she must shave daily.

Certainly, she wears powder thicker there than I have ever seen before, and even with ears plugged against the thunder of her footsteps you could track her recent passage through the Academy by the trail of powder crumbs she leaves. Though as to the hair of which the whispers speak – I have seen no sign of it save on her chin, perhaps, in certain lights, and I believe it is for some other reason that she wears this powder. If she had some affliction that caused her to sprout hair in unexpected places I swear she would flaunt it, not seek to conceal it, for it would add to the almost superstitious – almost? nay – *genuinely* superstitious awe in which she is already held. She recognises this, it is obvious, and constantly seeks fresh means of increasing it. From what the longer-established girls tell us, students can be called to her office at any hour of the night, and never know whether they are to be congratulated or chastised with such force as to leave them in the sanatorium *incommunicada* for a week, emerging strangely transformed from their former selves, as though they have passed through strange waters and seen strange lands.

The Countess supervises all expulsions in person too, and these, running high in the week before our arrival, we have heard, have now reached unparalleled frequency. Two of the girls I befriended on the train and had great hopes of later friendship with are already gone, despatched home without ceremony. Oh, forgive me for what I am about to write, Mama, for I know what further anxiety it will cause, but I have no other choice, for my own sake and for the sake of many others. One of these girls I befriended on the train, Mama, went with such speed that she left her rosary beneath her pillow in my dorm. And she would never have done this willingly, I am surer than surer, for I recall how she clutched it as the train swayed on a bridge, murmuring a prayer to the Goddess, and kissed it when we were safe across. She told me it had been given to her by her grandmother, and was the most precious of her possessions. I told my dorm mistress of this, and she promised to send the rosary after the girl, who (she assured me) had doubtless forgotten it in the shame of her early expulsion and her desire to depart the Academy so soon as she might.

But what did I see in the town yesternight, Mama, in the window of a little pawnshop we girls passed en route to the municipal swimming baths? That same rosary, I swear, for the beads were alternately amethyst and topaz and the dear little cross the same worn silver. My dorm mistress – one of the cruel-faced Bulgarians – had lied to me and sold the rosary after I handed it to her, and how could she do this at any normal school? If the girl has been truly expelled, I can just barely accept that she might forget her rosary briefly in her grief and shame. But I cannot accept that she would not write requesting it as soon as she were able. Yet my dorm mistress evidently felt secure in the disposing of the item, and I can only conclude that she fears no letter and no exposure of her crime. But if this is so, how can the girl have truly been *expelled*? No, she is, I very much fear, *sold* as 'servant girl' to some rich degenerate of Bucharest.

For was I not myself, within minutes of passing that pawnshop, stripping quite naked to swim with my schoolfellows beneath a gallery crowded with masked figures, some equipped with lorgnettes? I could feel their eyes raking my flesh, and would have complained to the sports mistress who supervised us, but was fortunately (for me) forestalled by one of my little companions, a Luxembourgeoise called Helena. The eyes in the gallery left me then, Mama, for Helena was plucked from the water like a minnow and stretched across the lap of that sports mistress, whose horny hand made spray fly from her wet buttocks. When she had finished, and poor Helena was shoved roughly off to snivel and rub her bottom without comfort as she trotted back to the changing room to dress in solitary disgrace, two or three in the gallery positively applauded, and a banknote fluttered down which the sports mistress, judging its flight to perfection, plucked from the air with a satisfied grunt.

When we returned, I compared impressions with one of the other girls who had accompanied me on the expedition, and found that hers chimed with mine. We were being *displayed* at those municipal swimming baths, Mama, like slave-girls on the auction block, and potential purchasers were eyeing us over before placing their orders. Those tales of Bucharest's decadence, which were so easy to dismiss as outworn and inflated in homely Reykjavik, seem more credible by the hour in Bucharest herself. But what can we do? The Countess, from all we hear, is high in the favour of the authorities here and a complaint by a single young foreign girl would gain no greater credence if it were made by a hundred. But forewarned is forearmed, and you can rest assured that I am on my guard. This letter will help guarantee my safety too, for once it is safe on its way to Iceland I have a threat to level against kidn . . .

[Letter breaks off here with an ink-splot.]

Letter of 21 November from Delivery Manager, Premium Grocery Supplies, Bucharest, to the Countess Caradul, Headmistress of the Academy for Underprivileged Young Women of the Lower Classes, Bucharest.

Dear Madame,

We are pleased to accept the terms in your letter of the 18th inst., and beg to place orders for the following girl-cheese for delivery by the 2nd prox.

Burduf – 10 gross
Dalia – 8 gross
Nasal – 8 gross
Telemea – 12 gross

Yours sincerely,

Cătălina Codrescu, pp. Disluminița Stănculescu.

Glossary

Abbreviations: adj. adjective; adv. adverb(ial); Fr. French; Gk Greek; int. interjection; Lat. Latin; lit. literally; Rom. Romanian; n. noun; phr. phrase; vb verb; W. Welsh.

Arglwyddi!: W. int. Lord!

Benodorous: adj. lit. meaning 'well-smelling', and used especially of the fresh odour of pussy-juice on the fingers or around the lips.

Bourgeoise: Fr. adj. belonging to the middle classes of *Fresh Flesh*'s universe (cf. *proletarienne*).

Buhă: Rom. n. owl.

Butchwife: (pronounced BUTCH-uff) n. The dominant partner in a lesbian marriage. Cf. femme-wife.

Callipygous: adj. with a beautiful backside.

Cap: Rom. n. heads (of a coin). Cf. *pajura*.

Cariad: W. n. dear, darling.

Ceteris paribus: Lat. phr. with other things (being) equal.

Champ de bataille: Fr. ph. field of battle.

Chelce: adj. pink, esp. as applied to the female genitals.

Clitoridilinctus: n. licking (and sucking) of the clitoris.

Cunnilinctree: n. one who is cunnilingued.

Cunnilinctr-ix: (pl. -ices) n. one who cunnilingues.

Cunnilingarium: (pl. cunnilingaria) n. a brothel specialising in cunnilinctus.

Da sau nu?: Rom. phr. yes or no.

Das Ewig-Weibliche: Ger. phr. the Eternal Feminine (Johanna Goethe).

Dea volente: Lat. phr. 'If the Goddess be willing'.

După a locului obicei . . .: Rom. phr. corresponding to 'When in Rome (do as the Romans)'.

Espionne: Fr. n. female spy.

Femmewife: (pronounced FEM-uff) n. the submissive partner in a lesbian marriage. Cf. butchwife.

Fluture: Rom. n. moth (in *Fresh Flesh*'s universe; in the Romanian of our universe, the main meaning of *fluture* is 'butterfly', 'moth' being *fluture de noapte*, or '*fluture*-of-night').

Fortday: n. fortnight, period of fourteen days.

Glart: adj. green, blue.

Ïe: W. yes, yea.

Introitus: n. entrance of the penis into the vagina or rectum.

Jumiter: proper n. the Goddess corresponding in *Fresh Flesh*'s universe to Jupiter.

Jus amoris: Lat. phr. 'juice of love'.

Liliac: Rom. n. nocturnal winged mammal; bat.

Mavrud: n. a red Bulgarian 'wine' (fermentation is not used in *Fresh Flesh*'s universe in polite circles).

Mens sana in corpore sano: Lat. motto 'A healthy mind in a healthy body'.

Overday: adv. overnight.

Pajura: Rom. n. tails (of a coin). Cf. *cap*.

Per vaginam: Lat. adv. phr. through the vagina.

Primigravida: adj. and n. (a woman who is) pregnant for the first time.

Proletarienne: Fr. adj. proletarian, belonging to the lower classes of *Fresh Flesh*'s universe. Cf. bourgeoise.

Puellar: adj. pertaining to girls.

Pussyhorn: n. the clitoris.

Quotinoctial: adj. lit. meaning normal, 'everyday' (lit. 'everynight').

Sal vitale: n. 'vital salt' (Italian): the Count's nonce-phrase for semen, punning on *sal volatile*.

Secundigravida: adj. pregnant for the second time.

Sowl: (rhyming with 'howl') 1. adj. yellow, light red. 2. vb. to make sowl.

Sowlhead: 1. n. a woman with red hair. 2. *–ed* adj. redheaded.

Spit-mother: n. a mother as the identical image of her twaughter (q.v.).

Treadle: n. a lever worked with the foot.

Twaughter: n. (tw(in)+(d)aughter) a daughter born by parthenogenesis as an identical clone of her spit-mother (q.v.). In the Europe of *Fresh Flesh*'s universe, women give birth to their twaughters at the *tweth* (q.v.).

Twenfer: n. a period of 24 hours.

Tweth: (also *tweth-year*) n. 1. the twenty-fourth year of life, during which 23-year-old women in *Fresh Flesh*'s universe give birth to their twaughters (q.v.). 2. a period of 23 years.

Un cri touchant de la victime nous annonce enfin sa défaite: Fr. phr. 'at length the victim's piteous cry announces to us her defeat'.

μη γενοιτο!: Gk phr. 'let it not be!' (A formula used often by St Paulina in the New Testament.)

Vace: adj. brown, dark red.

Via posterior: Lat. phr. back way, rectum.

Volens nolens: Lat. phr. willing (or) unwilling.

Vox e caelo: Lat. phr. a voice from heaven.

nexus

The leading publisher of fetish and adult fiction

TELL US WHAT YOU THINK!

Readers' ideas and opinions matter to us. Take a few minutes to fill in the questionnaire below and you'll be entered into a prize draw to win a year's worth of Nexus books (36 titles)

Terms and conditions apply – see end of questionnaire.

1. Sex: Are you male ☐   female ☐   a couple ☐?

2. Age: Under 21 ☐   21–30 ☐   31–40 ☐   41–50 ☐   51–60 ☐   over 60 ☐

3. Where do you buy your Nexus books from?

☐ A chain book shop. If so, which one(s)?

_____

☐ An independent book shop. If so, which one(s)?

_____

☐ A used book shop/charity shop
☐ Online book store. If so, which one(s)?

_____

4. How did you find out about Nexus books?

☐ Browsing in a book shop
☐ A review in a magazine
☐ Online
☐ Recommendation
☐ Other _____

5. In terms of settings, which do you prefer? (Tick as many as you like.)

☐ Down to earth and as realistic as possible
☐ Historical settings. If so, which period do you prefer?

_____

☐ Fantasy settings – barbarian worlds

- ☐ Completely escapist/surreal fantasy
- ☐ Institutional or secret academy
- ☐ Futuristic/sci fi
- ☐ Escapist but still believable
- ☐ Any settings you dislike?

_____

- ☐ Where would you like to see an adult novel set?

_____

6. In terms of storylines, would you prefer:

- ☐ Simple stories that concentrate on adult interests?
- ☐ More plot and character-driven stories with less explicit adult activity?
- ☐ We value your ideas, so give us your opinion of this book:

_____

_____

_____

7. In terms of your adult interests, what do you like to read about? (Tick as many as you like.)

- ☐ Traditional corporal punishment (CP)
- ☐ Modern corporal punishment
- ☐ Spanking
- ☐ Restraint/bondage
- ☐ Rope bondage
- ☐ Latex/rubber
- ☐ Leather
- ☐ Female domination and male submission
- ☐ Female domination and female submission
- ☐ Male domination and female submission
- ☐ Willing captivity
- ☐ Uniforms
- ☐ Lingerie/underwear/hosiery/footwear (boots and high heels)
- ☐ Sex rituals
- ☐ Vanilla sex
- ☐ Swinging
- ☐ Cross-dressing/TV

☐ Enforced feminisation
☐ Others – tell us what you don't see enough of in adult fiction:

_____
_____
_____

8. Would you prefer books with a more specialised approach to your interests, i.e. a novel specifically about uniforms? If so, which subject(s) would you like to read a Nexus novel about?

_____
_____
_____

9. Would you like to read true stories in Nexus books? For instance, the true story of a submissive woman, or a male slave? Tell us which true revelations you would most like to read about:

_____
_____
_____

10. What do you like best about Nexus books?

_____
_____

11. What do you like least about Nexus books?

_____
_____

12. Which are your favourite titles?

_____
_____

13. Who are your favourite authors?

_____
_____

14. **Which covers do you prefer? Those featuring:**
    (tick as many as you like)

☐ Fetish outfits
☐ More nudity
☐ Two models
☐ Unusual models or settings
☐ Classic erotic photography
☐ More contemporary images and poses
☐ A blank/non-erotic cover
☐ What would your ideal cover look like?

_____

15. **Describe your ideal Nexus novel in the space provided:**

_____

_____

_____

16. **Which celebrity would feature in one of your Nexus-style fantasies?**
    We'll post the best suggestions on our website – anonymously!

_____

THANKS FOR YOUR TIME

Now simply write the title of this book in the space below and cut out the
questionnaire pages. Post to: Nexus, Marketing Dept., Thames Wharf Studios,
Rainville Rd, London W6 9HA

Book title: _____

TERMS AND CONDITIONS

To be published in August 2006

CARNAL POSSESSION
Yvonne Strickland

Glamour model and writer of erotica, Joanna took the old house for peace and quiet. But her occupation attracts the lustful attentions of a perverse local coven, whose interests and practices are not entirely at odds with Joanna's strong but hidden sexual urges. Soon, under their influence, her bizarre fetish-fantasies become a reality of strict bondage and sexual power games.

£6.99   ISBN 0 352 34062 2

BIDDING TO SIN
Rosita Varón

Just when everyone is depending on her to win a vital contract, Melanie Brooks, a talented manager of Bermont and Cuthbertson's creative design team suddenly finds herself pitched into a tumultuous sexual adventure that makes her head spin and her backside sting. Her normal cool competence seems a thing of the past as the problems escalate out of control and she becomes immersed in an explicit world that threatens to sabotage her team's future.

£6.99   ISBN 0 352 34063 0

THE DOMINO ENIGMA
Cyrian Amberlake

At Estwych, Josephine had learned the value of obedience. She had tasted iron and leather; she had been abased and degraded and exalted to eternity. Her training had hardly begun.

Summoned by the double blank to a life of subjection at the hands of the unknown masters, Josephine must learn to surrender completely. To surrender her body – and her soul.

In this sequel to *The Domino Tattoo,* Josephine Morrow undergoes the hardest trials she has ever known – and survives the greatest rewards.

£6.99   ISBN 0 352 34064 9

If you would like more information about Nexus titles, please visit our website at www.nexus-books.co.uk, or send a large stamped addressed envelope to:
  Nexus, Thames Wharf Studios,
  Rainville Road, London W6 9HA

nexus

This information is correct at time of printing. For up-to-date information, please visit our website at www.nexus-books.co.uk

All books are priced at £6.99 unless another price is given.

- - - - - - ✂ -

Please send me the books I have ticked above.

Name   ....

Address   ....

....

....

.... Post code ....

Send to: **Virgin Books Cash Sales, Thames Wharf Studios, Rainville Road, London W6 9HA**

US customers: for prices and details of how to order books for delivery by mail, call 888-330-8477.

Please enclose a cheque or postal order, made payable to **Nexus Books Ltd**, to the value of the books you have ordered plus postage and packing costs as follows:

UK and BFPO – £1.00 for the first book, 50p for each subsequent book.

Overseas (including Republic of Ireland) – £2.00 for the first book, £1.00 for each subsequent book.

If you would prefer to pay by VISA, ACCESS/MASTERCARD, AMEX, DINERS CLUB or SWITCH, please write your card number and expiry date here:

....

Please allow up to 28 days for delivery.

Signature ....

Our privacy policy

We will not disclose information you supply us to any other parties. We will not disclose any information which identifies you personally to any person without your express consent.

From time to time we may send out information about Nexus books and special offers. Please tick here if you do *not* wish to receive Nexus information.   □

- - - - - - ✂ -